14

4

4

MOURNING THE LITTLE DEAD

MOURNING THE LITTLE DEAD

Jane A. Adams

This first world edition published in Great Britain 2002 by
SEVERN HOUSE PUBLISHERS LTD of
9–15 High Street, Sutton, Surrey SM1 1DF.
This first world edition published in the USA 2002 by
SEVERN HOUSE PUBLISHERS INC of
595 Madison Avenue, New York, N.Y. 10022.

British Library Cataloguing in Publication Data

Adams, Jane A.
    Mourning the little dead
    1.   Missing children - Fiction
    2.   Detective and mystery stories
    I.   Title
    823.9'14 [F]

    ISBN 0-7278-5855-6

Except where actual historical events and characters are being
described for the storyline of this novel, all situations in this
publication are fictitious and any resemblance to living persons
is purely coincidental.

Typeset by Palimpsest Book Production Ltd.,
Polmont, Stirlingshire, Scotland.
Printed and bound in Great Britain by
MPG Books Ltd., Bodmin, Cornwall.

Prologue

The day she heard about Helen had been heavy with the threat of storms. The wind that had blown from the sea all week, bringing with it a prematurely winter chill, had dipped almost to nothing and by evening the air crackled with a heated stillness that was unexpected for this late in September. Heat, and the promise of thunder. Naomi could imagine the stone-grey clouds gathering beyond the horizon and the yellow foam crashing and moiling upon the beach and dragging at the smooth worn stones.

In retrospect, she perceived that there had been a sense of expectation that day. She should have known something momentous was about to break. But that evening she had suspected nothing.

That evening, Naomi had the windows open, and the tall electric fan beating the stillness from the air while Napoleon's thick black tail beat another rhythm out on the wooden floor. She had switched the television on and lay slumped on the fat blue sofa beside the open window while the news played through the day's events.

It was a tiny snippet of a report. A few lines on the local bulletin, but Naomi felt the shock of it hitting like a fist in the stomach, winding her as effectively as a physical blow.

Police were searching for the body of Helen Jones. Twenty-three years on from the event, someone had confessed to killing her.

One

'**A**re you OK?'

She could imagine Alec's rather too handsome face creasing with concern. The grey-blue eyes clouded by one of those moments of seriousness he did so well.

'Yeah, yeah, I'm fine. It was a shock, though, I don't mind telling you. Where are they digging?'

'Lansdowne Road. You know, on the Bellingham estate. They were building it back when—'

'Yeah, I remember. Some of the new families had kids at our school.'

'I've brought you some wine,' he said. 'Thought we might send out for a takeaway. Or maybe you'd just like a drink right now?'

She smiled. 'I don't think I could eat. I'll get some glasses. What kind is it?'

'What? Oh, that one with the goat on the label. I remembered you liked that one.'

Naomi laughed then. Alec was a beer drinker for preference. He'd taken an interest in other forms of alcohol just to please her. It was typical he'd only remember the picture on the label.

'I'll find the glasses,' she said again.

'Here. Let me.'

'I can manage, Alec. I know my kitchen better than you do. Anyway, how do you think I cope most of the time?'

'Sorry,' he apologised. 'I just . . . well . . . You know.'

'I know.' She had long since given up being offended by well-meaning offers of help. Naomi crossed to the wall cupboard and reached to open the door, feeling her way carefully along the row until she came to the long-stemmed, pale blue glasses she had bought the week before. She knew they were pale blue because the friend who had gone shopping with her had told her so. Naomi had chosen them for the long, elegant stems and the satisfying shape that sat so comfortably in the palm of her hand.

In her previous existence, she had never given much thought to the way things felt. Now, it was her main criteria when it came to making a choice.

She held the glasses out towards him. 'Corkscrew in the drawer to your left. I'll let you do the honours.'

'Right you are.'

She could feel him smile, hear it in his voice. She leaned back against the kitchen counter and listened to the sounds of Alec rooting in the drawer for the corkscrew and then opening the bottle. The wine glugged impatiently into the glass and Naomi could imagine the deep-red glowing purple through the pale blue. She should have told him to let it breathe, she thought.

'So,' she asked him. 'What went on? The news was pretty vague; just that there had been a confession and they were digging for the body.'

'That's about the size of it.' He shrugged. She fancied she could feel it, but maybe it was just that she knew Alec and his body language all too well.

'Here, you want to carry your glass? Then I can bring the wine. Got it?' He waited until her fingers had curled securely around the stem and then moved towards the door. Naomi followed him into the living room. When he spoke again his voice came from across the room and she guessed he had settled on the sofa close beside the window. Napoleon's tail thumped steadily upon the floor, but the dog did not bother to get up. Naomi sat down in the worn leather chair beside the fireplace and reached out to check that the little table was where it ought to be. She set her wine glass down upon it.

'So tell me.'

Alec sighed. 'Not much to tell to be truthful. I got in this morning and the place was buzzing. Some woman had come in—'

'A woman? A woman confessed to killing Helen?'

3

'No, no. Look, hold on and let me tell. This woman had come in and demanded to see someone in charge. Turns out her father had just died and the confession was amongst his things.'

'You've seen it?'

'No.' Alec sounded slightly puzzled. 'They're keeping the whole thing tight. DCI Logan spoke to the woman and then spent the next hour closeted with Superintendent Phillips. His secretary routed about a half-dozen external calls, and next thing was a team was being assembled ready to dig up 43 Lansdowne Rd.'

'The residents. They're implicated?'

'No. Poor bastards have only been there six months. They've had to pack their bags and clear out. Phillips is having them put up in a hotel. Taxpayers' expense.'

'Why have them move out? I thought they were just digging in the garden.'

Alec shook his head, she knew that by the little pause before he said, 'No. Rumour has it the concrete for the floor was poured two days after Helen went missing. If so . . . Anyway, they've called in a team of builders to assist our lot. The news might have been low key this evening, but mark my words, by tomorrow it'll be reported as the next house of horrors.'

'They don't think . . . ?'

'Far as I know this is just about Helen. Look,' he added, 'I'd have come earlier if I could, you know that.'

'There was no need, Alec. Truly. But thanks anyway,' she added, realizing suddenly that she was glad he had. 'You know, I must have thought about her every day since it happened. I must have wondered, every single day, where she went. Was she dead? Was she alive or . . . I don't know . . . spirited away somewhere? We all *knew* she must be dead, but, you know, hearing it on the news like that it was still . . . shocking.'

'I know,' he said quietly. 'Yes, I *do* know.'

They were silent for a moment. A silence that grew like a shadow across the room between them. Not uncomfortable, but full of things that neither one had the nerve to say. Naomi broke it, asking. 'Who confessed, Alec?'

'No one's saying.'

'But there must be rumours? Who was the woman?'

'Oh, there are rumours. The mill's grinding them at the rate of three or four an hour. The woman, I don't know. The desk sergeant didn't recognize her. Said she was thirty, thirty-five. Dark-haired, well-dressed, pretty and smelt nice.'

'Don't tell me. That would be Bob Saunders.' Saunders had a fixation with the way people smelt. The result, probably, of dealing with too many sick drunks.

'Yes, it was Bob. He sent his best by the way. Guessed I'd be seeing you. But he didn't know her and she didn't give her name. She came in and said she was prepared to sit there all day until they found her someone in authority to talk to and that it was about Helen Jones.'

'She said that? That it was about Helen Jones? Bob Saunders wouldn't have known the name. He's not a local.'

'Well done, DI Blake! No, she said she'd come about the murdered girl. That she knew who did it. Saunders thought she meant that little kid out at Philby, so he went and fetched DCI Travers. Dick Travers is handling that one. Few minutes later, Travers left and dragged Logan into the interview room. The rest, as they say . . .'

The child out at Philby, Naomi thought. That had been almost a couple of months before. A six-year-old by the name of Sarah Clarke, found strangled only a few hundred yards from her home. It was still unsolved and Alec had told her privately that the investigation was on the skids.

'And nothing more than that? You must know something, Alec.'

'Wish I did. Like I said, they're playing this one close. My guess is either it's someone they had in the frame back then and they don't want him alerted, or they've got Helen's killer tied in to something else and, equally, they don't want him to do a runner.'

'The Philby child?' She shook her head. 'Nah, that would be pushing coincidence.'

'I agree. Or, it's someone in the family.'

'Helen's family? No, Alec, that's just daft thinking. Remember I know the Jones's.'

'People knew the Wests and Jeffrey Dahmer.'

5

'Now who's playing silly buggers?'

'OK. True. But you get where I'm coming from?'

'Sure. But you said the guy that confessed is dead. So there's no way he could run, is there?'

'Another score to DI Blake. No, if it *was* the dead man who made the confession, and remember, I don't know that yet, then barring him being an extra in *The Mummy Returns*, he couldn't run. Which means—'

'Which means he's someone whose name would be recognized. Who has a reputation to maintain.'

'Could be. Look, I'll dig around and see what I can find, but like I say, they're keeping stum.'

DI Blake, Naomi mused. Alec was the only one who called her that anymore. The only one who could get away with it and not make it sound like a sick joke. Somehow, coming from him, it was simply an expression of affection and respect . . . and a reminder of the time not so long ago when they had been colleagues. Of all her ex-work mates, Alec was the only one whom she could genuinely say had stayed her full-time friend, and, of course, much more than that. She had always been able to rely on him keeping her up to date about the goings on amongst her old colleagues. Who was screwing who – and if their wives had found out. Who was up for promotion; who was about to be scooted sideways to make way for some new-blood graduate on a fast track.

She had been resentful at first that he talked about the life she had left behind. Resentful because she was no longer a part of that world and couldn't find another universe to take its place. Then, she had been thankful that someone had seen through the façade and recognized her need to still belong, even if it was only at a distance.

But even after close on two years, it seemed so strange to be hearing second hand about events that she would once have been an integral part of. To be fishing for information she no longer had an automatic right to. Naomi knew that she would always find that hard.

'How did it go at the hospital?' Alex asked her, almost as if he knew where her thoughts had been.

'Oh, fine. Nothing new. They reckon the photo response

is about as good as it's going to get. I can perceive bright sunlight. I even get some sense of it being red, you know, like when you stare at the sun with your eyes closed. And I get some sense of shadows moving across if the light's bright enough behind whatever it is. That's about all.'

'Better though. I mean, than in the beginning.'

'And I'm supposed to be grateful?' She spoke sharply, with a sudden surge of anger that was quite out of keeping with the rest of the conversation.

She apologized at once. 'Sorry, Alec. I didn't mean . . .'

'Sorry? For what? Naomi . . .' He paused and she felt him change whatever it was he had been about to say and with a smile in his voice he asked her, 'I ever tell you how beautiful you are when you're angry?'

'Fool.'

'Got that in one.'

She heard him get up and the dog shift his position on the floor, the rate of tail-thump increase. Alec crossed over to where she sat and knelt down in front of her chair.

'Fool about you,' he said.

When Alec had gone, Naomi found it hard to get back to sleep. He had wanted to stay, but was due in court the following morning and they both knew from long experience that once he'd settled down for the night, neither would wake in time for him to get home in time to shower and change. Naomi lay still, listening for the front door closing and the car engine firing into life and then lay listening to the near silence of the sleeping town waiting for its sleep to come to her. When it didn't, she slipped from the bed and stood naked beside the widow, letting the cool of the night air play upon her skin.

She could smell the ocean, the salt and the damp scent of the mud flats out in the estuary. She heard the occasional car drive by on the main road or the swift footsteps of someone hurrying home, and in her mind she could see Helen Jones. Blonde and freckled with a turned-up nose and summer sky blue eyes set wide in her plump, pretty face.

Exact opposites the two of them, but friends since nursery. Helen: small, blonde, a little overweight and just at the age when she was worrying about it and reading all the fad diets in her mother's magazines. And Naomi: tall for her age and awkward with it, never quite knowng what to do with her overlong limbs. Naomi had feet which always felt two sizes two big and a body which was as thin and straight as a boy's, whilst her friend was already developing chubby little breasts that pressed against the fabric of her school blouse.

Helen, Naomi always swore, didn't have a serious bone in her body whereas Naomi was the solemn one. The one who took everything to heart, and that was just the trouble that morning: the morning that Helen disappeared from her life.

The two of them had quarrelled the night before. Argued over some imagined slight: Helen, daring to show more interest in her other friends than Naomi would willingly allow. Shy, uncertain Naomi, who always knew she needed Helen far more than her friend ever needed her.

'Never let the sun go down upon a quarrel.' Her gran had told her that, along with a dozen other such useful aphorisms. But that night Naomi, the grievance nurtured in her non-existent bosom, had been too wrapped up in that turbulent mass of self-pity that only a teenage girl can revel in, to take her gran's advice. And she had turned on her heel at the end of the road, walked away from her friend and not looked back.

It was typical that Helen should have waited for her the following morning. Helen, who was quick to forgive and who would most likely have thought nothing more about the entire incident. Helen, who waited until she was almost late for school.

Naomi, wishing she could let go of her anger but unable to lose face, even if only in her own eyes, had gone the other way.

Standing beside the window, staring out into the dark-ness she knew was there but could no longer see, Naomi wept for her friend and for herself and for the two children who had died on that day. Helen *and* the child Naomi. Naomi who had died a little death every time her friend's name had been mentioned. Every time the question hung upon the air, rarely said out loud, but in every look, every word that was spoken about her friend. The question: What

8

would have happened if Naomi had been with Helen that morning?

The little death every time a lead that had seemed promising had petered out. Every sighting of a small blonde girl that turned out to be another small blonde girl and not Helen until, little by little, Naomi had wondered if there were any part of her left to die.

Two

The morning, washed clean by the storm, was bathed in a brightness that Naomi could feel on her skin as she took hold of Napoleon's harness and negotiated the three steps down from her front door.

Someone called out a greeting and she turned her head, smiling as she replied and trying to figure out just who it was. Having moved to this house with its high front steps only a couple of months ago, she was still not too familiar with the neighbours, most of whom seemed perfectly nice, but were kept distant by that uncertainty of not knowing whether they should be straightforward in their offers of help or if she might see them as patronizing. Naomi was reminded of her own feelings about the old lady who had lived at the end of her mother's road. Sometimes, if she saw her out shopping, Naomi used to stop and offer her a lift home, but it had taken a fight with her conscience before she had finally taken the plunge and asked if she'd like a hand, not sure that Mrs Parks would see it as a friendly gesture or an insult to her independence.

There ought to be books of etiquette written, Naomi thought, and she added it to her list of stuff she'd do one day if ever life got so boring she had nothing else.

Napoleon was happy to be up and out, trotting along, matching Naomi's fast pace, with his tail held high and brushing against her side.

This part of her route was familiar now and she had come to trust the dog enough to walk almost as fast as in her sighted days. Took pride in timing herself until she could reach the end of the road in less that three minutes thirty-five.

Beyond the corner was a different matter. Naomi had deliberately moved to an area she knew well, only about a mile away from her childhood home and one which she could visualize easily. Even so, she was finding it hard to get to grips with matching the world she knew from her internal map with the one in which she had only her own feet and four borrowed ones to guide her.

Beyond the corner of the road, her pace slowed and the dog, sensitive to her mood and to the way she held his harness more tightly, slowed with her.

Since the accident her life had changed at its very foundations, and habits even at the most basic of levels. Instead of shopping weekly – or as her work allowed – at the local supermarket, where she stocked up more often than not on frozen ready meals that could be bunged in the microwave, Naomi now shopped locally in places where she could actually talk to the assistants. Simple things like going into a shop and being able to trust someone to weigh four red apples for you or pick the less ripe bananas had assumed an almost unreal importance. The local shops Napoleon could guide her to, knowing her habits and, Naomi was certain, understanding completely when she told him 'Bill's shop', or 'post office' and they usually ended up more or less in the right place. Anything further afield and Naomi still did not have the confidence to go it alone. To catch a bus or go into the centre of town she took a friend or her sister, thankful that Sue was a stay-at-home mum willing to spare her the time.

For someone as independent as Naomi had been, it hurt that she should have to ask for anything. But she was getting used to it. Slowly. And having Napoleon in her life made a difference that she had been totally unprepared for.

Ironically, blindness had been something that Naomi had always dreaded. If anyone had asked her, which sense would she be more scared of losing, then sight would have been it. Short-sighted as a child – seriously short-sighted as a child – Naomi was always the kid in the school photos peering through the regulation pink-framed National Health specs, in those days before it occurred to anyone that free frames didn't have to look as if that was exactly what they were. Her imperfect vision had always plagued her, and it was a standing joke at home that the first thing Naomi did in the morning was to put on her glasses.

11

As an adult, Naomi had switched to wearing lenses and discovered for the first time that she actually had rather beautiful dark eyes.

And then, she had joined the police force . . . and in quiet moments she could still hear DI Joe Jackson telling her, 'Use your eyes, Naomi. Before you do anything else, stand still and use your eyes.'

This morning she had letters to post. Cards for her two cousins. Twins, just a little younger than herself who had birthdays. She needed salad from the greengrocer's – where there was always a half-biscuit waiting for Napoleon – and steaks from the butcher two doors down – where there was always another biscuit waiting for Napoleon. When she had been working with the trainer, learning how to handle the dog, she had been reminded again and again that: 'Poly was a working dog and that treats given by others were a distraction and should be avoided.' But Napoleon was such an ice-breaker, handsome and glossy black – she could feel the shine on his smooth fur – and with such a puppy-like certainty that the whole world loved him, that people found him hard to resist. Often, they talked to the dog first, but that usually meant they talked to her too and Naomi found herself often pathetically grateful for the odd comments from strangers in a world which too often seemed frightening and isolated. In her sighted days, life had been something to be rushed through. Conversation, more often than not if it wasn't about business, was simply conducted on the run. These days, like this morning, she found herself relishing the time to spend walking in the autumn sunshine. The time it took to shop and talk and make contact, however unimportant the actual words might be, and though that compensated for nothing, Naomi felt that it was a lesson she should have learnt long ago, while she could still have *seen* what she was missing.

Finishing with the morning tasks, she walked down to the sea. Napoleon knew where she wanted to go as soon as she paused on the kerb outside the butcher's shop and he led her eagerly on to the promenade, his nose thrust into the seaward wind. They stood together, the dog's tail thumping slowly, his bulk pressed reassuringly against her as she stared intently out across the estuary, picturing the scene as it used to be in those growing-up years when she and Helen played on the coarse sand. She listened to the sounds of the ocean, to the late holidaymakers taking advantage of the sunshine and squawking like the seagulls as they ran into the freezing water of the North Sea.

Somewhere off to her left, where she figured the breakwater ought to be, she heard two girls, squealing and calling out to one another as they braved the cold. One of them was called Helen.

Alec arrived just after seven and Naomi busied herself with cooking while he buzzed around her trying to be helpful, but just getting in the way.

'So tell me.'

'Not a lot to tell. Have you been listening to the news?'

'Have I listened to the news? You joking? I've been waiting for every damned bulletin.' She turned around. 'You're not telling me you don't know any more than that?'

'Not a lot, Nomi. OK, I went to Lansdowne Road. There was a garden there once, now it looks like a map of the Somme. Oh, and they no longer have a living-room floor. By tomorrow, they'll need a hard hat just to be allowed through the front door. But so far, nothing. Not a sign.'

'The killer couldn't have lived there, could he? I mean, they were still building it.'

'That's right and there's now a whole street full of worried neighbours wondering if our man could have got the address wrong. After all, one half-built house is going to look pretty much like the next. There won't have been proper addresses, only plot numbers back then.'

'I guess so,' she shrugged, frustrated. 'But that's it? Still no names. No rumours?'

'Like I said yesterday, plenty of rumours. Quite a few names too, but even now they're admitting most are long shots, you know, lists of known sex offenders. Anyone who fits the basic profile. They've pulled the case records from when Helen first disappeared and got the civilian staff sifting through them for names of those interviewed at the time, but if you remember no one seemed to stand out even then.'

'There were three suspects,' Naomi recalled. 'Three men taken for questioning, but they were all released without charge, or at least, no charges to do with Helen.'

'That's right,' Alec confirmed. 'Russell Gibbs was one. Started life as a twocker, stole cars till he graduated to the odd burglary and was pulled in on the Helen Jones inquiry because of an alleged sexual assault on a thirteen-year-old girl.'

'Yeah, but he's long dead, isn't he? Someone knifed him, if I remember right.'

'Well done, Sherlock. Always said DI Blake had the memory of half a dozen elephants. Two years after Helen disappeared, he got the wrong side of a drug deal, so unless he's got a very inefficient solicitor, he's out of the frame.'

'Solicitor?'

'Oh, didn't I say? The confession was given to the daughter by the solicitor as per the father's wishes. Sealed envelope job with instructions it was to be handed over after the reading of the will or something.'

'Right, so she opens it thinking it's some personal message from dead daddy and discovers he was a child killer.'

'Now you're jumping the gun. We still don't know if "daddy" made the confession himself or implicated a third party.'

'True. I guess.'

'OK, suspect number two. Eric Kennedy. Remember him too, Sherlock?'

Naomi grinned. 'Here, take a look will you, see if the steaks are done?'

'Sure. How do you like yours these days? Medium rare, wasn't it?'

'Anyway it comes. The one thing I don't do so well is get the timing right.'

'Hmm. Looks dead anyway. Think it'll do. OK, where were we? Suspect number two.'

'Mr Eric Kennedy, arrested for indecency. He exposed himself to a couple of kids in the local park. Far as I know it was a one-off. Kennedy, if I've got this right, had learning

14

difficulties or something. Joe reckoned he was never much of a suspect anyway.'

'Ah, the famous DI Joe Jackson. A legend in his own lunchtime.'

Naomi shook her head. 'I never did understand why you two didn't get along.'

He shrugged. He was standing close enough for her to feel it. 'Can't get along with everyone. But no, he was right, there wasn't much of a case against the Kennedy boy.'

'Suspect number three,' Naomi continued. She reached for the salad dressing reflecting on how much easier it was to talk about Helen when she removed her involvement to this pseudo-professional level. 'Ian Holmes,' she said, giving the dressing a final mix before drizzling it carefully over the bowl of torn leaves. 'Here, could you put this on the table for me?'

'Napoleon is begging,' Alec informed her. 'Can I give him something?'

'Food,' Naomi told him firmly. 'Not chocolate, not whatever scraps you have wrapped up in that napkin in your pocket. At least, not until he's had something proper.'

'She's got wise to us, old man,' Alec told the dog. 'His food still under the sink, is it?'

He rummaged about in the cupboard, Napoleon in tow. Naomi said, 'Ian Holmes, he was number one for a while. He'd got previous for enticement and a minor sexual assault. Though he always swore the girl was willing and just kicked up after her parents found out, though that didn't alter the fact that she was under age. He didn't have an alibi for the time Helen went missing and his employers said he hadn't turned up for work that morning.' She sighed. 'Not enough of anything to pin it on him though. The best they had was circumstantial. I heard he left the area six months or so after.'

'We've checked him out. Jailed for rape five years after Helen. In and out of Her Majesty's Pleasure ever since. Still very much alive though, so he's not our dead man with the daughter.'

'That doesn't rule him out, does it? If the confession only implicated someone else, I mean.' She sighed, aware that none

15

of this moved them any further on. 'I don't know, Alec, where does that leave us?'

'Us?'

'Yes,' Naomi told him. 'Us.'

'It's not my case,' he said.

'And it's certainly not mine. That what you're saying?'

She felt him smile, the warmth of it in his voice. 'I wouldn't dare. No, where that leaves us is no further on than they were twenty-odd years ago.'

Three

The media circus had blockaded the entrance to Lansdowne Road. Local residents had taken refuge behind their net curtains and those who did have to venture forth had learnt to keep their platitudes to hand. 'Oh, it's a real shock . . . Nothing like that happens round here.'

The blockade parted reluctantly for the police car as it nosed its way through. Men and women, waving microphones or with cameras at the ready, bent to peer inside, but the lone, uniformed officer was too insignificant to warrant much of their attention. They watched him park his car at the head of the cul de sac and go inside the house. One or two shouted questions at his back. No one expected answers. There was a press call due that afternoon, most of them, old hands at the waiting game, knew they would have to wait until then.

A man stood across the road from them. He stood in shadow, half-hidden in the entrance of someone's drive, their privet hedge giving him the cover he wanted. He had been watching for about an hour, half expecting someone to come out of the house and ask his business, though it had become clear to him that there was no one home and he was screened from the neighbours by their own high hedge.

He had his hands pushed deep into the pockets of his raincoat and wore a dark grey suit beneath. He wore it comfortably, as though it were his everyday dress, the tie pushed right up to cover the top button of his shirt, the knot tied just so, and a white handkerchief protruding slightly from his breast pocket. It was an old-fashioned look, but it fitted him well as though he had been wearing it for years.

He was not a young man, neither was he old, though the prematurely greying hair and lined face added ten years to his forty-one. His eyes were pale. Grey-blue and watery in the unexpectedly strong wind. Hard to believe that the weather had been so unseasonably hot only the day before.

He shuffled his feet as though uncomfortable or undecided and glanced down at the polished toes of his black, lace-up shoes as though they would provide him with the answer to his unspoken question. Should he stay or should he go? Should he step out across the road and through the wall of journalists? Walk past nonchalantly, as though he had a right to be there and they had no right to question it? Have his 'no comment' ready on the tip of his tongue?

He wanted more than anything to be able to walk up that street, to pause outside the door of number forty-three and make certain that they had it right. That this really was the place where she had lain this past two decades and more.

But he knew he couldn't do it. A lifetime of invisibility had ingrained the habit so strongly that he would as soon strip naked and run down the beach as take that walk.

As he had done several times that hour he slipped the picture from his pocket and looked at it. It was crumpled with carrying and, to protect it, he had enshrined it in a little wallet of plastic and black leather. It showed two children, girls of twelve years old. They were both in their best dresses and laughing, neither looking at the camera, simply absorbed in some personal joke that one of them had told. In front of them on the table was a birthday cake, candles lit and ready to be blown out.

It was the last known picture to have been taken of Helen Jones.

Four

'*I*t's not a bad thing to cry. Sometimes it's the only way of getting your feelings out.'

His voice was soft and very gentle. She had never heard him raise his voice, not even in anger. Joe was always so even-tempered. So reliable, not like most of the adults she knew, who could blow at what seemed like the slightest provocation.

'I know,' she told him, 'but Mam keeps saying that it's been months now and I shouldn't keep walking round here with a long face making everyone else feel bad. She says they feel bad enough already.'

'I'm sure they do,' Joe told her gently. 'You know, Naomi, I've always thought it very arrogant of people when they say, oh look, you must have grieved enough by now. But they do have a point as well. Do you honestly think that Helen would want you to go on like this, tearing yourself to shreds, refusing to see your other friends, not going to school? Oh yes, I know about that.'

'She *asked you to talk to me, huh?*'

'That's right, she did. Your Mum's worried about you, and from what I've seen today, she's every right to be.'

Naomi said nothing, she looked away from Joe Jackson, biting her lip in disappointment. She had been so sure that when he called by that morning it had been a spontaneous thing. A real desire to see how she was doing. As a friend, not as her mother's messenger.

They had walked almost a mile along the canal towpath, down between the disused factories and out towards the open fields below the weir and the old mill.

'I thought you cared about me,' she said, her voice petulant and angry.

'I do care, Naomi. I really do and so do your mum and dad.'

'Oh sure. All they care about is I'm making it uncomfortable for them. They just want things back to normal.' She whirled around and grabbed Joe's lapels, clung on tight and shouted into his face. 'Don't they know it's never going to be normal. Helen's not here any more. Helen's not here and I am.'

'And you are,' Joe confirmed with slow emphasis. 'And so am I, Naomi, whenever you need me. Whenever, night. or day.'

DI Alec Friedman was officially off duty as was his colleague DCI Travers. It was early on the Friday evening and the pair of them were out on Philby beach, walking the scene ready for a reconstruction that would take place later that night.

Sarah Clarke had gone missing at around eight thirty on a summer evening seven weeks before. She lived only a street away from the sea front. A sea front lined with guesthouses and pubs and fish and chip shops.

Sarah had wanted chips. She'd gone with her older brother to the corner, a few hundred yards from where they lived. Bored with waiting in the queue, Sarah had gone to stand in the doorway and the last thing anyone remembered was her brother telling her off for swinging on the door. He'd turned to put salt on the chips, turned back . . . and Sarah was gone.

Her body had been found on the beach a couple of hours later, behind a breakwater and, despite it being a summer evening in a busy little resort, no one had seen a thing.

Alec glanced back towards the sea wall. A uniformed officer had been positioned a few yards back from the promenade rail. Alec stood close to the spot where the body had been found.

'See what I mean,' Dick Travers commented. 'You can't see him, he can't see you. The beach drops down towards the sea. Unless you stood right by the rail, you'd be effectively blind.'

Alec nodded. Travers had complained about this a number of times but this was the first time Alec had been here, to the murder scene, and seen the problem for himself. 'OK, so, half dark and well out of the way, no one would see the murder being done. Still doesn't explain why no one saw the kid being snatched. There were three people in the chip shop, not including the counter staff and the brother. God knows how many on the streets who *should* have seen a little girl being dragged away . . . It has to have been someone she knew. Someone with local knowledge too, bringing her here. You move fifty yards either direction up the beach and you're visible from the promenade.'

Travers nodded. There were frown lines etched between his eyes and he didn't look as though he'd known what sleep meant in a long time.

'We figured that lot out the first day,' he said dryly. 'We've had sweet FA since then.' He turned slowly, studying a scene he knew so well he could have navigated it with his eyes closed. 'How's this thing with Helen Jones?' he asked. 'Anything yet?'

Alec shook his head. 'I went out to Lansdowne Road again this morning. Nothing new, just a big hole where the ground floor used to be.'

'How's Naomi taking it?'

'Well enough. I saw her yesterday, I think she's been waiting for this a long time, but it's a shock all the same. Especially the way the news broke.'

'Press still not up to speed on the details, I take it?'

'Not yet, but it'll come out. Deathbed confessions make good headlines.'

Dick Travers snorted. The sound might almost have been a laugh. Then he stiffened. 'Didn't think she'd be here yet.'

'Who?' Alec turned. A woman stood close to the next breakwater. She wore a summer dress in a blue print fabric and a grey cardigan pulled tightly across her chest. Her hands tugged at it as though it were a shield, protecting her from the world.

'Mrs Clarke,' Alec guessed.

'Yeah. She's haunted the place.'

'You surprised?'

Travers shook his head. 'The first few days she spent on the promenade with a picture of Sarah. Just running up and down, shoving it in people's faces and asking if they'd seen her little

21

girl. The doc sedated her, but she just slept for a while and then she was out again.' He shook his head again. 'How do you tell her to stop doing a thing like that?'

'And Mr Clarke?'

'Mr Clarke shouted a whole lot and then made friends with the whisky bottle. Last time I saw him . . . he looked straight at me but there was no one there, behind the eyes.' Travers gestured emptily with his hands. 'You know the way it is.'

Alec nodded. They started walking towards the breakwater and the woman standing there. She waited for them, standing very still but her eyes never for a moment seeming to rest on anything. Her gaze darted this way and that as though she were afraid of what she might see.

'Hello, Maggie,' Travers said.

'I came to watch.'

'You think that's a good idea?'

She nodded violently. 'I have to see,' she said. 'If someone remembers anything. I have to see.'

'Ok, let's go on up,' Dick Travers said, nodding towards the steps that led back on to the promenade. He took her arm and together they walked back up the beach, Alec slowly bringing up the rear.

Five

Naomi had been out for most of the day. She worked twice a week at an advice centre in the centre of town, using her experience in the police force to give basic legal advice. What she didn't know, others at the centre usually did, and though it often frustrated her that she could not access this information herself by looking it up or searching the Internet, she still felt useful. For someone like Naomi who had always needed to feel useful, the advice centre was a valued outlet. She was seriously thinking of taking a counselling course and setting up a practice of her own.

People who came to the centre, often desperate, always anxious, were sometimes a little fazed by finding themselves talking to a blind woman. Some couldn't get over it and Naomi had learned to sideline these clients and pass them on to someone else very quickly. At first, she had let her annoyance show. Now, she shrugged her shoulders and got on with the next problem.

Other people actually found themselves more comfortable with someone who could not see their face while they bared their souls and Naomi was often genuinely upset by the depth of despair to which some of them had sunk. Today, a woman had come wanting advice on a debt problem; what had seemed a relatively simple threat of court action from a credit company. She had broken down, delivered her whole life history – warring partner, ungrateful kids and a miserable childhood, and Naomi felt both physically and emotionally exhausted after hearing her troubles and trying to offer advice.

Naomi had taken a taxi home. Napoleon loved travelling by car with his nose to the cracked open window and his ears flapping in the breeze. Naomi had built a relationship with a small family-run firm not far from her home. Her usual driver was George Mallard and they did their best to make sure he collected her on her advice-centre days.

George pulled up close to the kerb and helped Naomi from the car.

'Naomi?'

The voice was vaguely familiar but Naomi could not place it. She felt Napoleon lift his head to look curiously in the man's direction.

'Yes?'

'I'm sorry,' the voice said. 'I should have phoned or something.' He laughed awkwardly. 'I'm not usually so impulsive, you know. Oh, Lord, what a mess I'm making.'

But Naomi had placed him now. It was his manner that gave him away, and that shy, awkward laugh. 'Harry? Harry Jones?'

'Yes. I've come back, you know, because of Helen. When I heard, I knew I should come, couldn't let Mam face it all alone. Not again.' He paused. 'I heard . . . about what happened to you. I'm sorry.'

'So am I. But it's OK.' She reached out to pet the dog, stroking his silky ears. 'This is Napoleon,' she told Harry. 'Best friend anyone could ever have.'

'I went out there today,' Harry Jones told her. 'To Lansdowne Road, you know . . .'

'Where they're digging for Helen.'

'Yes. The press . . . journalists, television cameras. They were all at the end of the road. I stood and watched for a time. I wanted to walk up the hill and knock on the front door and say, "Look, I think you might have my sister in there. I want to see where that bastard buried her!" But I didn't. I didn't do a damned thing. I just walked away and went back home. Our old home, I mean.'

'They *will* tell you, as soon as they find anything, Harry. And I'm sure, if you or your mother really wanted to view the scene, the police could make some arrangement. Some relatives . . . some relatives have to . . . to see where . . . It helps to give them some kind of closure.'

'Is that the official language, Naomi? Closure?'

She smiled. 'I guess so.' She was wondering what he looked like now. In her memory he was a boy in his late teens. Sandy-haired, where Helen had been light-blonde. Freckled and pale-faced. Always tall for his age, he tended to stoop, to stand awkwardly as though his legs and arms had grown so fast that the length of them had taken him by surprise.

The man sitting opposite her smiled back, forgetting that she couldn't see. His hair was no longer sandy, but was now a steely grey and the freckles had faded or in places merged into awkward spots of darker pigment. He had lines around his eyes and crossing his forehead. They had been there since the year he had lost Helen.

'Great dog,' he said. 'You've had him long?'

'About eight months and yes, he is great. What have you been doing all this time? Your mum said you were training to be an accountant. I kept in touch for a while, then, we kind of drifted apart. I'm sorry about that.'

'She was sorry, too. I became an accountant. I got married.'

'You're married?'

'Divorced. She liked my boss more than she liked me. We have a son and he lives with me now. He *didn't* like my boss and when he got old enough to speak his mind I think it was more comfortable for everyone for him to move back to England.'

'They live abroad?'

'Florida. They moved to Florida after the divorce. Patrick used to come to me for the holidays. Anyway, I found another job, or rather, same job in a different company and there you have it really. The past two decades in a nutshell.'

Naomi laughed. 'How old is Patrick?'

'Fifteen. He's fifteen. Into computers, skateboards, desperate for a dog,' he added. He paused awkwardly and then said, 'He'd love to meet Napoleon. And you. I mean, if you'd like. I know Mam would love to see you, too.'

'I'd like that,' she said. A little surprised to find that she really meant it. 'Yeah, I really would.'

There was a long silence. Naomi could feel all the things he had really come here to say fighting their way out.

'I don't know any more than you do,' she said softly. 'Or, not much anyway.'

'Not much will do.'

Naomi bit her lip. 'It can go no further,' she told him. 'I mean, it'll all come out in time, but right now, this is confidential.'

'You don't need to tell me that. I know.'

'I have a friend in the force. He tells me that a woman came into the front office. Her father had died and left a confession behind.'

'I read in the papers, about a confession. I thought . . .'

'That the police had finally done their job?'

'Something like that. I couldn't understand why they wouldn't tell us who . . . I mean, if they'd arrested someone. Do you know who?'

Naomi shook her head.

'Meaning, you can't tell me?' He sounded disappointed.

'Meaning I don't know. Really, I don't know. They're not releasing the name and giving out very few details. This woman came in with the confession. It had been left with her dad's solicitor after he died. She took it to the police. Harry, I don't even know if the man confessed or if he'd been keeping it for someone else. Protecting someone. I know they've reopened the old files which could mean it implicated a suspect from back then. It could equally well just mean they're being thorough.'

'You know, day after day we'd wait for that knock on the door. First of all, it was the waiting. Would they find her, would she be all right? Then it was *how* would they find her? How did she die? You know, your mind goes through all the possible scenarios. Was she scared, in pain? Was it quick or did he—'

'I know.' She said it quickly. She couldn't bear for him to say the rest.

'Then. Have they caught him? Who was he? You know, I used to go out walking the streets, looking at people. I used to look into their faces and think, Is it you? Did you kill my sister? Do you know who killed her?' He shook his head. 'It felt like I was losing my mind.'

'I used to see her,' Naomi said quietly. 'When I came round to your house, she'd be there. Sitting in front of the television, running down the stairs. Sitting on the old swing in the back yard. In the end, I just couldn't face it, seeing her.'

'So you stopped coming round?'

'Yeah. I guess so. Your mam was so proud when I was accepted into the police force. You know, she came to my passing out parade.'

'I know. She sent me a picture.' His voice had a smile in it. 'You looked so serious. I mean, not a crack of a smile. We were all proud of you, Nomi. And I know Mam thought, you know, that you were doing it for Helen.'

'And now this.'

'And now this,' Harry agreed. 'Back to waiting for the knock on the door.'

Six

Naomi had come home after her probation and found herself serving alongside the man who had meant so much to her in her childhood.

'I'm so proud of you, Nomi.'

He had stolen a moment privately, just as she was about to go off duty. She grinned at him, felt the slight flush rising to her cheeks at this, Joe Jackson's praise.

'It's good to be back,' she said. 'When I applied for the posting, I didn't hold out much hope really. Thought I might be stuck in London for the duration. And then, I was scared you might not be here still and I wanted you to know. Wanted you to see me . . .'

She was waffling. Gushing, as her grandma would say. Joe had slipped from her life these past years, but never from her mind. She gathered that her parents had slipped a quiet word to him about overdependency – God, but she had resented their interference – because Joe's calls to her had become less frequent and his replies to her own calls and letters briefer and more distant.

But now, she told herself, it was all going to be different. She was . . . well, if not his equal, at least his colleague. And she understood, she really did, that he could not be seen to show any favouritism . . . any extra concern. But Naomi knew, and now he had confirmed it, that she was special to him.

She grinned at him again; not that she had really stopped. 'It's good seeing you again, sir,' Naomi said.

It was mid morning on Lansdowne Road and Geoff Holmes, resident at number 43, had come back to collect some of the family's possessions. His arrival had caused a flurry of interest among the waiting journalists, who did not recognize either the car or its occupant, Geoff and his family having been long gone before their arrival.

'Mr Holmes?' DCI Travers reached out to shake the man's hand. 'We spoke on the phone. I really am sorry about all this.'

He led the resident inside. The hall carpet had been covered by tarpaulin and boards and the furniture from the living room had been stacked in the kitchen at the rear of the house. No one had quite worked out what they were going to do with it should the excavations extend to there.

Geoff Holmes stared through the partly open door. What had been floor was now a gaping hole surrounded by smashed concrete.

'We'll make good,' Dick Travers tried to reassure him. 'But I'm sorry, Mr Holmes, this will have to be your last trip . . . you understand that this is a crime scene now.'

'I understand that this *was* our home.'

DCI Travers decided it was best if he didn't comment.

'She'll never come back here, you know. My wife, I mean. I don't think any of us could, not knowing . . .'

'We may not find anything. There may be nothing to find.'

'But you'll still have been here. We'll still know that you took the place apart, looking. That you lot touched our stuff, tramped through our home, ripped the place apart. It's like . . . like . . .' He gave up and turned towards the stairs. 'Everything I want to get is up there. I hope I don't need an escort?'

'No, of course not. I'll leave you in peace to get on, Mr Holmes. Just give me a shout when you're ready to leave. You understand I have to check all visitors in and out.'

'Visitors!' Geoff Holmes glared at him, then muttered something under his breath and stomped away up the stairs. Travers could hear him moving around, opening drawers, slamming cupboard doors. He sighed, knowing that nothing he could say or do would make it better.

A car pulling up outside attracted his attention and a moment later he was greeting Alec Friedman.

'Thought you were in court this morning?'

'A witness failed to attend. We've been dismissed while they chase it up.'

'Mr Holmes has come to collect some stuff. I've told him, anything else he'll have to send for. If it'd been up to me he wouldn't have been let on site, but Phillips had already cleared it.'

Alec shrugged. 'Got to keep the public happy, I suppose.' These days Phillips seemed more concerned with public relations than with police work. 'Not that there's anything to see,' he added.

'Except the bloody great hole in the living-room floor. Holmes reckons they'll not come back here, even if we find nothing.'

'I can understand that, I suppose,' Alec said. 'Naomi called me last night. She'd had a visit from Henry Jones. He wanted to know if she had any more on this that we were telling.'

Travers shook his head. 'Wish there *was* more to tell,' he commented.

'Like the name on the confession?'

Travers laughed. 'Nice try, Alec.'

'It's got to come out some time.'

'But not yet. When . . . if, we find Helen, and personally I don't hold out much hope on that, it will be time to release names. Until then, no name, no pack drill. My guess is that we're here on a very expensive wild goose chase. If that's the case, then there's no sense digging the dirt if there's no dirt to dig.'

'And if we find Helen?'

'Then we cross that bridge, don't we?' He shrugged and the two men fell silent as Geoff Holmes came down the stairs, laden down with bags.

'I'll get someone to give you a hand with those,' Travers told him, 'and I'll have officers keep the press pack at bay while you go through.' He gestured to the uniformed officer standing close to the door. The PC took several of the bags and Geoff Holmes nodded what might have been thanks. Alec got the feeling that the man simply could not trust himself to speak. He watched him go.

'And if we find nothing here, do we move on to the next house?' he asked.

Travers shuddered, 'Don't even think it,' he said.

Geoff Holmes drove off and the digging crew moved back in. Alec and Dick Travers moved outside to where they could hear themselves speak.

'Anything on the reconstruction last night?' enquired Alec.

Travers frowned. 'A couple of names we didn't have before. We've had two calls from neighbours who reckon that the man next door is a pervert or some such. No direct connection with Sarah Clarke's disappearance, but we'll check it out. And a possible . . . to say witness would be stretching it. A woman who thinks she might have seen a man shouting at a little girl. The child was crying, but at the time the woman thought nothing of it. She thinks the child might have looked like Sarah and she thinks it might have been on the right evening.' He nodded towards the marked police car standing a few yards away. 'I've told dispatch to dump it all through to the printer and seeing as you're here, you can follow up the witness and the suspicious neighbours.'

'Can't uniform do that? It sounds like a routine call.'

'I'd rather not under the circumstances. Both are on the Radleigh Estate. I don't need a repeat of last year.'

Alec flinched. Radleigh was what was commonly seen as a sink estate. A dumping ground for the local authorities, it was filled with broken families living on the poverty line and unemployed youngsters who hung around the street corners with nowhere to go and nothing better to do. It was a mire of tightly packed town houses and shit holes of high-rises, half of them sitexed up and left empty because even the hopeless still had some dignity left and to move to the Radleigh was often seen as the final move. You couldn't get any lower without climbing into the sewers.

Last summer, there had been a rumour – only a rumour – that some newly released paedophile had been placed in one of the flats. For an estate already so drained of life that is was tinder dry, the rumour had been enough. Fifteen nights of rioting; fifteen days of community relations nightmare.

Alec could see what Travers meant, but he didn't figure

that simply losing the uniform would fool anyone on the Radleigh.

'They'll still know exactly what I am,' he commented, 'and what I'm there for.' He shrugged. 'Our informants ready for a visit are they?'

'One won't give a damn. Viccy Elliot. Rathbone Street.'

Alec groaned. The Elliot clan, three generations of them, were so well known there was talk of naming the custody suite in their honour.

'The other doesn't want a visit. Mrs Anonymous.'

'There's a surprise. Both name the same man, do they?'

Travers nodded. 'Nothing on him our end. It's probably a no show but go and wave the flag. Discretely.'

'I'll do my best. Know anyone with a big dog I can borrow?'

'Scared, Alec?'

'Me? No. I just want something to guard the car. I like it with the hub caps on.'

Naomi had arranged with Henry to go and visit his mother. He collected her at ten and they drove the mile or so back to the streets where she and Helen had grown up.

Harry said little as he drove, he seemed awkward and tense. He asked if she had heard anything more from Alec, but it was clear from his voice that he had no expectations. It was only when he stopped the car that he said more.

'I didn't sleep well,' he told her, explaining his quietness. 'I woke up at two and Mam was crying. I heard her through the bedroom wall. I got up and made us all tea. We sat up for the next hour or two, drinking tea and trying not to talk about it. You know, it's only since having Patrick that I've really been able to understand what they went through after Helen. The thought of someone, anyone or anything taking my son away is more than I can bear. It was bad enough when he lived with his mother, but at least I could still talk to him.' He laughed briefly. 'God, but you should have seen the size of my phone bills. I could still go and visit him. I still knew that he was out there, living his life, playing with his friends, getting into trouble at school, doing the things kids do. But when we lost

Helen . . . it was final, but it wasn't final. You know what I mean.'

She felt him looking at her and nodded her head.

'She wasn't out there, being and doing or anything like that, but she wasn't anywhere else, either. There was no grave to visit. There was no finality. And last night, it just hit home. All these years, we've half expected her to walk back through the door. Somehow, we've still waited for her to come home and now I think we all realize that she never will.'

Alec parked directly outside the Elliot house, hoping he'd be able to keep an eye on the car. Uniformed patrols drove double-crewed on the Radleigh and he was conscious of being alone and just a tad bit exposed. Someone in the Elliot clan must have been watching from the window because the door opened before he reached it and Viccy Elliot, cigarette in hand, waved him inside, directing him through to the kitchen.

'Sit down, I'll make you a cuppa.'

'Er, thanks.'

She gave him a sideways look and then filled the kettle. A child took up station in the kitchen doorway, one finger rammed firmly up its left nostril and its gaze fixed on Alec's face. Alec wasn't certain what sex it was, only that it was small and mucky and still dressed in pyjamas, despite it being close on midday.

Viccy Elliot grabbed an ashtray from the window sill and sat down opposite Alec. She glanced over at the child. 'Go and play with yer brother,' she commanded. 'And git yer finger out yer nose.'

She shrugged elaborately. 'Kids,' she commented.

'One of yours?'

'No, that's Sandra's youngest. Sandra's one of mine. She's back at college, training to be a computer something. I told her, you've got a good brain, my girl. You get back to school and leave the little 'uns with me. She takes her Allen to the crèche now, but Kyle and Wayne aren't out of nappies yet, so they'll not take them.'

The kettle boiled and she got up to make tea. The remains of the breakfast pots still lined the sink, but the mugs she took from the cupboard looked clean enough. Viccy Elliot was a big woman with her hair pulled back from her round face and tied into a tight ponytail. She dominated the room and Alec knew from past experience that she also dominated her extended clan and a good part of the Radleigh estate.

She placed a bright red mug on the table in front of him. A tea bag still floated in the brownish water and she dropped a teaspoon into the mix. 'Take the bag out when the colour's right,' she said. 'Drop it in the ash tray. Take sugar do you?'

Alec helped himself to sugar. He said, 'Word is you're worried about one of your neighbours?'

She shuddered elaborately and flicked the ash from her cigarette. 'Bloody pervert.'

'What makes you think that, Viccy?'

'Anyone can see it. Lives on his own in Bentham House. Always creeping around, don't speak to no one. Spends ages just staring out of his windows, looking at the kids playing in the schoolyard.'

'And that's it?' He hadn't expected much but had hoped there might be a little bit more. And he had to admit, had he been a lone male, living on the Radleigh, he might well also have been accused of 'creeping around'. Nervously.

Viccy snorted her disapproval. 'You got kids, have you?'

'No, I don't have kids.'

'Then you won't get it, will you.'

'Get what, Viccy?'

'The nose for it. You get kids, you get a feeling about people. And he's no good. I'm telling you. You'll be going to do something?'

'I'll be talking to him, yes.'

'Talk. That's all you lot ever do.'

Alec took a deep breath. 'Viccy, I understand your concerns, but we none of us want a repetition of last summer, do we. It didn't do anyone any good, least of all the Radleigh.'

Viccy Elliot was not impressed. 'If anyone had taken notice in the first place, there wouldn't have been no trouble.'

'There wasn't anything to take notice of,' Alec insisted. 'The man you were all so set against had no criminal record.

He wasn't what you thought he was. He was just some guy who'd divorced his wife and had been re-housed here.'

'And why had she divorced him? Tell me that. She came down here, you know. Said he'd interfered with their kids. Their littl'un had told her so.'

'And as far as I know, there was no proof of that either. She withdrew her statement, Viccy. Admitted they'd been through a messy divorce and she wanted to get her own back. If I'd had anything to do with it she'd have been charged with wasting police time and incitement. There are still burned-out houses down the road that haven't been set to rights yet. I can't believe you'd ever want a repeat of that.'

Viccy Elliot regarded him with cold grey eyes. 'You've never lived anywhere like this, have you?'

'No,' Alec admitted. Childishly, he'd have loved to counter her with some story of a deprived childhood or a misspent youth, but he had none to offer. He'd had a comfortable childhood and an easy run from then on in.

'Then you'll not understand. No one out there looks out for us, so we do it for ourselves and we do it our way.'

Alec sighed and tried another tack. 'Why mention this man now? He's been here six months already. If you'd had worries, why not voice them before?'

''Cause we don't judge people the way you think we do. We just left him to it, let him be. Then he started taking interest in a young lass what lives on the landing below. Fourteen, she is, maybe looks a bit more when she's got her face on ready to go out, but he sees her in her school clothes, often enough. He knows.'

'Viccy . . .' Alec hesitated. 'Viccy, sometimes youngsters play up to older men. You've been mother to enough to know that.' Viccy had four female offspring that Alec could name. Feisty girls, like their mother, and two of them at least in frequent trouble with the law. The one she had mentioned earlier, Sandra, he hadn't known about, so maybe she was cut from different cloth.

Viccy Elliot glared at him. 'You think we don't know the difference,' she said. 'The girl's mam went up and told him to lay off and he just gave her a mouthful. Hangs around, he

35

does, waiting for her to come home and then we saw him on the telly.'

'I'm sorry?'

Viccy waved her cigarette impatiently in his direction. 'That reconstruction thing last night. You know about that little Sarah girl at Philby. He was in the crowd, watching every move.'

Seven

It was certainly not a crime to be present at a reconstruction, but nonetheless it was interesting that this man, whom Viccy was so insistent had shown inappropriate interest in one young girl, should be present at the reconstruction of another's murder.

Alec was fairly willing to bet that the second Radleigh caller had been the girl's mother. The girl's name, Viccy told him, was Emma Sanders and the name meant nothing to Alec, which probably meant that the Sanders had no history, police-wise. Alec knew the Radleigh well and was familiar with most of the regulars.

He left his car outside Viccy's house, only half-assured by her promise to keep an eye on it, and walked the hundred or so yards to the three-storey block known as Bentham House.

Bentham was low rise and therefore counted more desirable that many buildings on the Radleigh. It was also one of the few blocks that had provision for single residents, most dwellings on the Radleigh being designated for families only. The address he had been given was on the top landing but there was no answer when Alec rang the bell.

'He'll be at work.'

Alec turned to the woman who had just come up the stairs, hauling several bags of shopping.

'Work?'

'Yes. He got a job, couple weeks ago. Warehouse on the Murry Industrial Estate.' She lowered the bags to the floor and began to rummage for her key.

'I don't suppose you know where?'

She glanced sideways at Alec, still rooting for her key and

not really interested. 'Hammond's,' she said. 'That mail order place. He's a picker. The Job Centre sent him.'

She found her key and heaved the bags inside.

'Thanks,' Alec told her.

'Her downstairs, is it?'

'Sorry?'

'Making trouble for him? Calling you lot in.' She looked him up and down. 'Police or social, aren't you? Well, I'll tell you, Gary's done nothing to anyone here. It's that girl downstairs, throwing herself at anything in trousers. Her mam's been at it years and the girl's no better than she should be.'

'If you think he's so innocent, how come you're being so helpful?' Alec wondered aloud, but the woman shot him a withering glance and took herself inside.

The possible witness who may have seen Sarah Clarke with a man on the night of her death was only ten minutes from the Radleigh but might have been a world away. Neat streets of modern houses on the outskirts of Philby town with their tiny squares of cropped green turf in front and white net curtains defending them from the outside world.

Alec rang the bell and introduced himself to the woman who opened the door.

'Oh,' she said. 'I'm so glad you're not in uniform. The neighbours . . . well, you know how people talk.'

'Can I come in, Mrs Peters?' Alec asked, 'it will only take a few minutes, I'm sure.'

'Of course, of course. Would you like some tea?'

Alec declined and followed the middle-aged woman through to the lounge. She was a small woman with greying hair that had been over-permed. Little make-up and wearing a neat, if somewhat dowdy checked dress. He sat down at one end of a large green sofa while she took one of the chairs and Alec noted, almost absently, that the green of the sofa exactly matched the regency stripes decorating the fireplace wall.

'You called us, Mrs Peters. You might have seen something on the night Sarah Clarke was killed.'

She waved her hands ineffectually as though trying to push the thoughts away. 'That poor, poor child,' she said.

'Of course, it may have been nothing. But when I saw the television last night, I knew that I just had to ring. My husband said I should.'

'I'm glad you did, Mrs Peters,' Alec told her. 'As you say, it might be nothing, but it's better to be sure.' This was going to be a long haul, Alec told himself, wishing that this at least had been handed over to uniform and not to him. The Viccy Elliots of this world he could deal with, but middle-class, elderly ladies who reminded him of his Aunt Beatrice always managed to throw him off balance. In their presence, he felt like a child again, a child waiting patiently to be allowed to leave the table while the adults around him talked and ignored him and gave him no chance to interrupt.

'So, the little girl you saw, Mrs Peters. This was close to the fish and chip shop on Eldon Street? And what time do you think that would have been?'

Alec left almost an hour later little wiser than when he had arrived. Joan Peters had been walking down towards the sea front having arranged to meet her sister on the promenade. She was running a little late and so walked quickly and would like as not have taken no notice of the man and what she had taken to be his little girl if they had not quite literally crossed the path in front of her.

'He came barging across, holding the child by the hand and she was crying, you know, snivelling, not fully fledged crying. I remember thinking, Oh *there's* someone that can't get their own way. You know how children behave when you tell them they can't do something, or have something?'

Alec nodded wisely.

'Well, it was like that. He had her by the hand and she was dragging her feet and snivelling and he was telling her to come on.'

'Did he seem angry, Mrs Peters, or just irritated?'

She thought about it. 'Oh, not really angry. More frustrated, I suppose. They can be so vexing, children, and I just thought it was a father and daughter having a set-to. I used to hate it when mine showed me up in the street, so I looked away, I suppose. I didn't think the poor man would want me staring at him, but then, when I realized what night it was, I thought I'd better say something.'

'And before, when you first saw the news about Sarah's murder. You didn't think to mention it then?'

She looked embarrassed. 'You see, it was a Thursday.'

'I'm sorry, I don't see . . .'

'I usually meet my sister on a *Tuesday*. It didn't strike me until last night that the day was wrong. You see I met her this week as well and we had to change it to a Thursday – yesterday, you see – and we ran into all the fuss on the sea front and Margaret said to me "Just fancy, the last time we met on a Thursday that poor little thing was being murdered not a hundred yards up the beach!" She was exaggerating, of course, because as soon as we met we went down to the Elysee, that's the restaurant at the other end of the promenade, so we were much further away than that, but . . . well, that reminded me, don't you see?'

Alec did see. He pressed her for a description of the child and of the man. Both were vague. The child was blonde and dressed in jeans and a pink shirt, she thought. The man, well, not very tall, but not short either and also blonde. Medium build and ordinary, though she thought she might recognize him again and agreed that she should come to look at pictures at the station.

Alec left, feeling shell-shocked, and told her that someone would be in touch to arrange for her to look at the mug shots. And it would be worth showing her the TV footage from last night, too. See if she could pick out the man that Viccy Elliot had been so worried by. Gary Williams was his next stop.

The industrial estate where Gary Williams worked was only a short distance away. It had been built in the last few years and, apart from a few small units, seemed mostly to consist of warehouses and distribution centres for the big mail order companies and the supermarket chains.

If the man was innocent then Alec had no wish to screw up his chances in his new job, so he told the duty manager that Gary Williams was needed in connection with a witness statement he had made, something that needed clarification. A few minutes later Alec was interviewing Mr Williams in the manager's office.

'What's this about a witness statement? I never made any witness statement.'

'I know that, Mr Williams, but I didn't think it would go down too well if I told your manager this was in connection with Sarah Clarke.'

'Sarah Clarke?' Williams looked blank.

'The little girl who was murdered at Philby a few weeks' ago.' You must know whom I mean, Mr Williams. You were interested enough to attend the reconstruction last night.'

'The what? I don't know what you're on about.'

'But you were in Philby last night. Standing on the sea front. You were caught on camera.'

Williams shook his head.

'Let me remind you,' Alec told him. 'Big crowd of people. Police officers swarming like flies. A child from Sarah's school retracing her last known movements. If you looked hard enough you probably saw Sarah's mum in amongst the crowd. You could tell it was her because she couldn't stop crying from the moment it began.'

'I was there last night, yes. I didn't take much notice though, of what was going on, I mean. No law against going for a pint after work, is there?'

'Hardly your local, is it?'

'I met friends. Friends that live there. That all right with you?'

'And can I have their names, these friends?'

'Why? What's it to you?' He stood up suddenly, his hands clenching. 'It's that bitch downstairs, isn't it? Fucking cunt. She's had it in for me big time.'

'As it happens, this has nothing to do with Mrs Sanders, but since you mention her, maybe she didn't like the attention you were paying to her daughter. Emma is what? Fourteen, I believe.'

'Way she come on to me she weren't fourteen.' He shrugged uncomfortably. 'Look, I didn't know the kid's age. Thought she was a good couple of years older than that. Soon as I found out I sent her packing.'

'Even sixteen would have been a little young for you, I would have thought. What are you, Mr Williams? Thirty.'

'I'm twenty-eight. Not that it's got fuck all to do with you. Anyway, what's that got to do with the dead kid out at Philby?'

'You tell me, Mr Williams? Maybe your friends could shed some light.'

Williams turned towards the door. 'I ain't got nothing to say,' he told Alec. 'You want to talk to me, fucking well arrest me. I've got work to do.'

'I can do that, if it suits you better, Mr Williams, but I hardly think it would give a good impression to your new boss.'

Williams froze with his hand on the door. Then he seemed to make up his mind. The shoulders squared and he opened the door. 'I ain't done nothing,' he said. 'Now just leave me alone.'

Alec let him go. Williams' attitude was not what he had expected. Most people acted passively, showed concern when the police came to their place of work. They didn't in general display that much direct aggression and he didn't relish the thought of taking the man in alone.

Alec got up and crossed over to the door. Through the glass panel he could see Gary Williams talking to his manager. Alec took the mobile phone from his pocket and called Travers and minutes later a double-crewed car of uniformed officers was on its way to arrest Gary Williams.

Eight

*'Don't ever lose touch with the past,' Joe Jackson told
her. 'Don't cling to it so tightly that you can't move on,
but always keep your finger on the pulse of it. That way, you'll
never forget the lessons learnt. Or the important stuff, like the
people you shared it with.'*

It was strange to be in Helen's home once more after so long a
gap. Helen's mother had greeted her at the door, folding Naomi
in her arms as she had done all those years ago when Naomi had
still been only a child. Mari Jones had always been that kind of
a woman, warm and welcoming and overt in her emotions.

Naomi found herself on the verge of tears.

'I'm so glad you've come,' Mari told her. 'Especially
now.'

'I'm glad I came too,' Naomi told her, surprised at how much
she meant it. It had always amazed her that Mari had never put
any blame on Naomi for her child's disappearance. That just
wasn't Mari's way, though there had been times when the pain
of forgiveness had been so great that Naomi would almost have
been relieved had it been replaced by the pain of blame.

'Cool dog. Can I stroke him?'

The voice was young. Eager, but a little bit uncertain.

'You must be Patrick? Sure you can. His name's Napoleon.'

She felt him kneel down beside her in the cramped little
hallway and Napoleon reach forward curiously to sniff this
stranger before remembering that he was on duty and should
behave.

'Take his harness off,' she told the boy, 'then he knows
it's play time.'

'Great. He's brilliant. How long have you had him? How old his he?'

Naomi started to reply, but Mari was laughing and leading her through to the living room.

'Take him out in the yard, Patrick . . . If that's all right,' she asked Naomi. 'Harry, you make us all some tea. Nomi, there's a chair just near the door, it's a bit cramped, so watch your leg. I'll sit you on the sofa, if that's OK, there's a table next to it for your tea.'

Naomi allowed herself to be organized, putting out her hand to get her bearings when Mari stopped and gently turned her round. Once seated, Mari took her hand and showed her where the table was. 'We've had a change round in here since your last visit,' she said. 'Got a new three-piece. It's dark blue, like the curtains you used to like so much, though they fell apart long since.'

Naomi laughed. 'It sounds different in here,' she said. 'Bigger.'

'The book shelves have gone. We moved the whole lot upstairs to the little room, though now Patrick's here, they're in the way up there as well. Mac always loved his books, though. I couldn't just get rid of them.'

Mac had been Helen's father. A gentle man, Naomi remembered. Quiet-spoken and with a diffident manner very like Harry's. He had, as Mari said, loved his books and his pub quizzes and Mastermind on television, the one time in the week when he insisted on control of the programmes. He had died three years before, but Naomi had been in court the day of the funeral and her promise to herself that she would call round and see his widow had gone unkept.

'I wish I'd come before,' she whispered. 'Oh, Mari, I have missed you all.'

For the best part of an hour they talked, catching up on news and going over what they already knew about the search.

'A young man from the local station called round,' Mari told Naomi. 'He said that they were starting to look for her again. That some new evidence had come up and they thought they might know where she was. I couldn't believe it. After all this time.

44

'Then Detective Travers called me and asked if we could talk. He came to see us. Harry had arrived by then – I'd asked him if he could come, just for a little while. You know, it felt so strange. Anyway, this Detective Travers came here and told me that someone had confessed, but he couldn't tell me who. He asked question after question about what happened. Not just when Helen disappeared, but afterwards, when the police were investigating. That surprised me a bit, Naomi, I thought they'd have had all that on record.'

'They would,' Naomi confirmed, 'but it was so long ago the files would all have been archived. Files more than ten years old are stored elsewhere, we just don't have room for everything at the local nick. It might have taken a day or two to get them sent over and there would have been a lot to sift through.'

Mari nodded her understanding, then realized that Naomi could not see. 'That must have been why,' she said.

'What kind of things did he want to know?' Naomi asked her.

'Oh, what kind of things . . . he asked about Joe Jackson and if he'd been the investigating officer from the start. We talked about what happened the day Helen went . . . how long it was before anyone realized. I told him the school was really good like that. If the parents didn't phone in, then the school called the parents to say their kiddie wasn't there and were they ill. The school called me about half past ten.

'I came out of work and went straight up there. I couldn't understand it.'

Naomi nodded. She remembered as if it were yesterday.

'It was break time, just at the end of break, when you arrived,' she said. 'Josie was looking out of the window and she said, "Look, there's Helen's mum." You were hurrying up the path towards the entrance.'

'And I looked up, and saw you,' Mari continued. 'And then I knew . . . I knew for certain something was wrong. I'd thought at first that you and Helen . . . that you and Helen had bunked off together. When I saw you standing, looking out of the window like that and I saw your face, then I knew –' her voice trembled and Naomi could hear the tears in it – 'I knew even then that I'd lost her. That Helen was gone.'

Naomi was not sure who had suggested they walk that path, the way of Helen's final journey, but there seemed to be a consensus that they should. She let Patrick take Napoleon on the lead and she held Harry's arm. She could hear the boy and dog crashing through the bushes on the waste ground.

'Come out of the mud, Pat,' Harry complained. 'You're going to ruin your shoes.'

'They're my old ones, Dad,' Patrick shouted back. He sounded quite a way off and Naomi could hear him calling to Napoleon. She could almost feel the dog enjoying the freedom of running. In the distance, she could hear the voices of children drifting over from the schoolyard. Their squeals and yells carried on the light breeze.

She stopped still, trying to use the sound to get her bearings. 'Which way is the church?' she asked.

'Um, just over there,' Harry told her. 'Oh, sorry,' he took her shoulders and turned her around. 'Directly in front of you now.'

'Right, so the allotments are over that way and the little gap where we cut through to school was somewhere –' she raised her hand and pointed off to her left – 'somewhere over there.'

Harry took her hand and moved it slightly. 'There,' he said.

Naomi nodded. In her mind's eye she reviewed the scene. The waste land had once also been allotments but had been sold off for redevelopment which had never taken place. It was a hillocky, hollowed place, with the remnants of old gardens visible in the straggling brambles and the fruit trees and odd stands of self-seeded flowers. In summer it had been a place to play and make dens, but in winter it was left to the rabbits and foxes and the odd trail-biker, shattering the peace until the police were called.

The waste ground was almost surrounded by terraced streets and the rear view of the houses and their garden walls had been a familiar one. Mothers would shout for their children to come back, leaning over the garden walls and cupping their hands to make the sound carry. A Victorian church, red brick and sternly proper, filled the gap between the end of Helen's street and the iron foundry, derelict now and also earmarked for redevelopment that never happened. Beyond that was the doctor's surgery, the trees of the back garden tall enough to mark the boundary and the local shop with the maisonette above. A girl in Naomi's class had lived there. It had a fire escape running down the back of the building, the top of which could just be seen.

Then the allotments that remained and the path across the wasteland took a dog-leg into a copse and Helen knew from childhood experience that the view of anyone entering the copse was then blocked, even in winter, by the density of trees.

To the best of anyone's knowledge, this was where Helen had disappeared.

'Take me to the trees,' she told Harry.

'I brought him here,' Mari told her. 'That Inspector Travers. Showed him where Helen waited on the corner and then we walked the route. I told him it was hardly changed.'

Helen took a deep breath. 'If I'd met her that morning,' she said. 'If I'd just—'

'Then like as not they'd be looking for you, too,' Mari told her harshly. She reached out and took Naomi's hand. Her fingers were plump and soft, the wedding band tight on a finger which had once been girlish and slender. 'A man that could take Helen like that could have taken both of you, and one child gone is more than enough for anyone or anywhere.'

She squeezed Naomi's hand and the younger woman returned the gesture, but the old feelings had returned and were choking her. Blame me, please, she wanted to say. I'd almost rather you could hate me, at least . . . at least . . . But she couldn't think of an at least. It was her own failure that she could not face, Naomi knew that. Her own self-hatred that ate her and if Mari had added to that, in truth she didn't know if she could have gone on living.

'Who *did* confess?' Mari was wondering. 'I mean, surely they have to say sooner or later.'

'Alec says they want to wait until they find her,' Naomi said. 'If they released the name and it turned out to be some kind of fabrication, it would be really hard to retract, especially once the media got hold of it.'

'I suppose so. But, Nomi, who would fabricate anything like that?'

'I don't know, but people *do*. Every murder case has people confessing who couldn't possibly have anything to do with the case.'

'That's not likely this time though, is it?' Harry argued. 'I mean, surely they wouldn't start digging on Lansdowne Road without good reason?'

'I don't know. I'm guessing that there must have been something in the confession that tallied with the case notes. Something that wasn't generally known. I don't think they started digging until several days after they'd been given the confession. Travers would have had time to check at least the basic case notes by then, verify whatever it was.'

Patrick and Napoleon thundered up behind them. 'We're at the trees, aren't we?' Naomi enquired.

'Yes,' Harry confirmed.

Naomi let go of his arm and reached out, taking a few hesitant steps forward. The bark of the closest tree was damp beneath her fingers and grainy with moss and lichen. The ground was wet and soft here, her feet slid and Harry's hand was suddenly clenched around her elbow.

'I'm all right.' She moved away again. The trees seemed to close in around her and she lifted her face to gaze upwards with unseeing eyes into the leafless canopy and beyond to the bright blue sky. She could feel the heat filtered through the leaves, shifting across her face as the canopy shielded and then broke, the sunlight dappled on her skin.

'Is this where it happened?' Patrick sounded awed.

'Somewhere here. We're not far from the road and we're out of sight of the houses. She was seen, running into the trees, then she disappeared.'

'How big is the wood?'

'Not very. It's long and narrow and runs parallel with the road. It always seemed bigger because the trees are so close

48

together and in summer the undergrowth is dense. You have to push your way through the nettles and brambles, but in the centre there's a clear space, not big but almost circular. Helen loved it there. She called it our secret place and we must have come here nearly every day in the summer.'

'Cool,' Patrick said.

Naomi smiled. It must be hard for him, she reflected, caught up in this episode of family history. The ghost of Helen haunting the life of another generation.

'Can we see it? Your and Helen's secret place?'

'If we can get through.'

'I think I'll go back, if you don't mind,' Mari said.

'Oh, Mari, I'm sorry. I'm not thinking, am I?'

Mari squeezed her hand. 'It's all right, love, but I've not even walked around here if I could help it, not in years. Then I brought that detective here and now you, but I don't think I can go into the wood. Not today.'

'Will you be all right? Harry, you go back with your mum. Patrick can look after me.'

She could feel the boy shift uncertainly and imagined him looking at his father with a mix of eagerness and apprehension.

'I'll be fine on my own,' Mari objected, but Harry had apparently made up his mind.

'I'll make some tea for when you get back,' he said. 'Patrick, you keep hold of Naomi's arm.'

The boy nodded. He slid a nervous hand through Naomi's arm and took a deep breath. 'Which way do we go?' he said.

It was harder to get through the undergrowth than Naomi recalled, but then she had been much smaller then and could more easily slip through. Walking side by side with Patrick holding her arm proved to be impossible and in the end he had taken her hand, moving slightly ahead of her and telling her where to put her feet. As they moved on, his confidence grew and their trek became a game. 'Right foot forward about six inches then you can put your hand on the tree trunk while I shift the bramble. Hey, we should have brought the wood axe from the shed. Now, you can come forward a long pace, here, give me your hand again.'

Napoleon nosed against her leg and pushed through ahead of her.

'We could always get down and crawl,' Naomi said. 'Napoleon seems to be moving fast enough.'

'Yeah, but he doesn't mind the nettles! Watch your hand on that blackberry bush. It's got fruit on it. We'll have to come back when they're ready.'

'We'll come back, but you can pick the fruit,' she said. 'I'll just help you eat it.'

Patrick laughed, then, 'Wow,' he said. 'We're there, Naomi.' He took her hand again and led her into the centre of the clearing. 'Cool.'

He let go of her and she could feel him moving across the bright circle. 'Is it OK to sit down?' she asked him. 'No thistles or anything?'

'Oh, sorry. No, it's just grass there, or there's a log over here. It's dry.'

'I'll come over then. Keep talking and I can find you. Is there anything I'm going to trip over?'

'No, it's just short grass. And some rabbit shit . . . sorry, droppings.'

She laughed and seated herself on the fallen tree. 'What do you do with yourself all day? Isn't it boring for you here?'

He sat down beside her and she could feel him shrug. 'It's all right,' he said. 'I mean, Gran's nice and everything, but everyone's so upset and . . . you know. I feel like I should be serious all the time and when I laugh at something I feel kind of guilty.'

'I'm sure they don't mean to make you feel that way. It must be hard though.' She fell silent for a moment and then said softly, 'I remember, in the months after Helen went missing, I felt like that. I felt that my life had been sliced in half and only the sad part was left. My mum tried to get me out of myself and took me to see a comedy film at the cinema. Helen had been missing for about four months then and whether we liked it or not, life was back to normal for most people. I had to try so hard not to laugh. We watched the film and people all around me were laughing and giggling and, you know, just enjoying themselves the way people are meant to do. And I had to really work at not doing the same. I thought, if I laugh at this, I'm betraying Helen. I'm letting her down because Helen can't do that any more.'

The conversation was, she thought, getting a little heavy for a fifteen-year-old, but to her surprise Patrick nodded, he was sitting close enough for her to feel it when he did. 'I feel like that,' he said, 'but you know, everyone keeps telling me what a happy person Helen was. I think she'd hate it to know we felt like that.'

Out of the mouths of babes, Naomi thought absently. She smiled. 'Helen *was* a happy person,' she confirmed softly.

'Live for Helen, too,' Joe Jackson had told her only a little after that trip to see the film. She had reluctantly confided in him when her mother had asked him to have a word. 'And every time you laugh, think of it as laughing for Helen, too.'

Nine

A lec called her at home to say he would not be coming round that night.

'I didn't expect you would, I heard the news. You've made an arrest in the Sarah Clarke murder.'

Alec sighed. 'We've brought a man in for questioning, that's all. And *we* didn't release that information.'

'But you must have something on him to bring him in.'

'Rumour and more rumour and a distinct lack of cooperation when I went to ask him a few questions. Not a lot else. How was your day?'

'Interesting. I went to see Helen's mum. Harry picked me up. His son thinks that Napoleon is the best dog he's ever met and I suspect Napoleon is equally infatuated.'

Hearing his name, the dog shifted position and Naomi heard his tail begin to thump upon the floor.

'Traitor,' Alec said. 'You tell that double-crossing dog that I'm the man in his life. Look,' he added, 'I've got to run. I'll call you later or maybe tomorrow. Depends how things go.'

Naomi felt oddly bereft when she had put down the phone. In fact, it had turned into a far more pleasant day that she felt it had a right to be. They had returned to Mari's house after a couple of hours' absence to find Harry ready to come looking for them. By that time, she and Patrick had decided that it was worthwhile them becoming friends. Naomi had little to do with teenagers as a rule, but she liked this boy and by the time he had helped her back on to the path and they were heading for home, they had discussed everything from school – he hated it – to computer games – 'Final Fantasy rocks!' – to what it was like living back in England with his father – OK, a bit boring sometimes, but better than with his mum's husband.

Their lightened mood affected the others and the afternoon was spent with memories that had nothing to do with Helen's death. Old photos were pulled out and described in detail. Naomi remembered most of them. The parties, school plays and trips. Holidays and Christmases. Harry talked with unusual freedom and ease and Patrick questioned, taking advantage, Naomi guessed, of his father's unusual mood in order to fill in the gaps in his family history.

She liked Harry. Staid and somewhat formal though he was, she liked him and enjoyed his rather old-world manners.

Alec, well, Alec was different. Assured and sometimes flippant, and just as important as Alec the man, was the Alec of their shared past. And they had settled into an easy, relaxed relationship which she didn't think either of them thought was serious, but which nevertheless bound them and kept them from others.

She crossed to the window and felt for the clock. It had a large button on top and when she pressed it an electronic voice told her that it was nine twenty-five. Too early to go to bed, but even so, she felt tired. She made herself a snack and then showered, taking her time and making it last as long as she decently could. When she checked the time again it was half past ten. She got into bed, Napoleon settling himself on the rug beside her, and within minutes she was asleep.

Alec's time was dragging too, but for very different reasons. He had been cooped up in the interview room since four o'clock, taking time out only when the official meal break was called for his prisoner.

Since calling Naomi, his already shredded concentration had been further eroded. He sensed that it was not just Patrick and the dog that had hit it off so well. Naomi seemed quite keen on the company of Harry Jones.

Quite what she had said that had given him this notion, Alec couldn't say. It was more in her tone of voice, the lightness and almost overcasual responses to his questions.

He shook himself mentally, telling himself that it was all in his imagination and then remembering that Naomi was a very attractive woman and had never wanted for attention.

53

'So, Mr Williams, tell me again about the night of the reconstruction. You say you had no idea of what was going on. You don't watch the news? See the papers?'

'I didn't see *that* on the news.'

'And on August the twelfth, Mr Williams. You still have no idea where you were that night? I've given you some thinking time, yet you've still not given me any answers.'

'I've told you, I don't keep a fucking diary. I was unemployed all summer, days are just days. One like the next.'

'But that one wasn't like the rest, was it? Sarah Clarke died.'

'And I'm sorry for it, all right? But it's nothing to do with me. I *heard* about it. I heard about it, I don't know, the next day, but it was fucking weeks ago. Do you know what you were doing that day without looking at your fucking diary?'

'It was a Thursday,' Alec said.

'So you told me. Thoughtful of you, I appreciate the help, but like I say, one day pretty much like the rest.'

Alec sighed. He had hoped by now to have the tape of the television broadcast showing Gary Williams at the scene, but there had been a hold up that afternoon and the best the TV station could do was to promise to courier the tape over the following day.

And an hour ago a message had been sent in to him. There was trouble on the Radleigh Estate. Nothing very specific, just groups of youths wandering the streets and residents gathering outside the block of flats where Gary Williams lived.

Alec knew from his experience on the Radleigh that more trouble was simply a matter of time.

Naomi had fallen into a deep sleep and she dreamed about Helen. This in itself was not an unusual thing, few nights passed when Helen did not figure at least obliquely in her dreams.

This time though, it was different. She dreamed that she was walking the path that crossed the waste ground. She was able to see, though the landscape had a distorted look as though she were seeing it through a fisheye lens.

Ahead of her, a child was running. She was dressed in navy blue, a school bag slung across her shoulder and a scarf, blue and white stripes with an edge of red flying out behind.

Helen, Naomi thought. Dressed the way she had been on the day she disappeared.

Naomi had no sense that she quickened pace, but she found herself suddenly right behind the fleeing child. She could hear Helen's panting breaths and the splash of black shod feet in deep brown, puddled mud. In her dream, Naomi reached out for her friend. She reached and touched her on the shoulder; she could feel the slight ribbed texture of the gabardine raincoat beneath her fingers and the woollen scarf brushing against her hand.

'Helen!' Naomi called her name, urgently, willing her to stop, to turn around.

The change happened without her being aware of it happening, but suddenly, Naomi no longer stood behind. She felt the weight of the school bag on her shoulder; the warm softness of the scarf circling her neck and the cold mud splashing against her legs, seeping through the white socks.

'What . . .' Naomi, no longer Naomi, gasped for breath. The bag was heavy and made it awkward to run. She felt leaden, weighed down by the bag and the bulky coat and, Naomi realized for the first time, choked by Helen's tears.

They, she, were between the trees now. A sudden movement startled her and Naomi Helen glanced sideways into the stark grey wood. And someone spoke, a man's voice, though she could not hear the words.

'Sorry? What? I'm going to be late . . .'

And then she felt a hand around her wrist and the bag slipping from her shoulder and the tall trees turning above her as though, abruptly, they lost balance and slipped on their own roots and the world moved forward at twice the speed it had any right to do.

She felt the breath knocked from her body. Lungs burning as she tried to draw breath and then almost blackness as something hit her head.

For a time she could not reckon, her senses refused to make sense and the world spun and hands groped at her clothes and her body burned with pain and then she could see his hands, one of them red with blood, reaching for her throat.

Naomi struggled to wake up. She struggled at the unknown force holding her until reason impinged enough to tell her that it was only the bed covers tangled across her chest.

Napoleon whined, his wet nose nuzzled at her hand.

She slid from the bed, wrapping her arms around the dog, burying her face in the soft black fur and clinging tight, sobbing desperately and unable to control the shaking that wracked her body. She had never felt so glad of the presence of any living thing in all her life as she was at that moment, and so grateful not to be alone.

Ten

Alec called while she was giving Napoleon his breakfast. 'They've found Helen,' he said.

At first, Naomi said nothing. She realized that she had been expecting this ever since waking from her dream the night before.

'Of course you have,' she said.

'Are you all right?'

'I'm fine. Really, I'm just fine. Does her family know yet?'

'No. I've been asked to go, take you too, if you're willing. Travers thought it might help.'

'That was nice of him,' she said, genuinely grateful to have been officially included, though she had the feeling that Alec would have asked her to go with him in any case.

'How soon can you be ready? I can be with you in fifteen minutes.'

'I'll be ready,' she promised him. She fumbled for the cradle and replaced the phone, aware that her hands were shaking and her chest was tight. She had known for all these years that Helen must be dead, but to be confronted by the reality was another thing again. She felt herself flush hotly and then as rapidly grow cold. A trickle of sweat ran down between her breasts. She reached out for the coffee mug she had left sitting on the counter, reached out so suddenly that she misjudged the movement and sent it crashing to the floor. She was still trying to tidy up the mess when Alec arrived.

'What happened?'

'I dropped a coffee mug. A full one. Alec, can you check I've got all the pieces? I had to shut Napoleon in the other room while I cleaned up, he kept trying to help and I'm scared in case he cut himself.'

Alec scrutinised the dog. 'He looks fine to me. But you've missed some by your foot.' He bent, she felt the heat of him close to her and as he straightened again she found herself clinging to him.

Alec held her, stroking the short dark hair. He smelt clean: shower gel and shampoo and fresh laundry, and when he bent his head to kiss her she tasted coffee and mint. Normal things in a world that, this morning, felt so desperately unreal.

'We should be going,' he told her gently. 'I've called ahead, told them we have news.'

Mari sat very still. Naomi could feel the stillness in the woman's body. She wanted to reach out and clasp the older woman's hand, but she could feel the tension in her arms and guessed that she had her hands clasped tightly in her lap. To take one or even cover them with her own would, she suspected, break through the calm and Naomi didn't want to force Mari into a storm she might not be ready to face.

'There was no evidence of clothing,' Alec said. 'Even after all this time we would have expected some fragments, but, at first sight, there don't seem to be any. You've got to understand,' he added hastily, 'I've only the preliminary reports to go on. They rushed those through to us this morning.'

'And you say she was found last night?'

Alec nodded. 'The diggers were working through. We had two shifts going. Apparently, they found a tiny bone set into the concrete about five o'clock last night. Until we got our experts in, we weren't even sure that it was human, but it was decided that our people should work on through and about three o'clock this morning, they found what we believe to be . . . we found human remains.

'She'd been wrapped in black plastic and then a piece of what seems to have been carpet, then covered with wood and rubble. The concrete . . . the concrete was poured over that.' He paused. 'We're lucky,' he said. 'These houses were built on a kind of concrete raft. Beneath that, it was hardcore and general rubble and that protected the burial somewhat. If . . .

if the concrete had been poured into the footings, there's very little chance we'd have found anything.'

'You're certain it's her?' Harry asked.

'As certain as we can be. Dental records have been sent for. They were already on file as I understand it.'

Naomi felt Mari nod. 'Joe . . . Detective Jackson, that is. After she'd been missing for a while, he talked to us, said we had to prepare ourselves, like. He thought we should get ourselves ready, in case . . . in case, so we asked our doctor and our dentist to release the records and put them on file.'

She sighed. 'You know, that was a hard thing to do, it was admitting that our little girl would not be coming back alive. But Joe was right, it had to be done sometime.'

'We found this,' Alec said, reaching into his pocket for an evidence bag. 'It's described in the original files and it's what makes us pretty certain this is Helen.'

'What is it?' Naomi asked.

'Her bracelet,' Mari told her. 'That little silver thing with the bells all around the rim. You both had one, remember?'

Naomi nodded. 'Of course I do.' They had bought them at the same time from a little shop in town that specialized in incense sticks and temple bells and bright silk scarves sewn with tiny mirrors. They had bought matching Indian bangles, decorated with mock cabochons of coloured enamel and trimmed with tiny round bells that jingled softly. As kids they had loved these scraps of exotica. Jewellery had not been allowed at school, but they wore them religiously, too and from, slipping the bracelets safely into their bags through the day and donning them again the moment they got out through the cast iron gates.

'If the killer took her clothes,' Harry said, 'why leave the bracelet?'

'Because it was a tight fit,' Naomi told him.

She felt Mari nod agreement. 'Helen had such plump little hands,' she said. 'Nomi was always so tall and skinny and Helen was always the other way.'

Silence fell and thickened in the tiny room. The tension finally seeping out of Mari's body, enough for her finally to be able to cry. Harry knelt on the floor beside his mother and held her tightly, making those small comforting noises that people make when words won't work. Naomi heard Alec get to his feet, judging that it was time to go and she rose, too. 'Mari, we're going now,' she said. 'Call me,' she added, reaching out in Harry's general direction, but she received no answer. Alec took her arm and led her back to his car.

'Helen was strangled,' Naomi said.

'What?'

'Helen. The way she died.'

'I know what you mean. I mean, how do you know?'

He sounded concerned, suspicious almost. 'Naomi?' he prompted. 'How can you know?'

'I don't, not really,' she admitted. She sighed, realizing just how stupid this was going to sound. 'I had this dream last night,' she told him. 'It was so real, so frightening, and it wasn't just about Helen. This time, I *was* Helen. I was running away and there was this man and I . . .'

She trailed off, feeling Alec's frown even though she could no longer see it. 'Sounds crazy put like that.'

Alec was silent for a moment. 'I'm not surprised you dream,' he said. 'Look, Naomi, you know as well as I do that most likely you're right. If someone asked me to bet on how she died that would come pretty high on my list.' He paused. 'But you felt there's more to it than that?'

He was, she felt, making a great effort to keep the scepticism from his voice.

'Sounds crazy,' she repeated. 'Alec, I know it does.' She tried to smile. 'Most likely you're right. All the stress of the case being reopened and then hearing about the little Clarke girl. I guess it was all playing on my mind last night.'

'Yes,' he agreed. 'Well, I'd be more surprised if it wasn't getting to you.'

He pulled the car in to the kerb outside her house.

'You coming in?' she asked.

'Can't, sorry. Still questioning our so-called suspect.'

'Progress?'

'Not so's you'd notice.' He kissed her goodbye and stood playing with Napoleon's ears while she searched for her key, but she could tell that he was eager to be gone. Work filling up his mind.

'You'll be all right?' he said, but it was more of a statement than a question.

'Sure,' she told him. She heard him drive away even before she had gone inside.

Eleven

The trouble on the Radleigh Estate had escalated overnight and found its focus in the shape of Gary Williams' flat.

Broken glass crunched beneath his feet as Alec stepped into the hall. The glass panel in the front door had been smashed and the door itself wrenched off its hinges and kicked to matchwood.

They hadn't bothered to thieve, Alec noted, but it was pretty obvious that even before the intruders had done their remodeling, Gary Williams hadn't owned a whole lot of anything. What little he had, someone had tackled with a baseball bat or slashed with a knife.

Drawers had been emptied, bed covers shredded, cheap cotton curtains ripped from their hooks and trampled underfoot. The imploded screen of the TV set glared blankly at him from the corner of the room, a handful of CDs jammed into the void.

SOCO were dusting for prints, adding grey powder to the general mess.

'Anything?'

'Plenty, mostly partials.'

Alec nodded. Turning back towards the door he felt something slide beneath his foot. Glancing down, he saw that his foot rested on a photograph of two small children. They were smiling at the camera. The face of one, a little boy, was smeared with ice cream – he still held the cone in a grubby hand. The girl, a little older and a whole lot neater, had already finished hers with only a smear of raspberry sauce across her cheek as evidence.

'There were others on the bedroom floor,' the SOCO told him. 'I picked them up and put them on the bedside cabinet.

Alec carried the photo through to the bedroom and perched on the edge of the bed while he looked through the rest. The same two children appeared in several more and others too in what looked like a family group. A woman who bore a striking resemblance to the little girl stood hand in hand with Gary Williams. He wore a suit and she was dressed in a pretty frock with flowers in her hair.

Williams had mentioned no family. When asked if they should contact anyone for him, he had said that there was no one.

Thoughtfully, Alec slipped the pictures into an evidence bag.

'You there, Alec?'

'In here.'

Travers leaned on the door surround and surveyed the mess. 'Did quite a job, didn't they? What do you have there?'

Alec handed him the plastic bag. 'Family photographs, I'd say. He kept stum about that, didn't he?'

Dick Travers flicked through the pictures and then handed them back. 'Divorced?'

'Probably. Explains this place. And the chip on his shoulder, I suppose.'

'Unless the chip came first.'

'Unless,' Travers agreed. 'You talked to the neighbours yet?'

Alec nodded. 'Next door, a woman called Cathy Walton, she works the twilight shift, saw nothing. Downstairs heard nothing, saw nothing and don't give a damn either way. And I guess Viccy Elliot speaks for the whole community when she suggests that Gary Williams might not want to come back here.'

'She made a threat?'

'No, Viccy doesn't make threats, she's far too smart for that, as I say, she just makes suggestions. SOCO reckon they have prints, but you can bet your sweet life that they turn out to belong to the local kids. Minors only and under tens for preference. Just the odd big brother to make sure they do it right.'

'So. This leaves us where?'

Alec smiled, but there was no humour in it. 'Do you really want me to answer that?' he said.

Naomi had been unable to settle after Alec had left. Unwilling to be alone, she had gone shopping for things she did not really need and afterwards walked with Napoleon on the beach. The tide had just turned, the air fresh and salt-clean and very chill. She had taken off her shoes and dug her toes into the sand as she walked. Her arms were bare. The breeze from the sea raised goose bumps on her left arm while the right heated in the sun on the landward side and even the sound seemed split by land and water. Seabirds and waves dominating the seaward while from the land the sound of voices and cars dominated, mingling with the electronic music of the small arcades dotted the length of the promenade. She had learnt now to judge her position by the changing sounds.

She turned to face the sea, the cacophony of human noise to her back now, her focus on the waves crashing about her feet, sucking back the sand. Napoleon stood close beside her. She could feel as he lowered his head to sniff at the water and heard him snuffle in disgust as it got up his nose. He was never sure about the beach. He liked it when she walked, but standing still was never his idea of fun, especially in this stuff that stuck closely to his paws and caked in his fur. He avoided sitting down, disliking the feel of wet sand on his backside.

Naomi closed her eyes and turned her face to the sun. Red light flooded her retina, the only colour that remained in Naomi's universe and she welcomed it.

'*Race you down the beach.*'

'*The sea's too cold to swim.*'

'*No it's not. Just run in fast. Don't think about it.*'

'*How can I not think about it? It's bloody freezing.*'

'*Don't say that! Your mam will hear!*'

Helen giggled. 'She says it.'

'*Yeah, but she's a grown-up. They can do it.*'

Tiny bells jingled as the children ran by. No, not ran *by*, ran *through* her memories. She heard them splashing into the cold sea, squealing with delight and shock and daring one another to go further into the waves and in her memories she knew that

Mari watched them from the shoreline, glancing up every few minutes from her magazine, her fair hair shaded by a broad brimmed hat and her dress pulled up to let the sun get to her pale, overwintered thighs.

'Oh, Helen,' Naomi whispered. 'What would you have been by now?'

She turned around, listening now to the beachfront noises. Arcade straight ahead, children buying ice cream – 'You want raspberry on that, love?' – smell of candyfloss carried to her from somewhere off to her left. That meant the steps were almost straight ahead. She knew full well that she could trust Napoleon to take her there, but to establish this world plan in her mind's eye gave her great satisfaction.

Somewhere, in one of the kitchen drawers, she thought, there was a little tape recorder. In her police days she had used it to make notes to herself. She had a different use for it now. In order to make sense of what had happened to Helen, she needed to commit what she knew to . . . well at one time she would have sat down with a sheet of paper and made a list. What she knew, what she didn't know, how she could find out.

That was not a facility she had just now – she was getting to grips with the Braille alphabet, but it was a slow and unnatural process. So, she would use the tape. Note the things she knew, the things she didn't, and for the things she needed to find out . . . well something told her that Harry Jones might be her willing ally in getting to grips with that.

'My wife and kids,' Gary Williams said. 'Dead, almost two years ago. That massive pile-up on the motorway.'

'I remember,' Alec told him. Ironically this was the accident where Naomi had lost her eyesight, and for a while they had doubted she would survive. 'I'm sorry,' he added. 'I can't imagine how hard that must have been.'

'Yeah, well I should have been driving, you see. But I was late home, again. They went on ahead. Going to visit her mam's. I said I'd meet them there when I got off work. Sharon, well she wasn't best pleased, didn't like motorway driving. Especially not when it was getting dark. I thought, maybe if I'd been there . . . She and the kids were right in the middle of it. There was nothing left of the car, nothing you could recognize.'

Alec shook his head. 'I can't say about your wife and kids,' he said, 'but I was there that night and from what I saw, no one had much of a chance. The dead would have been dead no matter who was driving.'

Gary Williams said nothing, just held the pictures in his hands, staring at them. 'Those bastards,' he said at last. 'I don't care about the stuff. Didn't have much left. I mean, I drank anything I could sell. Lost the house. Lost the lot and I didn't give a fuck. But the pictures are all I've got left of Shar and the kids. All I got left.'

He looked up suddenly. His tone changing and the old belligerence returning. 'So. What now? You going to charge me with summat or what?'

'You can't go back to the Radleigh,' Alec told him. 'I've someone arranging temporary accommodation—'

'Like fuck I can't! Look here, I've finally got my head together and I've started again. I'm not going to be thrown out just because of some stupid wankers who can't see further than their own noses.'

'If you go back, it could give rise to a public order offence Mr Williams. I can't allow that.'

Williams stared at him. 'But you ain't charging me with nothing,' he said flatly.

'There will be no charges brought at this present time.'

'So. Let me get this straight. You come round to my place of work and you single-handedly fuck up my life. Chuck me back to the sharks without a word of apology and then threaten me with some bloody public order charge just because I want to go home.'

'I threatened you with no charge, Mr Williams,' Alec told him. 'I'm merely warning you of the consequences, should you—'

'That's not the way I heard it.'

'You have a complaint,' Alec said sharply, 'I'm sure the duty solicitor will be glad to advise you. Maybe, if you'd been a little more reasonable when I came to talk to you, there'd have been

66

no need to bring you in and you wouldn't find yourself in this mess. Look,' he continued in a more placating tone, 'I think you should consider the emergency housing. There's not a lot to go back to—'

'Emergency housing! Some hostel somewhere full of crack-heads and prossies. No thanks. Just let me out of here. I can take care of me own problems.'

Great, Alec thought. Just what the Radleigh estate needed. Viccy Elliot and her like would just love finding a few more excuses to sort him out.

Naomi listened to the evening news. She still used the television news in the evening rather than the radio, preferring the depth of reporting to the rather sketchy illustrations typical of the audio version. A woman reporter was telling the audience about the finding of Helen's body. She had a young voice and not one that Naomi recognized. She liked it best when she could match a face to the voice. Better still if the journalist was one she knew well enough to visualize what they were wearing. Naomi knew that it was an odd sort of preference, even stranger as she herself had never had a strong interest in fashion, but nowadays she delighted in her imaginings and loved it when she had someone present who could tell her, 'Oh, she shouldn't be wearing *that* colour!'

The young woman had a regional accent that Naomi could not quite place. It was overlaid with a veneer of BBC English. 'A man was taken in for questioning,' she reprised, 'but at a press conference about an hour ago it was announced that he had been released without charge and there are no further details at the present time.'

So they had to let him go, Naomi thought to herself. Alec would be disappointed.

She was sitting in her favourite place, on the sofa in the large bay beside the window. The windows were open to let in the evening breeze and the street below was quiet. The children's voices rose up to her. Two little girls chatting, their voices light and untroubled on the evening air.

'I think this is the place. Come on, I'll knock on the door.'

Curious, Naomi leaned towards the window. Their feet

shuffled on the pavement and she thought she heard something else. The light ringing of tiny bells.

Then she almost jumped out of her skin as the knocking came at her own front door.

Naomi sat quite still, her body rigid and unable to move, then the second knock seemed to break the spell and she pushed to her feet and, with Napoleon at her side, went to open the front door.

There was no one there.

She called out, 'Is there anybody there?' But there was no answer and no sound either of shuffling feet or of the children, having played a joke, running swiftly away.

And then she heard the metallic jingling coming from the step where Napoleon was snuffling curiously at something which lay there.

She bent down, feeling for the dog and then for the object he had found.

'Oh my Lord!' The object, slightly damp from Napoleon's curious ministrations, was a metal band. A bracelet, jingling with little bells.

Twelve

It was nine thirty on the Radleigh Estate and Gary Williams was attempting to clean up the mess.

Several times in the past hour he had been interrupted by someone banging on the door. The first time, he had gone to answer it, but there had been no one there, only the sound of laughter rising up from the stairwell and running feet upon the stairs.

He had cursed the 'bloody kids' he assumed were responsible and then let them take it out on the knocker the next time they'd hammered on the door. He assumed that if he ignored them, they'd eventually tire of the game and clear off.

The big window that had faced out on to the school field was broken, smashed from the inside by, he supposed, the same person who had wielded the baseball bat and smashed his television. He had seen the glass still strewn across the path when he had come back. No one had bothered to clean it up yet, any more than they had troubled to come and replace his window. It had been boarded up and a message said that the workmen would be round in the next few days. He wasn't about to hold his breath; broken windows on the Radleigh Estate didn't come as high priority on anybody's list.

The room was dark, illuminated only by an inadequate table lamp, rescued from the chaos in the bedroom, which the vandals had failed to smash.

When the knock on the door came again, Gary ignored it, taking note only when the knock came once more. Irritated now, Gary decided it was time to give whoever a real piece of his mind. He crept to the door and flung it wide. But it wasn't kids this time. His next-door neighbour stood outside his door, glancing nervously around.

'What do you want?'

'Oh!' She had jumped back, startled when he had wrenched open the door. 'I just wondered,' she said, 'if there was anything I could do?'

'Thanks. But I think they've already done it all.'

'Well, if you feel like that . . .' She turned away and prepared to go back inside her own flat.

Gary watched her go, her shoulders set defensively, and suddenly realized that he didn't want to be alone. He needed company, any company.

'Look,' he said. 'I'm sorry. Come inside before someone sees you.'

'Like who?' she asked. 'Only you and me living on this landing.' But she stepped quickly over his threshold, glancing back over her shoulder towards the stairwell as though afraid the kids who had tormented him might be hiding in the shadows.

'God, what a mess.'

'Thanks. I thought I was getting somewhere.'

She smiled. It made her almost pretty, though her eyes were sad and anxious. 'You could do with some light in here.'

'They even smashed the lightbulbs. Meant to do the job right.'

'I've got some. I mean, back in the flat . . . shall I?'

'Thanks. I'd be grateful. Leave the door on the latch. And, I don't mean to be cheeky, but any chance of you bringing a kettle and a couple of mugs? I'm dying for a cuppa.'

The kids knocked twice more but then gave up and Gary figured that it must be getting too late even for kids in the Radleigh to be wandering about. Cathy Walton helped him to clear away the rest of the mess and they drank tea and talked about how they had come to live on the Radleigh Estate.

'You must miss them so much,' she said when he showed the pictures of his wife and kids. 'Me, I've never been married. I looked after my parents. My dad was sick and Mum couldn't cope. Eventually, he died and she became really . . . her mind seemed to go. I mean, it's not that she's even that old, but eventually, I just couldn't deal with it. The doctor said I should have her put in a home. I didn't want to, but she didn't even

70

know me any more. Anything I said or did . . . anyway. The care home cost, she owned her own house and I had to put it on the market. One thing led to another and I ended up here.'

She frowned. 'You think there'll be more trouble tonight? I mean, there are police everywhere, but I don't suppose that will last, will it?'

He shook his head. 'Look,' he said. 'I appreciate this, you know, but I might not be the best person to hang around with. You know why the police took me in?'

'The little girl that was killed. Yeah. I know, but I don't believe it.'

'Why not? You don't know me from Adam.'

She shrugged uncomfortably. 'I don't know . . . I just don't believe it. I mean, you're not the type, are you?'

'Not the type,' he repeated thoughtfully. 'Is there one? The police think I might be.' He sat down in the slashed seat of the old armchair and took the pictures from his pocket. They were still in the evidence bag, Alec having slipped them back inside before he let Gary Williams leave.

'I lost my kids,' he said. 'You think I could take someone else's kid away?'

Alec and Dick Travers were in Superintendent Phillips' office reviewing the day. Whichever way you looked at it no one could say it had been a successful one. They knew now where Helen's body had been buried, but that only complicated matters in that they now had to open a second murder inquiry instead of dealing with what was still a technical missing person.

'It is still a cold case though, sir,' Alec commented. 'I can't, in all conscience, give it the same priority as the Sarah Clarke investigation.'

'I take it that's a sentiment you didn't share with Helen Jones' family,' Phillips chided him.

'I'm sure Alec has more compassion than that, sir. But that aside, I have to agree. Sarah Clarke's killer is still out there. If the confession is to be believed, the man who killed Helen Jones is cold in his grave and not exactly our direct concern.' Travers said, siding with Alec.

71

Alec's ears pricked up. It rankled greatly that he had still not been gifted with information about this so-called confession. 'You're assuming it's genuine then?'

'We have to. Now more than ever. It pinpointed the burial place. We have to take the rest of it seriously.'

'Rest of it? You're suggesting this concerned more than Helen Jones?'

Phillips shifted uncomfortably in his chair. 'I'm not suggesting anything,' he said.

Travers crossed to the hot plate and fetched himself more coffee, gesturing to Alec with his mug to ask if he wanted more. Phillips' office was the one place in the station where they could guarantee a half decent cup of coffee but Alec shook his head.

'You can't just sit on this,' he said bluntly. 'The rumour mill's turning stories that are probably twice as bad as the truth. It's bad for morale, you just holding back like this.'

Phillips tipped back in his chair and regarded Alec thoughtfully over the edge of his mug. 'Maybe, maybe not,' he said quietly. 'But trust us, Alec, for now this has to be kept under wraps, especially while the Sarah Clarke investigation is still ongoing. We give this free rein and you'd see morale sink through a crack in the ground and not make it back up again, believe me.'

Alec absorbed this. 'It was a copper,' he said, 'made the confession. It was one of us.'

It had been in his mind that this might be so ever since he had discussed it briefly with Naomi, but it was not something he had wanted to admit, even as a possibility.

Phillips set his mug on the table with a sharp crack. 'You'll keep your speculation to yourself,' he said sharply. Then shook his head. Alec could feel from the change of mood what was coming next.

'You already have a nice mess to deal with without finding another one.'

'Yes, sir.'

'In hindsight, you would have handled Williams differently?

'In hindsight, no sir. He was uncooperative and arsy. He

72

didn't give a good account of himself and didn't seem prepared to do so. I felt I had no option but to bring him in.'

'And you didn't think it prudent to speak with these friends of his first? Confirm his story about meeting them in Philby?'

'No. With respect, sir, I thought it best not to give him the opportunity to do a runner. He gave me the impression that he didn't like my questions and might not stick around for me to ask more.'

Phillips regarded him with a cold stare and then he said, 'So, let me get this right. You interview this man at his place of work, following on from some vague tip-off from a known troublemaker. And because he isn't all polite and public school, you call in the cavalry. His story checked out, I suppose?'

Travers replied, 'The friends he claimed to have met backed his story. According to them, they were walking along the promenade when they saw the crowd and the cameras. They went to look. The reconstruction was half through by then.'

'Either of you spoken to them?'

'No,' Alec told him. 'Uniform out at Philby.'

A video tape lay on Phillips' desk. He picked it up and took it over to the combined TV and video recorder that stood against the wall. The paint was peeling, Alec noted absently. The green flaking off to reveal the dirty cream beneath.

Phillips pressed play and the three of them watched in silence. The tape concentrated upon the little girl dressed like Sarah Clarke, walking down to the beach from the fish and chip shop. Alec noted Sarah's mother standing beside a WPC. She was crying and gazing hungrily at the child as though, if she looked long enough, this little girl might be transformed. The camera panned left, tracking her progress towards the steps that led down on to the beach and then pulled back to reveal the crowd. The event had been well publicized and large numbers of people had turned up to watch, to lend support, just to be there in the hope that somehow they might recall something about the murdered child.

'There he is,' Alec said and pointed at a man elbowing through to the front of the crowd. He pushed so hard that a woman next to him turned around to object. Another, with a baby in her arms, was forced to shift out of his way. It was hardly the action, Alec thought, of a casual observer, merely curious to see what was going on. This was someone who wanted to be in the thick of it.

'Watch him,' Phillips said, all of his previous irritation dissipated. 'It there's nothing to find, fair enough, but if he so much as breathes too hard, bring him in again.'

Thirteen

Harry came to collect Naomi the following morning with Patrick in tow, the boy eager to see Napoleon. Naomi was getting quite used to being upstaged by her sleek, black, four-footed companion.

The plan was that she and Harry would spend time in the newspaper archive; the news morgue would, she hoped, fill in some of the gaps that twenty-odd years of memory could not supply. Patrick was to take Napoleon to the nearby park; Naomi had armed herself with his ordinary lead, two frisbees and his favourite red ball. The dog recognized these off-duty signs and wriggled with excitement in the back of the car.

'He loves frisbees,' Naomi told Patrick. 'Occasionally he even manages to catch one. I tried playing with him on the beach a couple of times till I nearly took someone's head off. He's trained to ignore the ducks and other dogs, but he does beg for ice cream if he hears the van. Tell him no, OK?'

'OK,' Patrick agreed, but Naomi didn't believe him. She was glad that Napoleon would have this chance to play. It never ceased to amaze her, the change that came over the dog when she had put his harness on him: suddenly, Napoleon the rake would become Napoleon the responsible adult; conversely, he was quick to understand the off-duty moments.

'How is Mari?' she asked quietly as Patrick chatted to the dog on the back seat.

'Better this morning. I think she was glad that you were there yesterday. You know, we were talking about it last night and both of us thought it would have been good if Joe were here now. He'd have liked to see the job finished, as it were.'

Naomi nodded. 'It rankled,' she agreed. 'Even after he retired. I went to see him from time to time and he often said . . . I got the feeling he was still looking, you know, unofficially, long after he left the force.'

She thought about it for a moment and then smiled, recalling Joe's kindness to her both as a child and as a nervous young officer, terribly afraid of failing, trying too hard for the approval of her fellows. 'You know, I miss him,' she said. 'It's been three years now. I went to the funeral, but I didn't stay. You should have seen how many turned up though, just to pay respects even if it was only for a few minutes.'

'I finished Final Fantasy Nine last night,' Patrick said unexpectedly, his voice cutting into the silence that had fallen between them.

'What will you do now?'

He shrugged. 'Start again, I suppose. Do you play, Naomi . . . I mean, did you?' He sounded embarrassed to have asked.

Naomi laughed. 'Not much, no. But I used to like the arcade games. There's a Grand Prix one on the sea front and I regularly used to thrash Alec. He swore I could beat him even with my eyes closed.' She laughed again, realizing what she'd just said.

'Maybe you should try it?' Patrick suggested.

'Patrick, I hardly think . . .' Harry began.

'No, he's right. Maybe we should. It'd be a laugh if nothing else. We'll make a date, Patrick.'

'OK. Bet ya I win.'

They had reached the newspaper offices and found a place to park in the side street. Within a few minutes, Patrick and Napoleon had been dispatched to the park and Naomi had her hand slipped through Harry's arm.

'Something happened last night,' she said. 'Something really strange, Harry.'

'Oh? What?'

'I heard kids in the street and then someone banging on the door, but when I went down, there was no one there.'

Harry snorted. 'Little sods,' he said. 'Kids playing Knock Door Run, nothing strange in that.'

'No, no, I know that, but they left something behind. On the doorstep.' She slipped her hand into her pocket and withdrew the bangle. 'They left this.'

*   *   *

76

Gary Williams had lived in Philby with his wife and kids and that was to be Alec's first port of call that morning; his brief was to talk to the neighbours – ex-neighbours – and get some background. Last night had been quiet on the Radleigh. The police presence had been sporadic but high profile. Groups of youths had been reported hanging about on street corners and kids out late hanging around the flats, but nothing else.

During the day, the media presence had been felt upon the estate, but evening had seen it dispatched to the nearest decent hotel. They had returned this morning, apparently, queuing up to mount the stairs to the Williams flat, but getting no reply had returned to the task of getting background comments from mothers taking their kids to school or young men on their way to sign on, most of the workers having left and been at work long before the press fraternity had left their beds. The Radleigh was just that kind of place.

'Alec. Hold up there a minute.'

Alec turned to see Travers coming down the steps with a blue folder in his hand.

'The PM report?'

Travers nodded. 'They got the bone lady in,' he said, referring to the forensic anthropologist called to advise on skeletal remains. 'Not much we didn't know from the preliminary report. She's noted the crushing injuries that were probably post mortem, and so on, though they've managed to match a piece of the jaw to dental records, so we've got our positive ID.' He paused, 'Not that there was much doubt.'

'Good to get, though. It would be embarrassing . . .'

'Don't,' Travers told him. 'We've enough bodies without you even thinking that. But we've got a cause of death. Fractured hyoid bone,' he said, mentioning the little bone at the back of the tongue, and there was generally only the one cause of hyoid fracture. 'Manual strangulation,' Travers said.

Alec was thoughtful as he drove the coast road to Philby. He was not surprised at the PM findings any more than he had really been surprised at Naomi's conclusions – with or without a dream to help her. It was, as he had commented, an expected

77

result. But Naomi's insistence that her hunch had been, well, more than the result of experience, that disturbed him. He worried about her a great deal. Sometimes he thought that she was coping too well on the face of it and he often found himself wondering what was really going on in her mind. Alec knew, had their roles been reversed, that he would not have handled things anywhere near as well as Naomi seemed to be doing. He'd have joined Sarah Clarke's father, hiding in the whisky bottle and probably not bothering to crawl out again.

Thinking of Sarah, he realized that he had reached that point on the promenade closest to where her body had been found. He glanced sideways, out towards the scene, but even from the car could see nothing of the beach, just the line of grey water visible over the promenade railings.

Kids were swimming and splashing about in the water. Some appeared to be alone, though he supposed that their parents must simply be out of his sight. It disturbed him though and he had to ask himself whether he would have taken his kids to play there, on that stretch of beach, knowing that another child had been assaulted and strangled so close by . . .

Thinking about kids somehow led him back to thinking about Naomi again, and about himself. The clock is ticking, Alec old man, he told himself somewhat wryly. Thirty-eight and not even a single broken marriage yet. He wondered what Naomi would think if she found out just *how* she figured in his thoughts.

Gary Williams' previous address was a side street running at right angles to the beach and only half a mile from where Sarah Clarke had lived. Alec had not realized how close it was before and it got him thinking. It was possible that Gary Williams even knew the Clarkes – he'd been asked and denied this, but it was quite possible he had known them at least by sight. It was possible even that Sarah had attended the same school as the Williams kids. He made a mental note to chase that up.

Term had begun a couple of weeks before and as Alec left his car, he could hear the voices of children carried on the wind. A glance at his watch told him it was lunchtime.

Gary Williams and his family had lived at 23 Palmer

Road. The street itself was unremarkable. Terraced rows which reminded Alec of Mari's little house, though these had shallow bay windows giving shape to the front. Number 23 had an attic bedroom with a velux window, but was otherwise undistinguished. Shabby on the outside, but no more rundown than the rest of the row; houses close beside the sea but too small to be turned into B&Bs and not classy enough to capture the holiday market. And at number 23 there was no one home.

Alec peered in through the front bay window. A piano occupied the alcove on one side of the fireplace and a stack of shelves could just be discerned on the other. The floor was stripped pine and the furniture dark blue and cozy looking, grouped around a deep red kilim spread on the wooden boards.

He tried to imagine it in Gary Williams' time and failed miserably. It was hard to get a handle on what the man might have been like before.

'Can I help you? Didn't anyone ever tell you it's not right to stare through other people's windows?'

Alec turned. The speaker was an elderly woman with steel grey hair. She had a dog on a lead, some sort of terrier cross, Alec guessed.

'Any idea when they'll be home?' Alec asked her.

'I wouldn't tell you if I had,' she told him sternly. 'Who are you anyway?'

'Police,' Alec said, pulling out his identity card. The woman glanced at it.

'Police?' she echoed. She stepped back to have a better look at this unwanted visitor. 'I hope that nothing's happened to the Roberts?'

'The Roberts? No, nothing. I wanted to talk to them about the previous occupants. Do you live locally? Perhaps you knew them? Mr and Mrs Williams, the mother and children were—'

'Killed in that pile-up, yes, I know. But I don't think the Roberts would ever have met them. The house was repossessed, I believe. They bought long after Williams was gone.' She looked thoughtfully at him for a moment longer and then moved to open the gate of the neighbouring house. 'I'm going inside now,' she said. 'And I'm going to phone and check you are who you say you are. Then, I might talk to you.'

Alec stared at her. 'Fine,' he said. 'Do you want the number?'

For that he got a withering look. 'I'm quite capable, thank you. Such things as that, I keep beside the telephone.'

It was ten minutes before she opened the door again and Alec had retreated to his car, not wanting to get in, in case she should think that he had gone, but feeling oddly conspicuous, leaning against the door.

'You can come in now,' she told him, holding the door. 'I'm Phyllis Mole, Inspector Friedman. Mrs Phyllis Mole.' And she stood back to allow Alec to come inside.

Phyllis Mole's living room might have stepped out of the pages of *Homes and Gardens* – circa 1945. Through the open door at the end of the hall Alec had glimpsed the kitchen and the middle reception room – she had resisted the temptation to knock the two into one – and these looked as though they had at least made it into the 1980s, but this front parlour, as she called it, probably hadn't changed all that much since Mrs Mole, and the furniture, had been young.

She sat opposite him to pour the tea, from a pot covered in roses into cups decorated with more of the same.

'Now,' she said, 'you can tell me what you want with the Roberts.'

'With the Roberts themselves, nothing. What I wanted to know is, if the Williams family maybe left anything behind? Next stop was to have been the neighbours.'

'I heard it on the television,' she said, 'about a man being taken in for questioning about that little girl. And they said it was someone who lived on the Radleigh, but you weren't giving out his name. Now, my neighbours on the other side have relations living on the Radleigh Estate. Decent people,' she told him firmly. 'Not everyone who lives in that dreadful place is a vandal or a drug dealer.'

'No, Mrs Mole, I'm sure they're not.'

She nodded, peering at him thoughtfully, though it was

clear that she gave no weight to his agreement. 'They told my neighbours that the arrested man was none other than our Mr Williams.' She fixed him with eyes that were as steely grey as her hair, daring him to deny it.

Alec decided not to bother. 'Did you know the Williams family well?' he asked her.

'The children and the mother, yes. Lucy and Emory. Have you noticed how all the old names are coming back? Lucy and Emory were pleasant children. Well behaved and always remembered their please and thank yous. Their mother, Sharon, she worked hard and always made sure they were well turned out. And Williams himself, when he was working, he was a pleasant enough neighbour to have. I sometimes had little things that I couldn't manage myself. Gary Williams helped out a time or two. I paid him, of course, but it was convenient, knowing that there was someone close by that could be relied upon.'

'What kind of things, Mrs Mole?'

She frowned. 'Small things really. I had a blocked sink and couldn't get the U-bend off to clean it. Time was when I'd have done it myself, but as one gets older, one's knees tend to fail.'

She smiled for the first time, softening the steel. Alec returned it, warming to this stern old lady. 'And when the wind fetched my fence down last winter, he fixed it for me.' She sighed. 'Though by then, of course, the family was gone and he was about to lose his home. I knew the money I gave him would be used to buy more drink but –' she shrugged – 'I felt sorry for the man, knowing all he'd been through, and it isn't my place to judge the way folk deal with their grief.'

'Were they a close family?' Alec asked her.

To his surprise, she shook his head. 'No, Inspector, I don't believe they were. I think both parents loved their children and neither could bear to think of the children having to make choices between them. And I believe that they were still good friends . . . but the spark had gone, if you know what I mean. It was as though they all lived together because it was the con-venient thing to do. They shared the house and the children, but other than that, I believe that their lives were quite separate.'

81

'What made you think that?'

'Because even when they had the chance to be together, they didn't take it. There were no shortages of baby sitters for the little ones. I kept an eye on them from time to time – as I told you, they were easy children. And her mother and sister used to have them often enough. Even then, she would go her way, with her friends and he would go his.' She shrugged. 'It seemed like a lonely sort of life to me, but, I suppose, at least they stayed together for the children.'

Alec could not help but wonder how the children felt about this. The boy would probably have been too young to notice, but Lucy would certainly have been at that age when she might compare her own family to that of others.

'And you saw no signs of neglect,' Alec asked her.

'No,' she said firmly. 'I saw no sign of neglect, neither did I have reason to suspect abuse. Not that we can know what goes on behind closed doors, of course. But the children always seemed healthy and happy, well fed and well clothed, not like some who came to play with them.'

Alec had the sudden feeling that she was about to drop a bombshell – or at least, she thought she was.

'Like who, Mrs Mole? Like which children that came to play?'

'Like little Sarah Clarke,' she told him.

Phyllis Mole had clearly had this on her mind for quite some time. 'I called the police,' she said. 'Reported the bruises on her arms, but they said all they could do was to pass the information on. They wanted to know if I was related or if I knew the family doctor. I told them, no, that I didn't even know the child well, and that I supposed that her doctor must be someone at the group practice on Sandown Road.' She shrugged. 'I half expected someone to come around and talk to me, but no one did.'

No, Alec thought, the information would have been passed on, but unless there were corroborating reports, most likely it would simply have vanished into the system.

'Exactly when was this?'

'More than two years ago now. I never saw the child again to speak to. A week or so later, Sharon and the children were killed in that terrible crash and Gary fell to pieces. I went to the funeral and I half expected to see Sarah and her family there, but they didn't come.'

'But you've thought about her. Often,' Alec guessed.

The old lady pursed her lips and nodded slowly. 'It never ceased to amaze me how easy some folk find it to hurt the innocent,' she said. 'And how little conscience they seem to have about it. When I saw the news, I recognized her, of course. She was a plump little thing when I first knew her and in that news picture she's shed some of the baby fat. But I knew, even before they said the name, that it was her and when they said it was murder . . . I remembered the bruises and I called the police again.'

'You called again? After Sarah was killed?'

'That's what I've just said, Inspector. Someone, a young girl who sounded as though she should still be in school, she took my details and said thank you very much and that was it.'

Alec nodded. He knew just how many calls would have been generated and how easy it would be for a single piece of information to be buried. And a piece like this in particular, with no corroboration . . . Alec was all too familiar with how many times this happened. That a child was killed or disappeared and the calls would flood in, accusatory, vindictive and usually groundless, describing abuse and neglect that had to be investigated and which caused massive hurt. Usually, this was kept from the parents while investigators quietly looked into what, nine times out of ten, turned out to be unfounded lies.

Was Phyllis Mole just another vindictive busybody? Alec didn't think so.

'Mrs Mole, did you ever get a feeling for . . .'

'Who was doing it?' She shook her head. 'At first I thought it might have been the father, but I don't know.'

'And you are certain that this was not just accidental bruising?'

She smiled at him. 'I know, Inspector. I've had children of my own and sometimes they could have doubled for Dalmatian dogs, they were so spotty with cuts and scrapes and bruises. Especially if they'd been out on the beach and, Inspector, sometimes I think we must have spent our entire summers on the beach.' She smiled at the memory of it and Alec found himself smiling back at her again.

'No,' Phyllis Mole was adamant. 'Sharon was worried too. She pointed the marks out to me and asked me what I thought, said that Sarah had made up some cock and bull story about having to keep her cardigan on in case she got cold. The child forgot, slipped her cardy off and carried on playing, then got into a right state when she remembered what her mother had told her.

'The bruises were black, Inspector, and all around her upper arms. She had little sleeves on her dress that almost covered them but not quite, and when she moved and the sleeves rode up, you could see clearly. Someone had grabbed hold of her and dug their fingers in hard and left the mark of every one on that little girl's arm.'

Fourteen

A lec was thoughtful as he drove away. He had knocked on a few more doors but no one had been home. When he drove away, Phyllis Mole was standing in the front room bay window looking out at him and he wondered what she was thinking . . . and how much credence he should give to her words.

It was mid afternoon by the time he got back to the office and tracked down DCI Travers. Dick Travers listened as Alec reported what Phyllis Mole had said.

'We ran the usual checks,' Travers said. 'Nothing came through from social services or the health centre. Her doctor, if I recall, said he'd rarely seen the child. His records showed that he'd been called out when both the kids went down with chicken pox and Sarah had a high temperature . . . or maybe it was a locum went out. I think they use an on-call service, you'd have to check.'

He paused, frowned at Alec. 'Did Phyllis Mole leave her name or was she Mrs Anonymous?'

'She didn't say,' Alec was annoyed with himself for not asking. 'I get the impression though, that she'd have been upfront and the first time she called, she said she expected a visit, so she must have identified herself.'

Travers nodded. 'So, if Sharon Williams suspected enough to point it out to the old lady, then why didn't she act on it?'

Alec shrugged. 'Didn't want to get involved?' he suggested. 'That's the usual reason.'

'Then why draw attention to the bruises in the first place?'

Alec shrugged again. 'Sharp eyes has Phyllis Mole,' he said. 'And maybe Sharon knew that she'd do something. Save her the potential trouble.'

85

'Well, one thing's sure. We can't ask her. But we can have another word with our friend, Gary. Find out why he lied about knowing Sarah Clarke and her family.'

'Today?' Alec asked.

'No, leave it, Alec. I'd rather give our Mr Williams another night on the Radleigh. Think things over,' he smiled. 'We've got two surveillance units keeping obs on the flat, but they've instructions to be low profile. Unless anything serious starts, they'll stay put and observe.'

Alec raised an eyebrow. 'Serious?' he asked.

His boss shrugged. 'Word from above is not to antagonize the natives,' he said. 'So we wait and we watch.'

Alec took time to set things in motion as regards tracking down Phyllis' calls then headed off to talk to Naomi. He arrived just as Harry, Naomi and Patrick pulled up in Harry's car.

Napoleon was exhausted and flopped down on the living-room floor, refusing to respond to any of Alec's cajoling.

'What have you done to him?' Alec demanded.

'Three hours of walking and frisbees and playing ball,' Patrick told him. He didn't look in much better shape than the dog.

'So, where have *you* been?'

'Newspaper archive,' Naomi told him from the kitchen. 'We've been digging. I wanted to review the case and since I didn't have the case notes . . .'

'Oh? What were you looking for?'

'I don't know really. Just so many things I didn't remember clearly, like who else was on the team. That sort of thing.' She came through to the living room, her hands resting lightly on the door frame and her head turning as she got her bearings by listening to where everyone was. 'I know . . . I know. Not a lot of point. Now they've found Helen's body it's only a matter of time before they release the name of who did it, I guess. But, you know how it is. It was nibbling away at my brain and would carry on nibbling if I didn't do something. Where have *you* been?'

'Our man from the Radleigh,' Alec said. 'I was visiting his old neighbourhood.'

'Oh? And where's that then?' She came through the door, reaching out her hand towards him. He took it and pulled her into his embrace. Over her head he could see Harry in the kitchen. He looked their way and scowled, then turned back to the coffee he was making.

'Palmer Road, just back from the main promenade.'

'Palmer Road. I think I knew someone who lived there.'

'You did,' Harry said, coming though from the kitchen with a tray in his hands. 'Joe's brother lived there. I remember because our aunt Ida lives round the corner on Amy Street and Mum and I met Joe one time when we were visiting.'

Naomi shook her head. 'I was thinking of someone from school,' she said. 'Ingham Grammar took kids from Philby as well as here. I've this vague memory of going to a Christmas party there. Something like that.' She paused, frowning in her attempt to recapture the memory. 'I've a feeling Helen must have gone, too. I think your dad drove us. I didn't know Joe's brother lived there. I thought Ron Jackson lived here, in Ingham.'

'Not Ron. Another brother. I forget his name.' He pointedly handed a mug of coffee to Alec, forcing Alec to leave go of Naomi. 'How are you doing with your suspect? Has he gone back to that estate?'

Alec nodded. 'For the moment anyway. Nothing we could hold him on. We offered him safe accommodation, but he's refused it.' He sipped his coffee. 'If I were him, I'd be over the hills and far away by now.'

'Aren't you supposed to tell him not to leave town or something?' Patrick asked.

Alec laughed. 'Only in the movies. Fact is, we can't charge him and we can't tell him where to live.'

'Do you think he's guilty?' Patrick pressed.

'I think I've already told you far too much.'

'Nothing we couldn't have worked out from the news,' Naomi commented. 'Or not much more, anyway. Harry read the front pages to me earlier. Have you seen them?'

'I've seen them. More pressure for outing of known offenders. It's inevitable I guess, regardless of the fact that Gary Williams has never been charged with anything, let alone child abuse.'

87

'Well, why shouldn't people want to know?' Patrick asked. 'About people like that living close by.'

'Well, in this case because we've no real reason to think that Gary Williams *is* someone like that. He may well be an unpleasant, but otherwise innocent, party and as such we've got a duty of protection. Even if he were guilty as hell, we'd still have that same duty to protect; you can't let the mob rule, Patrick, however strong the provocation and much as it feels right sometimes – although I didn't say that,' he added, smiling at the teenager. 'And the other problem is that exposure drives people underground. They disappear and often the authorities have no idea of where they are or what they're doing.' He sighed. One thing everyone on the investigation wished was that they'd had bloody CCTV on Philby beachfront. Even if it hadn't picked up Sarah, it might have thrown up other leads. Told them who was in the area. He recalled vividly, when another little girl had disappeared from a seaside town in Scotland, the cameras had picked up more than twenty known paedophiles on that same promenade that day. Had he and Naomi been alone, he might have expressed that view out loud. With Patrick present, and Harry Jones, it seemed neither appropriate nor wise.

'You still think he's guilty though, don't you?'

Patrick was persistent if nothing else, Alec thought.

'Maybe,' he conceded. 'But guilty of what? Being an asshole doesn't automatically make him a killer.'

They sat down around the circular table, the copies of news reports spread across its surface. Napoleon snored softly, his legs twitching as he chased something through his dreams. The windows were wide open and the distant sounds of beach life drifted in as the wind changed and swept in with the tide: arcade music and children shouting amongst the fairground rides further along the promenade.

'Joe led the investigation,' Naomi commented, 'but I never realized until today just how many more folk that I knew also worked on it.'

'People tend to stick here,' Alec confirmed. 'Oh, you get the promotions out, but being regional HQ, it gives us a fair whack at internal mobility promotion and we can still stay local.'

'It's also a good place to get sidelined,' Naomi commented wryly.

'Maybe. Who were you thinking about anyway?'

'Well, for a start, there was Sergeant Miller. He was a young PC back then.' She turned to Harry. 'He's based at Philby now. Then our own DCI Travers. He'd just moved into CID as a DC. And old DS Lyman. He retired a few years ago but I worked with him in my first year. Nice man, but he never mentioned Helen or anything. There were probably others, but those two were mentioned specifically in the newspapers. I don't know, it seems strange, the way our paths cross time and time again with some people.'

'Didn't Joe tell people about you? Remind them, when you became a police woman?' Patrick asked.

'No. Thankfully, he didn't. It's probably not good to appear to have that much baggage. Joe and I talked occasionally about how we'd met and that sort of thing, but even Joe was a bit reticent by then. He saw it as a major failure.'

He also saw the Helen Jones case as what stopped him making DCI, Alec thought, but he said nothing.

'I'm surprised, you saying that. I got the impression that you were very open about all this,' Harry said. 'I mean to say, when Alec came to tell us about finding Helen's body, you came along, I thought, with official approval.'

Naomi nodded. 'Now, yes,' she said, 'but when I first came back here as a very green PC, I didn't want any of it to come out. I was naïve enough to think I might be treated differently. Singled out in some way. I was wrong. Later, I told friends about Helen. People talk; naturally they talk about what brought them in to the force and Helen was a big part of my reason. Joe Jackson was another. Then, after the accident . . . the papers did this big thing on the victims of the crash and someone got hold of the story about me and Helen'.

'I remember that,' Harry said quietly. It had been painful, both because of Mari's grief for Naomi and the way in which it had reopened their wounds over Helen.

There was a brief silence, everyone nursing their own thoughts until Harry said, 'Nomi, you should tell Alec about the bracelet.'

89

'Bracelet?' Alec asked.

'It hardly seems worth it.'

'Tell me anyway.' He reached out and covered her hand with his own. His right. There was a small callous at the root of the index finger. He had acquired it somewhere and kept it alive by picking it raw. Sometimes, when he touched her, it scraped her skin and, perversely, she had grown to like that. She felt she was touching the rawness of Alec himself. Whittled and picked clean, exposed.

Briefly, she told him about the children and finding the bangle on the step the night before.

'You're certain it isn't yours?' he asked her.

She groped in her bag for the chiming bangle that had been left behind and now lay it on the table. 'No, it isn't mine.' She went through to her bedroom and fetched her own from the bedside drawer and lay it beside its twin. 'See, *this* is mine. Green enamel. The other is purple, like Helen's.'

Alec turned them over in his hand. 'Bit too late to bag it, I suppose,' he commented.

'It was a bit too late last night. By the time Napoleon had finished with it and I'd fumbled it around in the dust, I don't think there'd have been a lot there.'

'No, I suppose not. Can I keep this anyway?'

'I guess so.' She felt oddly reluctant to let it go.

'Nomi, you should have called someone last night,' Alec said. He sounded concerned. Irritated, even.

'And told them what? That some kid dropped her bracelet on my doorstep?'

'There's more to it than that. Surely, you must have realized last night, there was more to it than that?' Alec insisted.

'No,' Naomi shook her head. 'Alec, I didn't realize. In truth, I didn't even think. I was too surprised, I guess. I went to the door and called out, but no one answered and I didn't hear anyone either.'

Alec thought for a moment, she could hear him turning the bangle between his hands, making the tiny bells chime softly. 'Can you remember what the kids were saying?' he asked her. 'You mentioned that one of them said something before banging on the door.'

She frowned. 'Yeah, something like, "This is the place" and I heard jingling, as if she was wearing it on her wrist.'

'Would you know them again? I mean, was there anything distinctive . . . ?'

She laughed. 'They sounded like kids. No, no, I know what you mean. Local, I would say. Early teens, bit younger. She sounded pretty self-assured and the footsteps weren't hurried or panicked or anything. Nothing like that . . . You know, I got the impression that the second child was younger, but I couldn't tell you why.'

'Oh? Try.'

'I don't know. Maybe her steps were quicker or something.' She shrugged. 'I really couldn't say, it was just an impression. Like I said, Alec, they were just kids.'

Alec glanced at his watch. 'I've got to go,' he said. He stood up and bent to kiss Naomi, making certain that he took his time about it. Time enough for Harry to harrumph uncomfortably and look away.

Once he had gone, Harry made more coffee. There was an empty feel to the day now, as though Alec had somehow taken their sense of purpose with him.

It was Patrick that voiced it. 'Well,' he demanded. 'So what do we do now?'

Naomi didn't answer. She'd been asking herself the same question. She felt suddenly deflated as though talking to Alec had reminded her how futile all this was: her little investigation, piecing things together for her own satisfaction when, in the next few days, she supposed that all the information included in the confession would be released and her gaps could be filled by official channels. It was habitual curiosity, she decided. Born of years of police work . . . and it was time she let go and found something else to do.

'*We* don't do anything,' Harry replied. He sounded heavy and defeated too as though his thoughts tracked Naomi's and made him feel just as bad.

'Oh, come on.' Patrick was indignant. He'd been enjoying himself with this inclusion into the adult world and he didn't want to give up the privilege.

'I don't think there's anything we *can* do,' Harry told him. 'The police will do their job and all we can do is wait.'

'Then why go to all this trouble?' Patrick demanded. 'You spent hours getting all this together. What was it, a big waste of time then?'

Neither adult replied. Naomi lifted her head to look in Harry's direction, symbolically meeting his gaze as if she could see his face. Her hands shuffled the pieces of paper, the photocopied sheets laying bare the memories of Helen's murder.

'They won't do much more anyway,' she said. 'If the confession is for real, they know who did it and he's already dead. In a few days at most, they release the information, close the case and that will be it. They've got the child out at Philby to concentrate on. Helen . . . I guess Helen will be a kind of bonus, when they catch the other man. And, I don't know, Patrick. I don't know why I went to all this trouble. It seemed important at the time. There were things I wanted to remember properly and, I guess, I wanted to feel involved.'

It was a hard confession to make. She felt Patrick shift uneasily in his seat and Harry get up, the chair lifted carefully so that he didn't scrape it on the wooden floor. Typically Harry, she thought absently.

'I'll make us some more coffee,' he said quietly. He patted Naomi's hand as he passed and she was reminded suddenly of Alec's touch. Harry's hands were soft, like Mari's, gentle on her own.

'I didn't mean to upset you,' Patrick said quietly.

'You didn't. I mean, really, you didn't, Patrick. I still find it hard to let go, to be shut out. My entire adult life was wrapped up in police work. My friends and colleagues were the same people. I lived and breathed it and I was good at what I did. It just feels so . . .'

She smiled, blinking rapidly to stop the tears which threatened. She could feel the boy reaching out to tidy the papers on the table. Shuffling and stacking them. Displacement activity, she thought. Harry made coffee, Patrick sorted paper. She . . . What did she do? Naomi was no longer sure.

'What about the bracelet?' Patrick asked her suddenly.

'What about it?' It was Harry who asked, coming back from the kitchen and setting the tray down with the same care he'd used when he moved the dining chair.

'Well, someone left it. Someone who isn't dead . . . it's kind of like leaving a message.'

'Oh, come on, Patrick.' Harry sounded vaguely impatient. 'I expect it was someone's idea of a practical joke. With all of this resurfacing –' he paused and sighed – 'there are some sick people out there who would see leaving the bracelet as funny, no doubt.'

But Naomi shook her head, Patrick's words having started a train of thought in her own mind. 'Alec was right,' she said. 'I should have thought more about it last night. It can't be that simple, Harry. Maybe Patrick is on to something and someone was leaving a message of some kind. The question is, what is it they wanted to say?'

Harry huffed impatiently. 'Someone remembered the bracelet; read about it in the papers and decided to play a rather sick joke. Alec's right about that, they should be hunting down whoever planned this thing and bringing them to book . . .'

Naomi's hands moved restlessly, flicking through the papers that Patrick had stacked so carefully, recalling their contents. Then she settled them once more upon the table. 'It wasn't mentioned,' she said quietly. 'Not anywhere. You read the accounts to me. There are descriptions of Helen's clothes, her school bag, even what books she would have had with her that day. Nothing about the bracelet.'

There followed a silence, but for the flap and shuffle of paper as the two of them looked for confirmation of Naomi's words.

'Well, all right,' Harry conceded finally. 'There's nothing here. But Helen wore that damned thing all the time. Same as you did yours. Anyone who knew her well would have assumed . . .'

'So why get two kids to dump its twin on my doorstep now?'

'Wouldn't it be difficult to find another one like it?' Patrick asked. 'I mean, yours and Helen's were bought years ago.'

Naomi laughed. He made it sound like the dark ages. 'No,'

she told him. The same little shop still sells the same junk it did when we were kids. In fact, it's all come back into vogue, the new age, Far Eastern sort of stuff. And, chances are, your dad's right.'

'See, Patrick. You read too much into things.'

'No, I didn't mean that,' Naomi told him. 'I mean, you're right about most of our friends knowing about the bracelet. But that doesn't answer the why part. Maybe it was a sick joke, like you say. But Harry, what if it wasn't? The only other explanation is that someone *knew*, knew for certain about Helen and about the bracelet and that it was still on her wrist when she died.'

Harry frowned. 'Isn't that quite a leap of logic?'

'Is it? Not really, I don't think. They must have known I would recognize it for what it was. But what I can't figure out is why. Not just why leave it, but why wait this long to come forward?'

'Come forward?'

'Oh, come on, Dad,' Patrick told him, the excitement in his voice unmistakable. 'They must have seen it when Helen was killed. They've got to have been there.'

Fifteen

A lec had returned to the office to catch up on paperwork. He had dropped the bracelet into his desk tray and it was lying there on top of his files when Travers walked in.

'Slipping, Alec? Shouldn't that be back in the evidence locker?'

'What? Oh.' Alec picked it up. 'It's not Helen's,' he said. He handed it over for Travers to see. 'It might well be evidence, but I'm damned if I could tell you what of.'

Travers gave him a quizzical look. He pulled up a chair and sat down, dumped the file he had been holding in Alec's in tray and examined the tiny bangle. Picking it up, it was clear that this was not Helen's. Hers had been well preserved, considering the time it had been in the ground, but it had also been bent out of shape and the enamel chipped and flaking.

'What's the story?' Travers asked.

Alec told him.

'Has she been interviewed?'

'Not officially, no.'

'I'll get someone on to it. You'd better give her a call, tell her to expect someone. Tomorrow, probably.'

'And what about this confession?' Alec demanded. 'Dick, you can't keep sitting on this. Not now you've found her. It looks . . .'

'I know how it looks.' Travers unfolded himself from the chair and stretched. 'Phillips wants a few more days. He's called a press conference for –' he glanced at his watch – 'about now actually. Take a look?'

There was a television in the corner of the office and Travers dragged it out and plugged it in. He flicked through the channels trying to find the news.

95

'. . . found the remains of Helen Jones,' Phillips was saying. 'The child's identity has been confirmed by dental records and personal items found with the body. Helen Jones, as you all know, disappeared on her way to school on the 17th March, twenty-three years ago. Her family asked me to relay that they are relieved to finally lay their child to rest and ask you to respect their need for privacy at this most difficult of times.'

'Fat chance of that,' Alec commented.

They watched in silence as Phillips fielded questions from the floor. Most concerned the confession. Phillips was evasive: Still further lines of inquiry to follow. A statement would be issued in the next few days.

'Think he'll do it?' Alec asked.

'Do what?'

'Handle the announcement when we have to tell them it was one of our own that killed Helen Jones.'

Travers looked at him, his face expressionless. 'Shooting in the dark, Alec?' he said finally.

Alec nodded. 'Yes, but it looks like I scored,' he said.

Harry, Patrick and Mari were also watching the news. 'I wanted to make sure he said it,' Mari told her son. 'About leaving us alone.'

'They'll take no notice, Mam,' Harry told her. 'It's a miracle we've been left alone as much as we have.'

She shifted uncomfortably in her chair. 'I know, but I still told him he had to say it.'

Harry shook his head. 'Come back to my place,' he said. 'Tonight. Or we could go away for a little while, just until everything quietens down.'

Mari frowned at him. 'And what good will that do? I want to be here to arrange the funeral as soon as they say we can. I want to be here to bring Helen home. There are still old friends around here, people who have the right to see her laid to rest, and I'll not have it said that I've not seen properly to my own.'

'No one would think that, Mam,' Harry protested. 'I just thought . . .'

Mari squared her shoulders. 'Some storms just have to be ridden,' she said.

A knock at the door put paid to further debate. Mari waved her son back to his seat. 'I'll go,' she said. 'It's probably one of the neighbours seen the news.'

Harry nodded. There had been a steady stream of visitors since he had arrived. Usually repeat visitors too, women and the odd man, who had known his family forever and wanted Mari to know that they were there. He watched his mother hustle through into the hall, wondering how she would handle things when they really were over and Helen buried and their lives once more changed forever.

Mari opened the front door and peered outside. There was no one there. She stepped out into the street and looked both ways, past the parked cars and kids playing in the road. In the distance, hurrying around the bend was a woman, dressed in blue, with dark hair. She was no one Mari recognized but it seemed likely that she must have been the one who knocked on Mari's door. Mari almost called after her, then she shrugged her shoulders and decided it was better to let it go.

As she turned to go inside a child's voice called out from down the street. 'Wait a minute, Mam!'

Mari stopped, one hand upon the door, and stood back, feeling the brush of clothing and whisk of long blonde hair as she ran on by.

Mari closed her eyes as tears pricked at the lids, wishing so hard that she could confide in Harry just how often she still saw and heard her other child.

Sarah Clarke's mother moved restlessly around the living room, straightening objects that did not need to be straightened; dusting, tidying, unable to be still. The television was on and her husband watched the news, leaning forward in his chair as though he needed to see more closely.

'It's going to be like this,' he said, 'isn't it? Like this, waiting bloody years for someone to catch the bastard.'

'They say he's dead,' his wife told him, her voice abstracted and distant. 'The one who killed that other child. Helen.' She said the name slowly, carefully, as though it were important to get it right. 'Helen Jones,' she said again.

Her husband glanced across at her and she watched as he

poured another measure of whisky into his glass. The evening sun glinted through the window, catching against the cut glass of the tumbler and breaking into a million, multicoloured fragments.

She blinked, realizing that her eyes were full of tears; tears distorting the light.

The door opened and their son, Sarah's brother, stood there, looking at them. No one moved, each one frozen in that captive moment. He closed the door again and Maggie heard him racing away from her up the stairs.

Sixteen

The day had begun with great frustration for Naomi. She had made a decision the night before that she should go and talk to ex-Detective Sergeant Lyman, the man mentioned in the news reports as being part of the investigative team under the command of Joe Jackson.

She recalled Lyman from her early days as a police officer and had worked with him closely on a few occasions, so she was reasonably certain he would remember her.

The address she had for him was an old one and she had no phone number. On calling directory enquiries she found that Lyman was now ex-directory and she had no means of calling ahead to see if the man still lived there, was home and wouldn't mind her coming over.

Frustration number one.

She had hope to call Harry and have him be her escort for the morning, but as she was about to pick up the receiver, Harry himself rang.

The press corps had returned in force, lining themselves up at both ends of the road and proving to be 'a flaming nuisance' as Harry put it.

'I can't leave Mari,' he told Naomi. 'They kept knocking on the door earlier, so we called the police. There's a patrol car sitting in the road now. I feel like a major crime scene.'

'How's Mari taking it?'

'Oh, far better than I am. Both sets of neighbours have taken up residence in the kitchen and they're all in there, drinking tea and pulling the world to pieces.'

Naomi laughed. 'Is Patrick OK?'

'Bored, but otherwise coping. You?'

'I'm just fine. Look, I'll talk to you later. You take care.'

Frustration number two.

Number three happened when she phoned her usual taxi firm and found that George Mallard was on his day off, but they knew who she was and that she was one of George's regulars and promised someone would be round in twenty minutes.

Finally, Naomi thought, she could be on her way.

It was after eleven when the taxi pulled up outside Lyman's house and the driver came around to help her out. 'You want me to wait until you're inside?' he asked her. 'George reckons to, doesn't he?'

Naomi laughed, he had evidently been well briefed. 'Thanks,' she said. 'And I'll ring when I'm ready to come home.'

She took a firm grip on Napoleon's harness and allowed him to lead her forward up the short garden path. The scent of roses filled the small front garden. They crowded against the edges of the path, pulling at her shirt sleeve. Napoleon stopped and sat down and Naomi reached out, looking for a bell or a door knocker. Finding neither, she rapped with her knuckles on the wooden door.

It seemed like a long time before he came and when he did, there was a silence long enough to fill Naomi with uncertainty once more.

'Detective Sergeant Lyman?' she asked finally.

'Yes, lass, it's me. I had this feeling you'd be along, you'd best come inside.'

Turning to wave to her taxi driver, Naomi followed her ex-colleague inside.

Geoff Lyman set the tea tray down upon a little table and Naomi could hear him pouring tea and arranging biscuits on a plate. He had said very little since welcoming her inside and leading her into what she thought must be the room at the front of the house. She had been here once before that she could remember and there were two reception rooms, with the kitchen beyond. The room was very quiet, just a clock ticking somewhere behind and above her head, and Napoleon snorting to himself as he settled at her feet. She had listened intently for a sign there might be someone else in the house – when she had come here the last time, there had been a wife in evidence, waving goodbye as they arrived – but there had been no sound this time that indicated anyone else's presence.

'I'm setting your tea down here, on the floor next to your chair. Can you manage that?'

'That will be fine. Thanks.'

'The . . . er dog, he won't drink it, knock it over or anything . . . ?'

'No. He knows better than that.'

It wasn't Naomi herself that he was uncertain how to talk to, she realized suddenly. It was the blind woman – sitting in his living room, with that very visible reminder of what she was snoring contentedly on his living-room floor – that he was having difficulties with.

'It's OK,' she said softly. 'I'm coping well, most of the time, and I don't expect you to say anything, because there's nothing you can say. I'm not here for the sympathy.'

'Sorry,' he said. Then: 'I'd forgotten how direct you can be.'

'That's OK, too. So had I.'

Geoff Lyman laughed briefly, but it cracked the tension between them.

'You said you'd guessed I'd come,' Naomi reminded him. 'What made you so sure?'

He waited for a moment before answering and she could almost feel him getting his thoughts in order. 'Dick Travers came,' he said. 'Asking questions about the Helen Jones case. He said there's been further evidence and they were going to start digging for the body.' He paused and in the silence she could hear him sipping his tea.

'He came back twice,' Geoff Lyman said. 'Asking questions about who had been involved in the investigation. Any gossip that had gone on. Anything I could remember that would not have appeared in the official records.'

'Like what?' Naomi wanted to know.

'Oh, God, lass, you know the sort of thing I mean. The conversations between officers that don't get annotated. The wild guesses and missed hunches. The bad jokes. Any disagreements among the investigating team. Everything. He wanted to know everything.'

'He came on his own?'

'Twice, yes. Once with Superintendent Phillips. Lass, there's not much I can tell you,' he added gently. 'You and I, we're no longer in the loop, as they say.'

The phrase was clearly not one of his. Phillips, she guessed. It didn't sound like Dick Travers either. 'And you resent that as much as I do,' she said.

'Maybe I do. But this time I'm also glad not to be involved. It's going to be bad, Naomi. Best prepare yourself.'

She looked up so sharply that Napoleon stirred. She angled her face so that, had she been able, she would have met his eyes. 'For what?' she asked. 'Prepare myself for what?'

'I can't tell you that. I gave my word I'd let them set the pace.'

'But you saw the confession,' Naomi guessed. 'You saw what it said.'

Geoff Lyman nodded slowly.

'You saw it?' Naomi asked again.

He spoke this time. 'Yes, I saw it. It was a typewritten sheet and it told them where to dig.'

'And you saw the name?'

'I saw the name.'

She sighed. 'I wish Joe was here to see this, don't you? Finally lay it all to rest.'

Harry stood in the front bedroom looking out through the net curtains at the scene below. The net impeded his vision of the journalists, but he had found that if he stood back a little and gazed obliquely through the gathered net, his view wasn't bad and he was fairly certain that he himself could not be seen.

A police car still sat at one end of the road, the other end now having been cleared of bystanders and reporters. The officers stood beside their car and chatted to the assorted neighbours who seemed intent on treating this as some sort of street party, Harry thought irritably.

The journalists themselves looked about as bored as Harry felt. They talked among themselves, having long since exhausted all input from the neighbours, and the police officer they had spoken to earlier had assured Harry that they wouldn't stick

102

around for long. It was a slow day news-wise. Digging had stopped at Lansdowne Road and nothing new had broken with regard to the other little girl whose death the police were investigating.

Harry tried not to think about what Sarah's parents were going through. He had been there already, to that limbo country which is no place to reside and yet which you cannot leave. The only difference being, he thought vaguely, was that they already knew that their child was dead. No false hope for them. No little glimmer of news appearing for just long enough to give hope, only to be dashed again on the rocks of reality.

Harry shook himself angrily. Why compare, either way was bad enough.

He had hoped to be able to see Naomi again today and felt guilty that the majority of his irritation was because this was not likely to happen now. He was frustrated too at the realization that her relationship with Alec was more involved than Harry had first thought. Naomi was the first woman to have really caught his interest since his ex-wife left him and Harry found himself deeply and shockingly jealous of this other man.

Mildly jealous of his son, too, who seemed to have founded such an easy relationship with this woman. Harry never found social contact easy; especially contact with women and most particularly women that he liked.

A small movement off to his right caught Harry's attention. A woman had come into the street from the church end, the end cleared of people. She wore blue and she was alone. She stood, watching, half hidden by the church fence. Her position reminded Harry of his own that morning when he had stood at the end of Lansdowne Road. He watched her curiously. She fitted, vaguely, the description of the woman his mother had seen hurrying away the previous night, but she was not familiar to Harry.

His mother had stated firmly that the woman she saw was not local and Harry saw no reason to distrust her opinion. His mother had a radar instinct for such things and Mari had insisted that the woman she had seen was 'not from round here'.

A brief flurry of movement off to Harry's left pulled his attention back to the other end of the street as another police car arrived. When Harry looked back, the woman had gone.

Seventeen

It was nine in the evening when Alec arrived at Philby
to rendezvous with the plain clothes unit who had been
keeping Gary Williams under observation. Williams had left
home an hour before and driven to Philby, parked on the
promenade – permitted after seven – and then wandered down
on to the beach.

He seemed to have no eventual destination in mind. The
tide was out, the wet beach ribbed with ripples left by the
retreating waves. Gary Williams didn't follow it. He stood for
a while above the high-water line, gazing out to sea, the evening
thickening around him as the mist rolled lazily inland and the
sky darkened and blurred through the slow moving fog.

He had turned inshore just before nine and Alec had arrived
just as Gary Williams turned into the end of Palmer Road and
stood outside number 23.

'What's he doing now?' the officer, DC Stoppard, standing
beside Alec wondered. Gary Williams had been easy to follow.
Walking slowly, with his hands shoved deep into his pockets
and a distracted air about him, he had looked neither left
nor right – certainly not back – and though Alec and DC
Stoppard now stood in shadow some distance away, Alec got
the impression that they could have come right up to him and
he still would not have turned around.

'His old address,' Alec said.

There were no lights burning at number 23, the family who
lived there presumably out or having an early night. Next door,
Phyllis Mole was sitting in her chair, watching the television.
She had her back to the window, the top of her grey head
just visible, and Alec wondered what he would do if Gary
knocked at the old lady's door. He had no reason to prevent

Gary Williams from visiting an old neighbour, but all the same, he didn't like the idea.

As though she had heard him, Phyllis chose that moment to move, get up from her chair and cross to the window to draw the heavy curtains.

She saw Gary Williams and he saw her and for a second or two they stood, looking through the glass, frozen. Then Phyllis drew the curtain closed and blocked the man from view. Alec decided it was time to move.

'Nice evening for a walk.'

Gary Williams turned. He seemed unsurprised and unconcerned by Alec's presence.

'I thought so.'

'You know them, do you? The new people?'

'What? Them that live there now? No, I don't know them. I just wanted to look.'

'Is that I *really* don't know them?' Alec asked him, 'or I don't know them like I didn't know Sarah Clarke?'

Gary scowled at Alec and began to walk back down the street. 'I don't . . . *didn't* know Sarah Clarke. I told you that.'

'She used to play with your kids. Visited your house.'

'So did lots of kids. Mine were popular. Had plenty of friends. How the hell am I expected to remember one?'

'Oh, I'd have thought you'd recall this one, especially considering what happened to her.'

'And I told you, I'm sorry for the kid. Sorry for her people. I know what they're going through.'

'So you deny knowing the Clarkes?' Alec persisted. 'You don't recall little Sarah coming round to play? She'd have been a little thing, only just having started school. A child that age would need supervision, I would think, especially with your two being small as well. Maybe you played with them? Your two and Sarah. Her mum and dad came to pick her up, maybe. Or you dropped her home. Come on, Gary . . . why lie about something we could check as easily as that?'

Gary Williams swung around so swiftly that Alec took an involuntary step back. 'Check, did you? I can tell you how you checked, copper. You came and talked to that nosy old fart we used to live next door to. Always poking where she wasn't welcome. Stirring it.' He swung away again and resumed his walk. Striding now so that it took Alec a step or two to catch up with him.

'What's your hurry, Mr Williams? Worried about something she might have said, are you? I'm surprised you're here at all, Mr Williams, considering what happened to your flat last time you were away.'

'And whose frigging fault was that?' He halted suddenly. 'Look, you. Charge me, arrest me again. Take me in, but you've got sweet FA. I came out, I needed some air. Fresh air, without you stinking it up. Now arrest me, or push off.'

This time Alec did not follow as he walked swiftly away. Stoppard mooched up behind him. 'Mortimer's on him, sir, reckons he's back in his car. Likely he's going home.'

Alec nodded, debating in his mind whether or not he should take up Williams' challenge or let him be for the night.

'What's his game, d'you reckon?' Stoppard asked him. 'There's more to this than just wanting a little walk.'

'Sure of it,' Alec agreed. Wearily, he rubbed at his face. The fog had poured inland now, filtering down the narrow streets and chilling his skin. 'I think another chat may be in order,' he said. But, he decided, he would talk to Travers first.

Naomi was alone. She had dragged one of the sofa cushions on to the floor and sat on it with the dog close beside her on one side and a bottle of red wine on the other. She had already made her way through three-quarters of the bottle and had every intention of finishing the rest.

She had hoped that Alec would come round or at least call, but when the phone rang earlier, it had been Harry.

She found that she had little to say to him, too absorbed in matters that she could not discuss with him. The journalistic presence had diminished during the afternoon and by evening had dissipated entirely. He hoped it would stay that way.

'I've been trying to persuade Mam to go away for a few days,' he said and Naomi knew that he wanted some input from her. Something reassuring or encouraging, though whether she thought they should stay or go, she wasn't sure and couldn't really be bothered to work out. She felt too distracted with her own thoughts to pay any mind to his and, though she felt guilty when the call ended and Harry was clearly put out by her attitude, she didn't have the will to call him back and try again.

Naomi wasn't sure exactly what had put her in this mood, but suddenly the whole situation seemed so utterly over-whelming.

The dog licked her chin and whined inquiringly. She lay her head against the dog's soft neck. His fur was thick and soft beneath her cheek. She wept softly, crying alternately over the dog's neck and into her wine.

Harry and his mother were watching the ten o'clock news. Patrick had already retreated to his room to play on his PlayStation and think about getting ready for bed. He was clearly bored – he had voluntarily spent part of the day doing school work – and Harry couldn't blame him. Harry himself was feeling at a loose end. There was so little to do here and Harry was used to being busy. When he had come home, it had seemed the only and obvious thing to do. Now he was here, Harry wasn't sure either what use he was or what Mari needed from him. Never terribly eloquent where emotions were concerned, he knew that his mother was probably getting more support from her long-time friends and neighbours than she was from him. Guiltily, he admitted to himself that he would be so relieved when Helen's body was finally released for burial and things could get back to something like normal.

He trapped the thought before it could be allowed to develop, shifted in his chair, trying not to look at Mari when she glanced curiously at him, afraid that by looking into his eyes she might guess his thoughts and feel ashamed by his lack of feeling.

It wasn't that he didn't care, Harry argued with himself, as he watched some aspect of the Middle Eastern war filter into his consciousness; more dead and dying for their families to mourn. It was simply that all his adult life he had been com-pelled to care in a way that should not have been demanded. It was as if the murderer had not just denied Helen the right to grow up, become a woman, have children and a future of her

108

own, but that he had somehow imprisoned all of them, refused to let them move on, or forgive or even forget . . . just a little. Just occasionally . . . just for a brief time.

Harry shook himself mentally, but was really jolted from his thoughts when someone rapped hard on the front door.

'Who the devil's that?' Mari asked. 'At this time of night.'

'I'll go,' Harry told her, glad of the excuse to move. It was probably, he thought, either a late-working journalist hoping to get a jump on the rest, or a neighbour, come back for another round of late talks.

They had already locked up for the night and it took a moment or two for Harry to unchain the door and fiddle with the deadlock. When he pulled the door open, it was neither his neighbour not was it an errant reporter. The woman who stood there was dark-haired and dressed in blue and Harry was taken aback by his shock of recognition.

'I had to come,' she said. 'Forgive me, but I just had to see you.'

Eighteen

It was late, but Naomi's lights were still on and Alec rang the bell, hoping she would still be awake.

She came to the door with Napoleon in tow, dressed in a nightshirt and robe. Her feet were bare and her short dark hair rumpled and untidy. She had been crying, her eyes red-rimmed and her face blotched with tears and when he kissed her, her mouth was heavy with the flavour of wine.

'Naomi?'

She leaned against him. 'I hoped you'd come.'

Awkwardly, he reached behind him to close the door, Napoleon trying to help and sniffing expectantly at his pockets.

'Sorry, old man,' Alec told him. 'No snacks tonight.'

He turned Naomi around and steered her back into the living room. An empty wine bottle stood beside the sofa and she had started on a second. Alec sat her down in the nearest chair. He hesitated for a moment, choosing whether he should get another glass and join her in finishing the bottle or make them both some coffee. He decided from the look of her that she'd had far more than enough already.

'Stay put,' he told her. 'I'll get us both a drink.'

'Wine over there.'

'Not wine. You've had enough of the red stuff. Have you eaten by the way or did you down all that grape juice on an empty stomach?'

She giggled like a child.

'Not a good sign when you laugh at my jokes,' he told her. 'Now be good, let go,' he added as she reached for him again. 'Let's get you sobered up a bit and then you can tell me what you've been drowning.'

She was asleep by the time he had made the coffee, curled up in the chair with her bare feet sticking awkwardly from beneath her robe. He went through to the bedroom, fetched a blanket from the cupboard and draped it gently around her, then stood in the kitchen doorway, mug in hand, watching her sleep.

Napoleon sat back on his haunches, his back end wagging so that he shuffled across the polished floor.

'What's going on, old lad?' Alec asked him. 'No, I don't suppose you're any the wiser either.' He sipped his drink. 'You hungry,' he added, 'or is that a stupid question?'

He returned to the kitchen, fishing bread and sandwich ingredients out of the fridge. Honey baked ham – half a slice for the dog – smoked cheese, cranberry sauce and chopped dill pickle. She had two kinds of bread – squashy supermarket white and kibbled wholewheat. He took a slice of each and spent time arranging the filling artistically between them. He ate, sitting on the sofa, watching Naomi and thinking about Gary Williams and Phyllis Mole.

'God, how long have I been asleep?'

'About an hour. You missed the most wondrous construction, didn't she, old man? Ham and cheese and cranberry and a little dill pickle, very finely—'

'Oh, don't,' she protested. 'It was all right up until the pickle. Any coffee left?'

'I'll make fresh. You go and have a shower, make yourself feel better.'

'Thanks. Sorry, not good company, am I?'

He kissed her gently. 'I'd rather be here with you asleep than . . . well . . . than.'

'Mmm . . . Bad day?'

'I've had better. Yours?'

'On a scale of . . . I'd say I hit a minus ten.'

'That good? Shower, coffee, tell me about it? Yeah?'

'Yeah. No. Alec,' she ran her hands through her already tousled hair. 'God, but I'm going to feel rough, aren't I?'

'Probably.'

The phone began to ring. Alec glanced at his watch. It was half past one. 'Who the hell's that?'

'Can you get it, Alec? I don't want to talk.'

'This time of night, it's bound to be for me.' He snatched the

111

receiver from the cradle and barked into the phone. 'Friedman. Oh, Harry, it's you. Sorry, I thought . . .' He fell silent and listened, glanced at his watch again. 'We'll be there. Half an hour.' He glanced at Naomi, taking in her tousled hair and still reddened face. 'Forty minutes, max.'

'What's going on?' Naomi asked him as he lowered the receiver, an odd look on his face.

'We're going to Harry's,' he said.

'At this time of night?'

'Yeah, and you might want to shower and tidy yourself up. Penny Jackson's there. Joe's daughter.'

Nineteen

G ary Williams arrived back at his flat just after one. He had been driving since leaving Alec, aimlessly looping in ever decreasing circles between Philby and the Radleigh Estate.

Everything was quiet when he returned to his flat. He resisted the temptation to wave at the officers on obs in the next block then knocked quietly on his neighbour's flat and slipped inside as Cathy cracked open the door, leaving the lights off in her hallway.

'Well?' she demanded.

'Yeah, you were right. They had me followed all the way to Philby and all the way back here. I led them around for an hour or so, just to keep them guessing. *He* was there. At Philby. Bastard.'

'He won't let up, will he?'

Gary Williams shook his head. 'Maybe you're right,' he said. 'Maybe we should do it.'

'What you got to lose?' she said, touching his arm. He looked down at her hand, but let it lie, though his gaze shifted to some distant point above her head. His eyes hardened.

'It's a chance to make a fresh start, Gary,' she said. 'Get away from here.'

He nodded slowly and before he could change his mind, she picked up the phone and began to dial.

It was well after two by the time they arrived at Mari's house. The street was silent and dark, street lamps pooling their light on the ground in front of blank windowed houses.

Harry must have heard the car because he opened the door as

Alec pulled up by the kerb, the sudden spillage of light almost shocking in the surrounding black.

Harry reached out and clasped Naomi by the arm. His voice was cracked and tense as he spoke to her, almost ignoring Alec.

'She's been here so long. I don't know what to say to her any more. Nomi, she says Joe wrote that thing. She says he might . . . that he killed Helen.'

'We'd best go inside,' Alec said, 'before we wake the street.'

Mari was sitting in the living room. As they went through, Naomi could hear her voice, but not the words at first. She sounded thick and muffled as though she had been crying or had her face hidden in a handkerchief. Naomi, who had sobered rapidly when Alec had explained about the call, began to feel her head tightening again, the beginnings of the hangover she knew was inevitable, beginning to bite.

'Mari?' she said.

'Over here, love. Come and sit down. I'm sorry to drag you both out at this hour but Harry thought . . .' She sniffed again, her voice breaking. Naomi reached out towards her and Mari took her hand and drew her down on to the sofa.

'What's going on?' Naomi said.

She heard a second voice then, one she did not know, but which was twinned with Mari's in the emotional stakes. 'I'm Penny Jackson,' the other woman said. 'And I came here because . . . because I thought you ought to know, all of you, just what the police aren't saying. Oh God, I wish I didn't have to know either.'

'You're saying that DI Jackson made that confession?' Alec asked her, his voice quiet and controlled, contrasting with the atmosphere of confusion and pain.

The woman must have nodded, Naomi thought, because Alec began again.

'You brought this so-called confession to the police?'

'Yes, yes, that was me.' She took a deep breath as though trying to regain control and when she spoke again she seemed in some measure to have achieved it. 'I'm sorry,' she said. 'You must all wonder what kind of mad woman came here tonight.'

'Why did you come?' Alec again. Slightly abrupt, Naomi thought.

'Why?'

'Yes, why.' Alec paused. 'Forgive me, Miss Jackson, but if it had been *my* father that might be guilty of this appalling thing, the last place I'd want to be would be with the victim's family.'

'I had to do something,' Penny Jackson said.' I didn't know what else to do.'

'OK,' said Alec. 'Then let's start at the beginning. Suppose you start by telling us how you came by the confession and why it took three years after Joe Jackson's death to come to you?'

When her father had died, Penny explained, he had left everything to her, including the house. Penny had never married, but she'd been in a long-term relationship, which had broken up about a year before Joe died. She had moved back home and remained there.

'It's a big house,' Penny went on, 'and prices have been going through the roof this past year or so. I decided to sell up, find something smaller, maybe right on the coast. Dad had an extension built to make the kitchen bigger and also so that he could have a garage. The people who want to buy asked me if the foundations had been laid deep enough, or something, for the next floor to be built on top. I asked our solicitor to get the deeds and plans out of storage for me. This . . . confession . . . it was in with those.'

'Any idea why?'

'No. No, of course I don't. Dad was normally a really methodical man, but it wasn't filed with his will or any of the personal stuff that came to me after he died. It was stuck in a storage box with the building plans, just as though it didn't matter a damn who found it or when.'

Her earlier emotional storm was threatening to break again. Beside her on the sofa, Mari sat tense and still, though she had kept a hold on Naomi's hand.

'How long did it take you to decide what to do?' Alec asked her.

'Oh, I knew what I had to do. Straightaway I knew that. As

soon as I read it I knew what it was all about and that I had to show it to someone. It was a Sunday by the time I'd had a chance to look at the plans and found the letter. I didn't think there'd be anyone available on a Sunday night, so I waited and I didn't get a wink of sleep. And on the Monday I took it in and asked to see someone in charge. The rest you know.'

'What was in it?' Naomi asked her. 'Penny, what did the letter say?'

'I've already told Mari what it said,' Penny told her. 'I'm sorry, but I don't think I could go through that again.'

'It said that he had killed our Helen,' Mari said softly. 'That he had strangled her and hidden her in the foundations of a house on Lansdowne Road; he thought it was number 43. That he was sorry, it hadn't been meant to happen like that, but sometimes that's just the way life is.'

Mari took a deep, quavering breath. 'Isn't that how you said he worded it?' she questioned. 'That he was sorry, that our Helen was dead, and that was just the way it was.'

The silence remained for a long time, unbroken by anything except Penny's quavering breaths and Harry, standing in the doorway, shifting slightly from foot to foot.

Mari said nothing more. She didn't move and seemed hardly to be breathing, so still was she close against Naomi's arm.

'I've felt so utterly alone,' Penny said quietly. 'And I know it was a stupid thing, coming here tonight. I'm sorry, truly, deeply sorry, if I've caused you more pain but I had to do something, talk to someone. Ever since I took that paper to the police . . . I thought I'd get some support, some help . . . I don't know what. But something. Instead, I've just been pushed aside and totally ignored. Treated like *I've* done something wrong. It wasn't me who did any-thing. It was him, it must have been him. The letter said so.'

'You seem very ready to be convinced,' Alec told her. 'Did it never cross your mind that the confession might have been a fake, or a plant or some stray piece of evidence your father shouldn't really have had?'

'Of course it did.' Anger replaced pain now. 'You really think I wanted to believe that my father was a killer?'

116

Naomi felt Mari wince. Harry shifted his position once again and came to sit on the arm of the settee.

'I wanted them to say to me, Penny, we don't know what this is, but it has nothing at all to do with Joe. But then they started digging and they found her, didn't they?'

She got abruptly to her feet. 'I'm going now,' she said. 'I'm sorry to have bothered you. I just thought . . . I just wanted . . .' She began to cry again. 'I never should have come,' she said.

Alec had walked her to her car, checked again that she felt well enough to drive and then returned to the others.

'How long has she been here?' he asked.

Harry came in with a tray of mugs and a pot of tea. 'Since just after ten,' he said. 'I shouldn't have let her in, I suppose, but I was so taken aback. Then she didn't seem to want to go.'

'You could have told her to,' Alec observed.

'Yes, I suppose, but it didn't seem polite.'

'I'll bet double-glazing salesmen have a field day in your house.'

'Hmm,' Harry said. 'I can't help the way I am. I know it won't do on occasion, but I can't help it.'

'It's the way he was raised,' Mari said quietly, coming to his defence. 'But it was getting too much. I wanted her to go away and then I couldn't stop listening to her. She went on there, talking about Joe, telling like he wasn't the man we thought he was but how she never thought it would be this bad. That he'd do anything like . . . like what she reckons he did to Helen.'

'What do you think she's playing at, Naomi?' Harry asked.

Naomi shook her head. 'I don't know,' she said. 'Maybe she just needed absolution. But, Alec was right, if I'd been in her place, the last thing I'd have done was come here. God, I'd probably have burned the thing.'

'Would you though?' Alec asked her. 'Or would you be so shocked that you acted as Penny Jackson did? On that same kind of impulse.'

'Was it impulse?' Harry demanded. 'She admits she had at least a night to think it over. I don't call that an impulsive act, more one that had been considered and well thought out.'

'Did Joe ever talk about his daughter?' Mari asked Naomi.

'Yes. He mentioned her from time to time. What she'd been doing and so on. She's a year younger than me, I think. I remember that, 'cause she took her A levels the year after I did and Joe said how well she'd done. He was proud of her, if that's what you mean. I don't know how close they were.' She frowned. 'I don't know, Mari, Joe was quite a private man. He didn't talk about much except the job, even when he was off duty. I got the impression that he and his wife didn't always get along, even that there was another man, but I couldn't tell you more than that. I know they finally separated, then divorced.'

We talked mainly about me, she though, realizing this suddenly. We hardly ever talked about Joe and after those first few months, didn't even talk much about Helen.

She closed her eyes, a reflexive action when she was trying to focus on something, even though there was no longer anything to block out.

'I can't remember much at all about Penny,' she said finally. 'Except that she was an only child and Joe saying that his wife had decided they wouldn't be having any more.'

There was another movement from the doorway and the slow thump of Napoleon's tail against her leg told Naomi who it was.

'Hello, Patrick,' she said quietly.

'Hi, Naomi.'

'Pat, back to bed with you. Have you any idea what time it is?'

'Bet it's cold on the stairs this time of night,' Naomi said. 'I used to freeze my backside off, sitting there, listening when my parents rowed.' She smiled. 'They didn't do it very often, but boy, when they did. I could sit on the stairs and hear every word.'

'Patrick?' Harry questioned.

'Yeah,' the boy admitted. 'I heard. I heard and then I couldn't sleep but I didn't want to come down. I knew you'd just send me back up.' He moved further into the room and squeezed into the seat beside Naomi. 'I want to know what's going on, Dad,' he said, his voice so earnest that Naomi felt herself melt in sympathy.

'I think he has a right,' she said softly. 'There've been too many secrets, Harry.'

She heard him sigh, a great outrush of breath that seemed to deflate all arguments he might have formulated. 'I'll get you a drink,' he told his son. 'Warm you up, but frankly, I don't know that I can take much more of this tonight. I don't know what's worse any more. Knowing or not knowing. Either way . . .' he hesitated, not good with words that offered such emotional betrayal. 'Either way,' he said finally, 'it hurts like hell.'

It was after four when Naomi and Alec arrived back at Naomi's home. The plan was to grab a few hours' sleep and then for Alec to track down Phillips and talk things through. It was not an interview that Alec looked forward to.

They had talked and talked until words had become just empty noise and all anyone wanted was to escape into sleep, even Patrick, who had been drooping against Naomi's arm. Even Napoleon seemed subdued, not liking this change in his routine.

Naomi had been silent and thoughtful all the way home. 'Penny for them?' Alec said, then laughed at the unintended irony. 'Sorry,' he said, 'I guess a Penny's what they're worth.'

She smiled at him. 'I guess so, too,' she said, but what she had been thinking all the way home was what an impact Joe had exerted upon her life. From the child, frightened and guilt-ridden, to the teenager who had, if she was honest, an almighty crush on this big, safe man. To the young police officer, bowled over by the thought of working with her hero. There had been little in her life that had not in some way been linked to or influenced by Joe Jackson and she could not believe – would not believe – that now all of her beliefs and hopes and dreams and actions – all her adult life virtually – had been built on such flawed foundations.

'He didn't do it, Alec,' she said slowly. 'Not Joe. There has to be another explanation.'

119

But Alec said nothing and Naomi reminded herself that Alec and Joe had had a feud going on all the years she had known them both. Something neither of them acknowledged publicly or made a big thing of in their professional lives, but which was palpable every time the two men met.

Alec, she realized, had no difficulty at all in believing.

Twenty

Saturday dawned clear and cool but with the promise of warmth in the watery sun. Naomi stood beside the window sipping her morning tea and feeling the cold breeze blowing from the sea across her bare arms. It raised gooseflesh, chilling her until she retreated and closed the window, stood still in the sunlight through the glass, enjoying the warmth of it as it eased the chill from her flesh. It was bright enough for her to have some small perception of it: red through her eyelids when she closed them. Shadowed red, dim and unsatisfying, but welcome nonetheless.

She felt exhausted, and from Alec's reluctance to leave her bed this morning figured he must feel the same, not, she noted with a wisp of satisfaction, that he was ever eager to leave.

Irritated with herself that she should allow such frivolous thoughts to filter through even for a second, she turned away from the sunlight and returned to the kitchen where she had left Alec in charge of cooking breakfast. One thing she still did not have the confidence for was frying eggs.

She could hear him chatting to the dog, Napoleon replying with thumps of his tail upon the floor and a whole range of canine vocalization that he usually reserved only for Alec. Little chirps of noise that sounded more bird-like than dog-like combined with excited panting and questioning whines.

'You and that dog solved it yet?' she asked.

'No, but give us another half hour or so. We plan to revise the theory of evolution next week, if you care to join us. Put dogs right up there with the primates on the evolutionary tree.'

Napoleon arfed happily.

'You see, he agrees with me.'

'You bribe all your stooges with bacon rind, do you?'

'Damn, caught us out again, old man. But you're wrong, Nomi. Actually it was sausage. Now you sit down and I'll bring breakfast.'

She laughed, shaking her head at the pair of them and went to find the table, feeling her way around it with her free hand until she came to her chair.

This was all delaying tactics, she knew. This domesticity of Alec's. He didn't want to get on with the day any more than she did. Bed seemed even more tempting that ever and a day in bed spent with Alec, the more so, but even had last night not happened, that would have been impossible.

Alec set her plate down in front of her. 'More tea?' he asked, heading back to the kitchen.

'Please. Think you'll still be able to make it this afternoon? Sam will be really disappointed if you don't.'

'I'll be there.' He returned to the table and sat down. She heard him refilling her cup and the clatter as he picked up his cutlery and began to eat. Alec was satisfyingly noisy about everything, she thought. Much easier to keep track of. Harry, on the other hand, did everything with an exaggerated quietness that she found intriguing. Around Harry, she found herself straining to hear, to make out the restrained sounds that went with his actions. To interpret every little nuance as if it were speech.

'I'll make it just after three with a bit of luck. Sure you're OK for getting over there?'

'No problem, Paul's coming to get me at twelve. The hordes are due at half past one, Sue's taking them swimming. Apparently there's some special floating toys available Saturday lunchtimes. We'll all be getting back before three anyway.'

'We? You're going too?'

She shook her head. 'Not going in the water, but Sue wants as many bodies as she can to help them get dressed and so on. I can still put socks on and fasten shoes.'

'Sounds like great fun,' Alec said dryly. 'A bunch of four and five-year-olds, all wanting to pee at the same time and getting their laces stuck,' he continued, but he said it fondly. He was in truth very close to Naomi's sister Sue, her husband Paul and their two boys and it had become an

122

accepted thing that Alec was included in any invitations that Naomi had for family events.

'What do you think Phillips is going to say?' Naomi queried.

Alec snorted. 'What can he say? He can hardly deny everything now, can he? I've got to admit, I'm pretty peed off at being kept out of the loop like this. I mean, I was to start with, but especially now.'

'Are you glad it's Joe?' The question came out unbidden and she regretted it immediately.

'What sort of a question is that? How can I be glad there's any suggestion it was a police officer? Especially one with Joe's rank. Look, Nomi, I didn't like the man, but I don't want to think anyone I've worked with could do something like that.'

'I'm sorry,' she apologized. 'I don't even know what made me say it.'

'Of course you know.' He had softened his tone but the irritation still showed. 'You asked because you know we hated each other's guts and I've never told you why.'

'And will you tell me? Now, I mean. Alec, I know you've always held back because you know how I feel about him. How important he was to me, but now . . . Alec, things are going to come out whatever we do, I'd kind of like any other revelations to come from the horse's mouth.'

She heard him lay his cutlery down upon his plate and lift his mug of tea from the table. Delaying tactics again, Alec, she thought.

'I'll tell you,' he said finally. 'But not just now. Now I've got to go and face Phillips before I put it off altogether.' He got up from the table and came round to her side, kissing her gently on the top of her head and then, when she lifted her face, on the cheek, this second kiss more absent, his mind already somewhere else.

'OK,' she told him, 'but Alec, like we agreed last night, there are already too many secrets. Don't hold out on me any more.'

The morning had been taken up by clearing breakfast away and

123

getting ready for the afternoon. Paul had collected her and she had joined a dozen noisy kids and assorted parents in their trip to the swimming pool.

Naomi had loved to swim before. She had tried a few months ago, going with her sister to a quieter, women-only session that the pool held in the evenings. But even that had been too much; the noise level, echoing and confusing. The lack of clues as to where she was in the water, how far from the end of her lane, how she could keep to her own space. It was all too much to take in, even with Sue to guide her.

She promised that she would try again but thus far she had not done so. She suspected that this birthday treat had been arranged in part for Auntie Naomi to go back to this place that had confused her so much and get acclimatized before Sue started on her next round of persuasion.

And Naomi was something of a novelty. 'Sam's-auntie-that-can't-see' was soon in demand to persuade small damp feet into socks and untie knotted laces. Still, Naomi was glad to get out of this place of amplified confusing noise and back to her sister's house.

'You look exhausted,' Sue told her. 'That wasn't too much for you, was it?'

'No, I was up all night. Or most of it.'

'Oh yes? Alec stayed over again, did he?'

'He did, but that wasn't . . .'

'Oh, no, I'm not having that. You're going bright red.'

'I am not!' Naomi laughed. 'I always say I'm not going to rise to the bait and I always do, don't I?'

'Course you do,' Sue said as she squeezed her arm. 'Years of sisterly conditioning. Alec will be coming, won't he? Sam's been asking.'

'He'll be here,' Naomi told her. 'He had to see his Super this morning, but he promised to be here around three.'

'Superintendent Phillips on a Saturday. That's enough to ruin anyone's weekend. Something new?'

She was saved the problem of replying by the doorbell ringing. 'Oh, that's probably Mam and Dad,' Sue said. 'Sam, Rickie, Granddad and Grandma.'

124

And she headed for the door, leaving Naomi a moment or two to prepare herself for the parental onslaught.

Alec arrived at half past three to be given a paper plate piled high with sandwiches and cake. 'I hope you saved me a jelly?' Alec said as Sam offered him a balloon.

'My mum put spiders in the jelly,' Sam told him happily. 'Yours is green.'

'Excellent!' Alec approved. 'Red jelly, with green spiders. Life is now complete.'

He sat down next to Naomi who seemed to have acquired a child and several dolls, all piled on to her lap. 'Having fun?'

'You better believe it. How did it go?'

'Oh, I was flavour of the month. First, I disturbed him at home, then I broke the wondrous news.'

'And? Is it true, what Penny told us?'

'It's true. Or it's true she took the letter to the police at any rate. I told Phillips that if he didn't speak to Helen's family then they might well be looking elsewhere for information.'

'You mean the press? Alec, Harry and Mari would never do that.'

'I know that, you know that. Lord, Harry would sooner run along the beach naked.'

'Naked,' said the little girl on Naomi's lap. She giggled.

'Right . . .' Alec seemed somewhat at a loss. 'Maybe we should take a walk around the garden?'

'Oh no you don't.' Sue's voice floated across to them as they started to get up. 'It's cake-cutting time.' She came over and kissed Alec on the cheek. 'Just accosting your man, big sister.'

'I'm sure he won't mind.'

Sue leaned over to her. 'Just let Sammy blow his candles out, then you can be relieved of party duty and I'll let you talk shop.'

'Naked!' came a little voice down by Naomi's knees. 'Naked. Naked!'

'If you are, you'd better put your clothes on,' Sue told the child. 'Come and have some cake.'

'Cake! Cake!'

Alec sighed heavily. 'You all right?' he asked.

'I'm all right.'

'Not too tired?'

'Too tired for what?' she asked wickedly.

'Lord, you can always tell when you've been around that sister of yours. Full of ideas you are.' He put his arm around her and squeezed, pulling her as close to him as was decent in a room full of excited kids. She leaned in to him, enjoying the warmth and hardness of his body pressed against her own.

'One two three, blow and don't forget to make a wish . . .'

'Too tired for what?' Naomi asked again, her voice drowned by the singing of happy birthday to her nephew Sam.

'I've taken the liberty of inviting Mari and co. to meet at your place later,' he said. 'We can always get a takeaway or something after.'

'After what?' Naomi asked.

'After Phillips has come round and talked to us all,' Alec said.

Twenty-One

At three fifteen on the Radleigh Estate a car pulled up outside the block where Gary Williams lived. There were two men in the car and they were not local, Viccy Elliot was sure of that. The car was too good for a start, no one on the Radleigh owned anything as new or upmarket as that.

Viccy Elliot had ample opportunity to observe the slew of journalists who had wandered through the Radleigh in recent days, knocking on doors and asking for opinions from young mothers on their way to and from school. For the most part, they had been the same faces as had tracked over their estate when the so-called riots had broken out over that pervert the other year.

Riots, Viccy Elliot said to herself. If they thought that was a pigging riot . . . and those two in the car . . .

She did have a pretty good idea what they were and she hadn't remembered seeing either of them before . . .

A small movement at the corner of the flat, a man's head peering warily out from the shadow of the red brick wall. Suddenly Viccy realized whom they had come for.

Gary Williams broke cover, the first time Viccy remembered seeing him out in daylight since the arrest, and threw himself into the rear of the car, an overnight bag stuffed in just ahead of him.

And then another figure came running from the direction of the flats, this one looking about her nervously. She caught sight of Viccy just before getting to the car and for an instant she froze, the two women meeting eye to eye across the narrow road. Then Cathy Walton did a very stupid thing. She had the temerity not just to smile at Viccy Elliot – a wide, Cheshire cat grin that really rubbed her face in it –

but she also raised her hand and gestured in Viccy's direction with a single upraised finger.

Viccy Elliot was a forgiving woman, but some things, from some people, would never sit right.

'Fucking bitch!' Viccy Elliot exploded as the car sped away.

Twenty-Two

B y five forty-five everyone concerned had piled into Naomi's living room and Patrick was helping Alec with coffee. Phillips had been unhappy at the boy being present, but Harry had told him in no uncertain terms that he was not about to leave Patrick on his own in the evening, not knowing how long they'd be away or who was still hanging about outside their house.

'Most of the journalists have gone,' Harry admitted, 'but after last night, I wouldn't want to be on my own, and I don't see why my son should be.'

Phillips, though clearly displeased, gave in to the fait accompli and Patrick seated himself on the floor at Naomi's feet, with Napoleon's head resting across his legs.

'I want to see what he wrote,' Mari said, speaking for them all. 'And don't give me any bolony about you not being able to authorize it, because I know you're in charge on this and you damned well can.'

'Mrs Jones . . .' Phillips began, but Mari was not to be silenced. She had things to say, emotions walled up for years that had suddenly broken out through the dam and she was ready for battle.

'Don't you Mrs Jones me,' she said. 'My daughter died more than twenty years ago. She never got the chance to become a woman. She didn't even get the chance to grow up, and if the confession is right and that man took her life from her . . .' Her voice broke and she choked on a sob.

'Mam,' Harry said softly. Naomi could imagine him holding her hands, groping in his pocket for a handkerchief. 'Mam, let me . . .'

'No Harry, no. This was my fight first and I'm going to have

129

my say. We trusted Joe Jackson. Trusted that he cared about our Helen and about finding her killer. He was there, all the way through, supporting us, caring for us, or so we thought. He got through to Naomi there when her mam and dad had given up hope of her ever getting hold of life again. He was there for us even after the case had been run down and all the files on my Helen's death packed away to gather dust. I need to know, I need to know for my own sanity and my own peace of mind. Not that I'm ever going to have peace of mind again after all of this. I need to know if he wrote that awful letter. I want to hear if what he said was the same as she said it was. So damned callous I couldn't hear Joe saying that, not ever. I need . . . I need to see that confession or whatever it was and if you don't show me, my God, I'm going to raise Cain.'

'Wow,' Patrick said softly.

Wow, Naomi thought. She had become so used to the Mari she knew. Soft-spoken, strong in her own quiet way, but so much in control of her emotions. This was something new and she could feel the tension of Mari's speech infiltrate every corner of the room.

Phillips cleared his throat and shuffled uneasily in his chair. 'I understand, Mrs Jones—' he began to say, but he got no further.

'No, Mr Phillips, you don't understand or you wouldn't be trying to flannel me like this. You don't understand because you didn't lose Helen. You didn't go through years and years of wondering. Of seeing her in your head every night when you went to sleep. Of falling asleep imagining what the bastard who took her might have done. Seeing her in your dreams killed every which way you could imagine and a few more besides that you didn't want even to imagine, so that when I found out that she was strangled, you know what, Mr Phillips, I was almost relieved. At least now I could imagine the worst and know it couldn't be . . . couldn't be.' She stopped there and took a deep breath in, the sobs rising in her throat to choke the words.

'Mam,' Harry said again. 'Mam, I never knew.'

'No. No one knew. That was just the trouble. Mac thought it best not to talk about it. He couldn't bear to do so himself, so he wouldn't talk to me. And the thought of telling you . . . you're our child, Harry. And even when you grew up, you were still our kid, frozen like Helen and I couldn't put that much grief on you.'

'You think it wasn't there?' His voice was sharp. Uncharacteristically so. 'Mam, if you think I did any less . . . Mam, I'd go out at night looking. I'd sit where I could watch the waste land, just hoping whoever it was would come back and that I might somehow know it was him if he did. God, you think you were the only one to dream?'

He fell silent and the room with him. Even the dog had caught the mood and lay motionless with his big black head resting on Patrick's thigh.

'Why don't you want us to see it?' Patrick asked at last. 'Whatever's in it can't be worse than Dad and Nan imagine, could it? I mean . . .' he seemed suddenly taken aback by his own temerity.

'No,' Phillips told him quietly. 'I don't suppose it could.'

Naomi heard him draw something from his pocket. It rustled and crinkled when he unfolded it. A copy then, she guessed, not the original. That must be locked away somewhere. Phillips' voice was quiet as he began to read out loud:

I make this statement on October the 19th 1979. I want to set the record straight, though, God forgive me, I don't have the courage to come out with it now, knowing how many are going to be hurt. It's my hope that all of this will come out long after I am gone and if luck is on my side, I don't have to be there to face the consequences when the shit finally hits the fan. It seems to me only right that everyone, whoever they are, should have the right to a decent burial and for their family to know where they are laid to rest and it's because of this that I write this now.

You'll find the body on the Lansdowne Road. The houses were just half-finished when I was looking for a place to leave it and it seemed appropriate, knowing what I know about the place. There was only a plot number there at the time but I've been back since and

131

think the house must be number 43. I'm sorry for those who'll be living there when this is found. It won't be pleasant for them.

I won't ask forgiveness. What's the point? I didn't mean for this to happen, but sometimes life has a way of getting away from you.

'It's signed at the bottom, Joe Jackson, Detective Inspector. And it's dated October 19th 1979,' finished Phillips, his voice weighted with sadness.

'My God,' Harry said.

Mari began to cry, softly, almost as though she wanted no one else to hear.

Naomi sat in stunned silence. Vaguely, she heard the paper rustle again and Alec's voice. 'Typewritten,' he said. 'An old portable by the look of it. What do Documents have to say?'

Phillips cleared his throat. 'They agree,' he said. 'We're working on the model and so on. Nothing firm yet.'

'Is it his signature?' Naomi wanted to know. 'No one could have . . .'

'Forged it? I'm sorry, Naomi, Documents are convinced it's contemporary with the letter being written and it matches. We've pulled records from other cases for comparison and his daughter provided us with other samples. There's very little doubt.'

'Very little?'

'None.' Phillips amended. 'Naomi, I wish there were.'

The clock ticked noisily in the silent room. No one moved. It struck the hour and Naomi counted automatically. Six o'clock. The sharp ringing of a mobile phone suddenly shattered the uncomfortable peace.

'Excuse me,' Phillips said. He spoke briefly into the handset. Listened, spoke again. 'I've got to go,' he said.

Naomi wondered if he really did or if the phone call was just a blessed excuse for him to escape.

'I'm sorry, Naomi,' Phillips said. In her confusion she wasn't sure what he was sorry for; having to leave or her mentor having murdered her best friend. She nodded, not trusting herself to speak.

132

Alec left with Phillips after giving her the briefest kiss goodbye. 'I'll call you later,' he said. She had known that he would not be staying that night, but even so, she hated that he had to go.

The silence continued in the room after they had left, the slamming of the front door only serving to emphasize it.

'I think I want to go home,' Mari said at last. 'Naomi, love . . .'

Naomi nodded. 'It's OK,' she said, thinking, no it's not. Nothing will ever be OK again.

'Can I stay?'

'What? Sorry.'

'I said, can I stay?' Patrick repeated. 'I can sleep on the couch.'

'Patrick, I don't think . . .' Harry began.

'No,' Naomi told him. 'I'll be glad of the company,' she surprised herself by saying. Then surprised herself again by finding this was true. The thought of being alone with her thoughts was not an appealing one.

'I've a spare bedroom anyway,' she told Patrick. 'You'll have to help me make up the bed, but you're welcome to stay.'

'Well, if you're sure,' Harry said. He sounded doubtful, but also oddly relieved. 'OK, Mam, let's get you home. I'll call later,' he promised. 'Make sure everything's all right.' Naomi nodded. She stood in the centre of the living room, listening to the sounds of their departure, of Patrick showing his dad out and then coming back upstairs and closing the door. He stood for a moment, just inside the doorway. Naomi could feel his pent-up energy and frustration reaching out to her across the room.

'I want to walk,' she said. 'I can't stay cooped up here.'

'OK. How about down to the sea? I've hardly seen it since I've been here.'

Naomi smiled. 'I'll get my coat,' she said. 'It's likely to be windy this time of night. You have one?'

'Yeah. You think dad'd let me out of the house without?'

'Right,' she said, suddenly desperately energized. Urgently in need of action, any kind of action. Something to do that had

133

nothing at all to do with Helen or the pain of it all. 'We'll take a walk on the beach and then you can thrash me at that arcade game we talked about.'

'Great,' he agreed and she knew instinctively that he felt the same. 'And . . .' he hesitated as though what he had to say was a secret he wasn't certain he should share. 'I'll tell you about my world,' Patrick said.

Penny Jackson sat on the top step in her father's house, half-hidden by the balustrade that ran across the landing. Below, through the turned spindles, she could see down into the hall and the living-room door just at the corner of her view. She had long lost track of the numberless nights she had sat up here, perched in this corner of the landing, listening to her parents' voices in the room below.

Sometimes there would be just a low murmur of conversation against the background noise of music or the television and she would go to bed happy, knowing that they were talking and at peace with one another. Other times, far too many times in Penny's memory, the voices would be raised in anger, snatches of their conversation rising up on waves of rage to break about her on her cliff-top step.

The arguments always followed the same pattern. They were always about The Job, her mother pronouncing the words as though they were writ large in capitals, and the way it ruled Joe's and therefore all of their lives.

'You're a good man, Joe,' her mother said, 'but you're a bloody street angel.'

'What's that supposed to mean?'

'Exactly what it sounds like it means. Out there, you're Mr Wonderful. Mr Compassion. Mr I Care. But I ask you, Joe, when was the last bloody time you brought that compassion home?'

'Out there are people who need me.'

'And we don't?'

'It's not the same.'

'Isn't it?'

'You know damned well it's not.'

'Sometimes, Joe, the only way I think we'll get you to notice

134

us is if we wind up dead. Would you see us then? The great Inspector Joe Jackson—'

She remembered how her mother had broken off then. The sharp recoil of her father's hand slapping her mother's face and the soft crying that followed.

And her father's voice. 'Oh God, I'm sorry, love . . . Oh God, I'm sorry . . . I just didn't mean . . .'

And then the phone ringing and her father coming slowly out into the hall, drawing a deep breath before he picked it up. 'Jackson . . . Oh, hello. No, of course it's not a bad time. That's all right . . .'

Knowing it was Naomi, or if not Naomi some other voice in the night come to take her dad away.

'You're going out again?' Her mother's voice, thick with crying. As Penny leaned as far as she dare, her mother's face visible, the cheek red, the fingermarks on her pale skin.

'I have to go. She's going through a rough time . . .'

'And we're not?'

'Leave it, Lydia. Leave it, please.'

She heard her mother begin to cry again and her father open and then softly close the door.

'Are you all right?' Bill's voice from close behind her dragged Penny momentarily back to the present.

'Yes. I'm OK.'

'Oh no, you're not.' He sat beside her on the step and held her tight, drawing her against him, the warmth and comfort of his arm across her shoulder almost more than she could bear.

'Still watching the ghosts?' he asked her softly and she nodded, her cheek rubbing against the rough fabric of his woollen sweater.

What about me? The child, Penny thought, her pain reaching into the mind of the adult and stirring the memories afresh. What about me? Doesn't she have a mum and dad of her own? Why does she have to steal mine?

Twenty-Three

A lec arrived on Sunday morning just as Naomi was about to get breakfast ready. He had a holdall with him and a bundle of newspapers tucked under his arm.

'Can I stay for a few days? I can go and find a hotel if it's a problem, but I don't think now is a good time to be at home.'

'Stay? Of course you can. You should know that, but a "hello Naomi how are you this morning" would be nice first.'

'Sorry.' She heard him drop the bag to the floor and the papers after it. He reached out and drew her into his arms, kissing her firmly on the mouth. 'Hello Naomi and how are you this morning?'

She smiled and lay her cheek against his chest. 'That's better. Now, what's going on?'

'Alec's in the papers,' Patrick announced. 'Wow.'

'What?' Naomi lifted her head and looked in the boy's direction. 'What do you mean, Patrick?'

'Gary Williams sold his story,' Alec told her. 'He's made claims of police harassment and yours truly has been named as chief persecutor. Phillips gave me a call about an hour ago. I threw a few things into a bag and came over here.'

'What if the reporters know about Naomi being your girl-friend?' Patrick asked. It seemed like a fair question.

'We just hope they don't,' Alec told him. 'If we find an outside broadcast unit camped on the doorstep later on, well, I'm afraid she'll just have to marry me.'

'You sound very cheerful about it?'

'No point not being, really.' She felt him shrug. 'No, I'm completely pissed off, I'm also hungry, 'cause I missed breakfast and I'm sorry to land this on you.'

'Don't be. Patrick, read them out for me while Alec earns his keep.'

'OK.' She heard him flop down in the kitchen doorway and spread the newspapers on the floor. 'I'm here, is that all right?'

'For now, yes.' He'd got used to giving her updates on where he was standing, what he was doing and if he'd left anything on the floor. She found it both amusing and rather touching.

'"I've been hounded out of my home, my job, my life, claimed Gary Williams, thirty-six, yesterday, in an exclusive interview with the Sunday Star".'

'Oh, brother,' Alec moaned. 'I suppose he claims I did the hounding?'

'Sort of. I'm getting to that bit. "Gary Williams, whose life has already been touched by more tragedy than . . ."'

'Spare us,' Alec said. 'Just give us a resumé, Patrick. I don't think I can cope with the journalese.'

Williams had really gone to town. His life story seemed to have been one of unmitigated woe – broken home, absent father, mother who was a binge drinker – culminating in the loss of his wife and children two years before.

'It is sad though, isn't it?' Patrick interrupted himself.

'It's bloody awful,' Alec agreed. 'I pity the man, but that doesn't stop him being a scrote and a toe rag.'

'What's a scrote?' Patrick wanted to know. 'Anyway, he says that you've victimized him, spread rumours about him all over the Radleigh Estate.'

'That *I've* spread rumours? Nice one, Gary.'

'He says that because you've spread all these rumours and dragged him away from his job and made all these unfounded accusations that his flat was wrecked and he was forced to flee the Radleigh in fear of his life.'

'I take it that last bit's a direct quote? Naomi, I'm going off the idea of bacon.'

'Tough, it's half cooked now. Since when did you let the media put you off your breakfast?'

'Since now. I'm not usually the star attraction.'

'There's a good picture of you,' Patrick told him. 'Look.'

137

Alec looked and groaned. 'Me and the venerable Viccy Elliot,' he told Naomi, 'looking far too friendly.'

'Really? I wonder when that was taken.'

'Oh, I can work out when it was taken,' Alec told her. 'The question is, who took it?' He sighed impatiently. 'OK, go on.'

'He calls the residents of the Radleigh Estate a load of in-bred animals,' Patrick continued. 'He said they haven't got a brain cell between them and all they're good for is wrecking other people's lives and living on a place like the Radleigh.'

'That's good, coming from someone who lost everything pissing it against the wall,' Alec observed. 'And it's going to go down really well when Viccy and her mob hear about it.'

'That's about it,' Patrick told him. 'Pictures of Gary Williams.' He held them up for Alec's inspection. 'And a woman called Cathy.'

'The neighbour.'

'Right, she says they're animals, too.'

'Subtle, but it lacks variety. She should think up her own insults. She won't get very far recycling Gary Williams'.' He groaned and flopped back against the kitchen counter. 'Great way to start a Sunday morning.'

'Can you move the stuff and lay the table for me?' Naomi asked Patrick.

'Sure.'

Alec handed him the cutlery and then went back to the stove to fry eggs. 'Make the most of it,' he said, his irritation really showing through and his attempts to laugh the whole thing off rapidly turning sour.

'What?'

'The peace and quiet.'

'You reckon there'll be more trouble on the Radleigh?' Naomi commented.

'You can bet your life,' Alec said.

The rest of the morning was, however, surprisingly quiet. Over breakfast they told Alec about their walk the evening before and how they had stopped at the arcade on the way back.

'Lord, it's months since we went in there,' Alec laughed.

'Months? No, it's a couple of years. The last time was before . . .' She didn't need to finish.

'She nearly thrashed me though,' Patrick was clearly impressed.

'You know, it was funny,' Naomi said. 'I remembered what sounds the game made when I did different things. I mean if you'd asked me before, I'd have looked at you stupid, but it was weird. I knew it made a kind of buzzing noise when I got close to the enemy and if I'd scored a near miss it kind of whined. It was fun,' she finished.

Alec reached across the table and squeezed her hand. He swallowed down the emotions suddenly blocking off his throat and found himself at a loss for words.

The afternoon was punctuated by a phone call from Harry and then a brief visit when he brought round Patrick's PlayStation and drawing stuff.

Mari was unwell, he said, when Naomi asked him how his mother was feeling. He had persuaded her to go to bed.

Harry was clearly worried about his mother. He stayed for long enough to assure himself that his son was happy and Naomi not tired of having him around, and then he left.

After Harry had gone, the boy disappeared into the spare bedroom and hooked up to the portable TV Naomi had in there. It was the last they heard of him for a while, just the faint sounds of the game filtering out through the bedroom door.

'He's a nice kid,' Naomi said. 'I'm glad he was here last night. We went walking on the beach. You know, he told me he wants to design computer games when he grows up. He's designing this . . . world . . . heroes and monsters and maps. Even a language. He's not the kind of kid I'd expect Harry to have.'

'I'm sorry I wasn't here. I was up to my ears in paperwork till after eleven. Unpaid overtime.'

They were just relaxing into the idea that Alec's assessment of further trouble had been wrong when his mobile phone rang, the sound painfully intrusive in the quiet room.

Alec listened and Naomi leaned closer to him so that she could catch the controller's voice on the other end. The expected trouble on the Radleigh Estate had at last begun.

*   *   *

By the time Alec and Superintendent Phillips reached the Radleigh Estate things were getting nasty. The evening light had been thickened by black smoke from a pile of burning tyres set light on the end of Needham Road, the main drag through the estate and the road that crossed between Viccy Elliot's house and the flats.

The other end of the road had a living barricade. People were crowded there to a depth of four or five and their mood was angry. Defiantly so.

'What's happening?' Phillips demanded.

'Stalemate at the moment, sir. The two officers we had on obs in the second block are still holed up on the top floor. The crowd's gathered around the ground floor entrance. We can't reach them and they can't get down.'

'You've maintained radio contact? What's their condition?'

'They've barricaded the door. They're not happy, sir.'

Phillips pursed his lips and frowned.

'When did this flare up?' Alec asked.

'It's been like this for about an hour,' the officer told him. 'Been building all day, though, from when the news broke this morning. Seems the residents object to being called animals.' He sounded as though he agreed with Williams' assessment.

Alec ignored him. Not the most helpful of attitudes, he thought. He began to make his way towards the human barricade. A low wall surrounded the front garden of the house at the end of the road and Alec clambered up on to this, looking over the heads of the crowd and down towards the flats. She was there, in the thick of it, as he knew she would be.

Glancing back, he saw the first of the outside broadcast crews arrive, pulling up to join the little knot of newspaper journalists already gathered.

'Viccy!' Alec shouted. 'Viccy Elliot! I want a word.'

The crowd, almost beneath his feet, surged and rumbled. 'Say please, copper.'

'What d'you want our Viccy for? She ain't done owt.'

Viccy Elliot turned and looked his way. For a moment, Alec thought that she would not respond and then she spoke to someone close beside her who ran toward the crowd.

140

'Alec! What the hell are you doing?' Phillips shouted at him.

Alec jumped down from his place on the wall and as if by magic the human barricade parted before him and closed up in a solid wall behind as he passed through.

Viccy Elliot was waiting for him on the other side, arms folded over her considerable chest. Black smoke hung in a solid wall behind her at the other end of Rathbone Street and even here the air was chokingly full of it. Alec coughed and groped in his pocket for a handkerchief. Viccy Elliot seemed unmoved. A forty-a-day smoker, Alec reckoned. Maybe she was used to smoke.

'Bit thick for you?' she asked him.

'Just a bit. God, Viccy. Whose fool idea was all this?'

'Kids lit the tyres,' she said. 'We told 'em it was a stupid move, but kids will be kids.' She shrugged, looked critically at Alec's watering eyes. He was aware that the crowd behind him had shifted focus. He was now it.

'Can we go inside?' he asked.

'No, I don't think so,' she told him. 'Owt that has to be said can be said out here, in plain sight.'

Plain sight, he thought. The smoke was filling the street now. 'What started this?' he repeated.

She huffed at him in a way that momentarily reminded him of Harry. 'Them up in the flats not tell you?' she demanded. 'Too busy with their binoculars watching Emma Sanders get undressed with her curtains open, most like. Or her mam turning tricks.'

'We know he left,' Alec returned evenly. 'Left in a car with his neighbour and two men. And I read the papers. I know what he said, but Viccy, is that worth all this? You'll be proving his point, nothing more.'

'Bloody journalists,' Viccy Elliot snapped back. 'Bloody perverts.'

'Aw come on. The man was questioned and released. There were no charges brought and no evidence of him doing anything beyond having a mouth on him and if that was a crime, Viccy, I'd be pulling in half the kids on this estate on a daily basis. Viccy, I may be being thick here, but

141

Gary Williams is gone and you lot did smash his place up. I did arrest him. The man thinks he has a grievance, he has the right to say so.'

The look she gave him told him that Viccy Elliot thought he was more than thick. 'Liar,' she said.

'Liar? What am I meant to be lying about?'

Viccy Elliot snorted at him. 'Coming on all Mr Reasonable,' she said. 'Williams was here now, you'd want to wring the bugger's neck same as the rest of us.'

Alec shook his head. 'Too many witnesses, Viccy.'

That earned him a grudging half-smile. 'We ain't animals,' Viccy told him.

'No, Viccy, no you're not,' Alec agreed. And certainly not inbred, he added to himself. Viccy's brood had four different fathers to Alec's count.

'You can bet she put 'im up to it,' Viccy Elliot continued. 'That woman what lives next door. Not the sense for something like that, Williams hadn't.' She wriggled her shoulders and re-crossed her arms. Emphatic body language in the Viccy Elliot vocabulary, Alec figured.

A shout from the walkway outside Williams' flat attracted Viccy Elliot. She looked up and then gestured towards Alec. 'You'd best be out now,' she said. 'I can't promise to look after you no more once things really get going.'

'Get going? Viccy . . .'

'Shift yourself,' she said. 'Like now, copper.'

'Viccy, what about our men in the other block?'

Viccy had already turned away. She turned back now and gave him a none too gentle shove back towards the battle lines.

'They'd best have the sense their mothers gave them and just stay put,' Viccy Elliot said.

Alec was never certain how he made it back through the human barricade. Things happened very rapidly after that. He realized with a pang of gratitude that Viccy had somehow ensured him safe passage back to the police lines and he was thrust unceremoniously through a rippling, surging crowd and spat out the other side. He fell, stumbling at someone's feet and felt himself lifted and shoved on again, fetching up this time on the other side of a line of officers dressed in full riot gear, standing behind a wall of shields.

So that, Alec figured, was what Viccy meant when she talked about people really kicking off. They'd been waiting for the tough guys to arrive and now they were here, the Radleigh would see it as a declaration of war.

'Alec, what the fricking hell you think you were doing?'

'Talking to Viccy Elliot.'

'And who the hell is Viccy Elliot?'

A sudden roar of sound erupted from behind them. The residents of Needham Road surged forwards and abruptly broke ranks. Like water flowing through a ruptured dam, they came flooding out, a vanguard of young men, all armed with stones and baseball bats and behind them . . .

'Petrol bombs,' Phillips shouted.

Alec whirled and grabbed Phillips' arm. They might be behind the shield line, but he had been in riot situations before. He knew how far and how fast the flames could spread. 'Sir, get back behind the cars!'

Another roar went up from the crowd. The shield line rammed forwards towards them. Glass smashed on the tarmac and flames spread outwards. Someone screamed and an officer staggered backward, breaking formation, flames shooting upward from his calves as he fell back.

Alec pushed Phillips back towards the main police lines and then he ran.

Twenty-Four

A lec ran to where the officer had fallen. The ranks had closed behind him. He was rolling on the ground and beating at his legs with gloved hands trying to put out the flames. By the time Alec reached him he had nearly succeeded.

'You all right?'

'Yes sir, flame proofing. Buggers topped the petrol with old engine oil, didn't they? Sticks better. Gave me a few nasty moments there.'

His voice was raised over the shouts from both sides and the drumming of batons on shields as the second rank moved up, breaking around Alec and the fallen officer as if they had been stones in a river. Two paramedics followed on behind, taking advantage of the extra cover they had offered.

'I'm all right,' the officer repeated, shouting to make himself heard above the din, at the same time struggling back on to his feet. He bent to recover his shield but Alec had him by the arm. 'No, you're not,' Alec shouted back. He ducked involuntarily as some lighted missile he could not identify hurtled over their heads and smashed against a police car. 'Frigging hell! Look, you'll get yourself checked out first. Now go.'

He was a young man, Alec noted, as the paramedics led him away, eager to be as far from the action as their duty allowed. 'Too bloody young,' Alec muttered. 'I was never that bloody young.' He took off at a smart jog to where he had spotted Travers crouched behind the open door of a marked car.

'He all right?'

'Yeah. He will be. I don't know which of us was shaking most.' Alec paused, looking back towards the lines and the ensuing chaos. 'Where's Phillips?'

144

'Back in the van. It's a while since he's been at the sharp end.'

Alec nodded, crouched lower behind the shelter of the car as another missile crashed only feet away from them.

'Sensible man,' he commented. 'I had a chat with Viccy Elliot. You know her?'

'Of course I do. She the ringleader, Alec?'

More like the ringmaster, Alec thought, but he shook his head. 'Couldn't say. At the heart of things certainly, but I'm not sure anyone has overall control here.'

'She say anything about our men? Last I heard they were holed up behind the barricades.'

'She implied that they'd be safe so long as they stayed put,' Alec told him.

'You believe her?'

'Far as it goes, yes, but as I just said, that implies someone is in overall control of this mess and I'm not taking bets.'

Travers nodded. Alec watched as a third line of riot police pulled up from the rear, jogging forward before splitting into two wings that started to push down the sides of the street. Their aim, Alec saw, was to confine the crowd, filter down through the front gardens and come around behind. He didn't give them a cat's chance. Travers' radio spluttered. Alec leaned in close to hear. Through the mix of noise and static he picked out that the officers holed up in the flat were getting panicky. Bricks were being hurled in at the windows. Alec could hear the breaking glass and the thumps as they hit the floor. He frowned, trying to recall the exact layout of the estate, of the flats. Trying to think of another way to get the men down.

'Alec, can they get out on to the roof? Is there access?'

Alec frowned. 'You're thinking helicopter.'

Travers nodded.

'The police chopper's not equipped for rescue.'

'No, but we've got the coastguard not ten miles from here.'

'Great if they can get out, but Dick, I don't see how. There's no access as far as I know and bugger all to climb.'

The radio crackled again. This time the officer in the flat was on speakthrough. He sounded scared, rhythmic thudding

145

behind the voice told Alec that someone was trying to break down the door even before his words confirmed it.

He reached into the car, grabbing one of the stab vests that had been left on the seat and struggled into it.

'Alec? What the hell?'

Alec cut down behind the row of cars to the left-hand side of the road, closest to the flats. He didn't have a hope of cutting through the lines either of police or rioters. Instead, he dodged through an entryway between two blocks of houses and came out in the rear gardens. The sound was lessened here, muffled by the walls. Lights were on in the house and he hoped that no one chose that moment to look out into the yard.

He hurled himself over the fence between gardens and then back up the next alleyway, coming out further up the street. The wall of noise rose up to meet him, blocking his path with its solidity.

Alec pressed himself against the wall. Before him was a mêlée of struggling bodies. Blue-clad police, hampered by their shields here in this close combat, with no room to use their batons. A group of three had been pinned against a garden wall. Others had been pushed back into the front gardens of the houses, their opponents falling with them over low walls and stumbling through broken gates.

Alec Friedman, you should have your head examined, he told himself, trying not to admit how truly terrified he really was.

He ducked back through the entryway, resisting the urge to go over the back fence and make his escape through the back gardens of the street beyond. Instead, he cleared the fences that separated the next two gardens and went back down the next alleyway towards the road.

It was better this time. He'd come out behind the worst of the fighting. He shoved his way through the stragglers and out into the road just a bit beyond Viccy Elliot's house. She wouldn't be in the street, he was almost certain of that. Having seen things set in motion, Viccy would be content to watch.

A moment later, he was hammering on her door.

'Viccy! Get the fucking door open. Viccy!'

Heads turned his way. Eyes focusing upon him. A knot

of young men and boys broke free from the main group and started to run towards him. Alec hammered louder, cursing himself for the fool he was.

Then the front door opened, Viccy Elliot stood upon the threshold. 'You mad?' she asked him.

Alec nodded, his mouth too dry for the words to come out. He swallowed hard and licked his lips with a tongue that seemed impossibly parched. 'Viccy, you've got to call them off.'

She shook her head. 'You're touched,' she said. 'What the frigging hell you on about?'

'The flat. Our men up in the flat. Breaking down the door, your lot are breaking down the door.'

He was surrounded now. The breakaway group standing in a tight circle. The one closest to him carried a baseball bat; he had a rag tied about the lower half of his face. Another held a claw hammer; he was bouncing the flat end softly against his palm. Alec could feel the closeness of the rest, their body heat seeping through his clothes, they were so close. He felt chilled, his legs giving way beneath him, his stomach dropping to a point somewhere between his knees.

'Viccy. You don't want this,' he managed, hoping to hell that it was true.

For a long moment, an eternity of seconds, she just stared at him. Then she shook her head. 'You lot, come with me,' she said. 'And *you*,' this to Alec, 'I don't want your frigging corpse on me conscience.' She glanced backward over her shoulder and Alec was aware for the first time of the kids crowding behind her in the narrow hall. 'You lot stay put,' she told them. 'Listen to Sharon and do like she tells you. If I find any of you went outside while I were gone, I'll thrash your hides.'

There were ten in the motley group that Viccy Elliot led across the road towards the flats, picking their way through the rubble. The flats stood at right angles to the road, two long, three-storey interruptions to the flow of houses. There was no fighting here, the police lines not having pushed through that far. Instead, a straggling opposition made up of those torn between their instructions to trash what was left of

Gary Williams and his neighbour's flats and an eagerness to rush out and join the main fight.

And it was quieter here, silence compared to the pandemonium in the main street. Alec could hear the crash of glass and splinter of wood and other noises harder to identify but which spoke of people bent on absolute destruction.

A bigger group, rowdier and, Alec noted, mostly drunk, crowded the stairway of the second block. The two officers were on the top floor, this block a mirror image of the first, their position had been perfect for observing the Williams residence.

Alec had gone beyond being scared now. He tagged along in Viccy's wake, baseball bat and claw hammer behind him, though whether as escort or protection Alec didn't want to think. His mobile rang, he heard it dimly beyond the sounds of shouting and raucous laughter and, even more dimly, he realized that it had rung before. He reached into his pocket and switched it off, feeling for what he hoped was the right button.

'Hey, Greg, what the hell you lot doing?' Viccy Elliot demanded.

The one called Greg leaned over the upper balcony and grinned down. 'Viccy. Darling. Come on up and join the fun.'

He was obviously drunk. Very drunk.

'It's *mam* to you,' Viccy told him tartly. 'Now let me through.'

She disappeared into the flats, leaving Alec and his guard alone.

'You wish you were there, don't you?' Patrick asked her.

'I don't know. I mean, not the situation. I've been there and it's crap. It's the lowest, Patrick, it really is. You wonder what the hell you're in the force for. You know, facing that kind of blind hate and knowing that you're no longer a person. You're a uniform. An object. A target for them to hurl their stones and the spit and . . .' she broke off and smiled self-consciously. 'But yeah, being there would be better than sitting here trying to figure out what might be going on.'

'Do you love Alec?'

'Do I . . .' she laughed. 'Getting personal, aren't we?'

She felt him shrug. He was sitting beside her on the sofa, Napoleon lying across their feet and snoring quietly.

'My dad likes you a lot, you know that?'

Naomi didn't know what to say. 'I like him too,' she said at last. 'Harry, I hope, will be a good friend.'

She had the feeling, the strong feeling, that this was not what Patrick wanted to hear, but it was the best that she could offer. She liked Harry, yes, but she hadn't really thought of him in that way. She couldn't think of him the way she thought of Alec . . . the way she enjoyed thinking about Alec. She felt a slight touch of colour rising to her cheeks.

'You're blushing,' Patrick said abruptly.

'You notice too much, you know that?'

Patrick laughed. 'So you do like him, I mean more than just as a friend.'

'I never said *that*. I wasn't thinking about him, honest.'

'Look, you're going even redder now.'

'I am not!' But Patrick was giggling now and she couldn't help but join in. She grabbed the cushion from the end of the settee and whacked him with it, repeatedly, until he was laughing so hard he could hardly breathe.

Naomi put the cushion behind her. 'That'll learn you,' she said.

'Nan says that. It makes Dad cluck his tongue, you know the way he does. "That'll teach you, Mam, not learn",' he mimicked, imitating Harry so perfectly that Naomi almost choked on her laughter.

Then she bit her lip. 'Helen used to do that, too,' she said softly. 'Correct Mari like that and Mari would pretend to be annoyed and chase her down the yard.'

It was a minute or so before Patrick said anything more and when he spoke Naomi was shocked to hear him trying not to cry. 'Is there anything Helen didn't do?' he asked.

He had wept then, silently and angrily, and Naomi had let him be, not knowing what to do. She felt the dog move, shifting himself to sit in front of the boy and then Patrick slid down on to the floor, putting his arms around the tough

149

black neck as Naomi had done the night she last dreamed about Helen.

At last, when she felt that the sobs were past their worst, she shifted over and reached out towards where she thought Patrick must be. Her hand found a tangle of longish hair and the smoothness of Napoleon's lush coat all tangled into one. She stroked them both, feeling tears pricking at her own eyes, sharply aware of just how lonely Patrick must be, trapped in this piece of history that didn't seem about to let any of them go.

'She didn't draw,' Naomi said at last. 'She didn't make worlds, create heroes or monsters or wonderful legends the way you do. She didn't ask the kind of questions you ask or suffer from self-doubt. I did that, Patrick, not Helen. I did those things.'

'You know what I wish sometimes,' he whispered and she could feel the tension in his body, the tightness of holding this in, this thing that he was about to say. 'I wish sometimes that there'd never been a Helen. If she hadn't existed she couldn't have gone away.'

'I wish she never existed,' Penny whispered. They were lying in her bed, moonlight streaming in through the open window and the branches from the apple tree tapping softly against the glass.

'I wished and wished that she had never existed, that Naomi had never existed either. That those other people that he said always needed him would just go away forever. Vanish like they'd never ever been. I just wanted him here. And then I thought, after what my mother said, I thought, what if I were the one that was hurt or disappeared or caught up in some of the Joe Jackson kind of trouble that had nothing to do with bullying at school or not passing my spelling test or getting into trouble when I couldn't understand my homework.'

'He didn't mean it,' Bill told her gently, his hand softly tracing the line of her body, resting for a moment in the hollow of her waist before moving on. 'He never meant to hurt you.'

'I know,' Penny said softly. 'Really, I do know.' But when it happened, she thought, her mind clouded with that dark place where she hid even from herself. When the bad thing came, the great Joe Jackson was still no more within her reach than he had ever been.

'When I lived with Gerry and my mum,' Patrick was saying, 'I felt I was always kind of letting them down, you know what I mean?'

'Not unless you tell me,' Naomi said. She was sitting beside him now, the three of them, woman, boy and great black dog, wrapped in a tangled pile of arms and paws and soft dark hair. When Patrick spoke, she could feel his cheek moving against her shoulder.

'It wasn't like Dad thinks,' he said. 'That I didn't like him, Gerry, I mean. I did like him and that kind of made it harder. He had two kids from his previous marriage and they used to stay a lot of the time and I liked them, too. We email each other all the time when I'm at home and talk on chat. But I don't like to talk to Dad about it. I think he might be hurt, you know?'

'I know.' She wanted to tell him that Harry wouldn't be hurt by this friendship, that he wanted what was best for his son, but she didn't think this was the time.

'It was just that Gerry and Paul and Adam, they were different to me. They were good at sports and they loved the sea . . . Naomi, are you scared of anything?'

'Oh yes,' she said. 'I could give you a whole long list of things I'm scared of.'

'I hate to swim. I don't do it very well. I can sort of manage a width if I try really hard, but I don't like it. I'm pretty crap at it and they were really into all this scuba diving and . . .'

'And you were different. That's all it is, Patrick, you were just different.'

'And I missed my dad,' he admitted at last. 'I miss my mum now, but she didn't need me the same way Dad needs me. She was always doing stuff, you know, and I got all mixed up. It was like, she was never there anyway and all the time it was Gerry trying to help me fit in and Pauli and Adam . . . they phoned the other day, Gerry phoned, talked to my dad and said if I wanted to stay for a few weeks until this was all over then he'd arrange everything. Dad asked me and I talked to Gerry. I told him I'd like to come but not right now. I told him Dad needed me right now and I wanted to help him.'

A lot to take on at just fifteen, Naomi thought. 'What did Gerry say?' she asked.

Patrick was silent for a moment and she could feel him swallow convulsively to stop the tears, his jaw shifting against her arm, his face half buried in her sweater.

'He said that he was proud of me,' Patrick said quietly.

It seemed like forever. Alec dared not move, dared not even look at his watch. He felt like some trapped animal whose only hope of survival was in keeping still and concentrating only on his own silence.

Drifting up from the road, the noise and crash of battle continued. Sirens wailing though the night as reinforcements arrived. Neon blue bathing the landscape, lighting the night like summer.

Around him, the men said little. Some smoked, some shifted restlessly. Others drank, keeping topped up with both alcohol and anger.

'Oi, you, come on up.' Viccy's voice. Viccy's head poking over the balcony.

Baseball bat and claw hammer served as escort as Alec climbed the stairs. On the balcony a group of twenty or so stood around, all eyes fixed on Alec as he emerged from the stairway. The flat door was splintered and Alec could glimpse behind it the wardrobe the captives had used as a barricade.

'Tell 'em who you are,' Viccy commanded. 'Tell 'em they can come out and get the hell out of here. We've no fight with them, only that bastard over there.' She jerked her head back towards the opposite block, as though the spirit of Gary Williams might still be hiding inside.

Feeling oddly foolish, but not sure how else to approach this, Alec knocked upon the door. Down below, vans with their sirens wailing, filled with reinforcements, screamed into the space between the buildings. Phillips, complete with bull

152

horn and surrounded by officers carrying shields, emerged from cover and began to shout.

'Oh, shut the fuck up,' Alec muttered. He banged again upon the broken door.

It was some time before PCs Dobson and Wake emerged from their prison, blinking in the sudden brightness of dragon lights trained upon the balcony.

Alec had reached that point where fear had gone to be replaced by overwhelming weariness. Whatever happened now, he just wanted to get it over with. The adrenaline rush that had carried him this far was long since burned out, to be replaced by dull thoughts, such as the amount of paperwork his little escapade would generate.

'It's all right,' he told them. 'Everything's just going to be fine now.' He turned them towards the stairs, urging them down then glanced back towards Viccy Elliot who was standing in usual Viccy pose with her arms crossed once more across her chest.

'Thanks,' he said and, absurd as he knew it to be, found himself sticking out his hand for Viccy Elliot to shake.

To his profound surprise, she did. Her clasp was as fiercely strong as any man's.

'You're nuts,' she told him again, just in case he had missed it earlier. 'Totally touched.'

Downstairs, the crowd had parted and the officers walked though, urged behind the shield line and into the relative safety of the armoured van. Phillips lowered his bull horn and stared at Alec. Alec glanced at his watch, then shook it and looked at it again. The numbers changed even as he watched. It felt like days, but only a scant half-hour had passed since he had first taken cover with Phillips behind that first shield line.

Twenty-Five

A lec arrived midway through the Monday morning, filthy and smelling of smoke, exhausted but too hyped up to sleep.

'You stink,' Naomi told him frankly as he kissed her.

'Sorry. I'll get in the shower.'

'Give me your clothes and I'll get them in the machine.'

'Thanks,' he said. 'I . . . um . . . I might be on the news.' And disappeared into the bathroom before she could question him further.

There was a bulletin at eleven. She tuned into it with Patrick. 'Looks like the whole place burned down,' Patrick said.

'What do you mean?'

'All these piles of stuff on the road. They're still smoking and there are loads of fire engines and bricks and stones and broken glass all over the road. There's a riot shield, it's lying in someone's front garden.'

The anchorwoman began to report and Patrick shut up so that Naomi could hear as she reprised the Gary Williams story and showed library pictures of the riots two years before that had flared up over such a similar event.

There was a reference to a couple of officers on observation who found themselves under siege but, said the anchorwoman, they had no details as yet about this, beyond knowing that both escaped without injury.

'Local police find themselves at full stretch,' she went on to say, 'and reinforcements were called in last night from Barsford and Felton. Officers I have spoken with this morning, though reluctant to say that morale is low, emphasize the difficulties of dealing with situations like this one on the

154

Radleigh, with all the high-profile allegations against the police that have undoubtedly fed the bad feeling which already existed here.'

'That's a cock-eyed way of putting it,' Alec commented, emerging from the bathroom.

'Nothing about you yet,' Patrick told him, slightly prematurely.

'At the centre of these allegations is Detective Inspector Alec Friedman, the police officer who arrested and subsequently released Gary Williams, the man whose residence on the Radleigh Estate sparked this last round of troubles.

'Currently, as well as the riots, police here at Ingham and five miles down the coast at Philby are investigating two murders. The killing of Sarah Clarke, the six-year-old whose body was found on Philby beach and in connection with which Gary Williams was originally brought in for questioning. Also Helen Jones, who died more than twenty years ago and whose remains have recently been discovered in a house on Lansdowne Road.'

Then followed more library pictures showing police in overalls carrying spades into number 43.

'Rumours concerning a belated confession, which reportedly told police where to dig for Helen's body, are rife in this small community, though so far police are refusing to release any information regarding this so-called confession or to comment on the claims that the murderer is now deceased.'

'Feeling better?' Naomi asked him as Alec came over and sat down beside her.

'Some. Hungry though.'

She squeezed his hand. 'We'll have an early lunch. Bad was it?'

'I've had better days . . . nights. Whatever.' He had leaned his head back against the sofa and slumped down. She could feel his fingers growing slack against her own and a moment later his breathing told her that he had gone to sleep.

Phillips arrived an hour after Alec and announced without ceremony that it was Alec he had come to see.

'What is this?' Naomi asked him. 'An incident room?'

'Sorry,' Phillips told her. 'Is there somewhere we can talk? In private.'

'Oh, sure,' Naomi told him, unable to keep the note of sarcasm from her voice. 'Patrick and I will hide out in the kitchen.'

She only partially closed the door and as Patrick helped her with sandwiches she made no attempts not to hear the conversation from the other room.

Phillips was trying to clear Alec out of the way.

'You've got TOIL time built up, Alec. Paid leave, too. Take some time out.'

'What and make it look like Gary Williams has a case? I've done nothing wrong. Push me out and what kind of statement are you making?'

'This has nothing to do with Williams,' Phillips told him in a furious whisper. 'It's about last night's little commando action. Alec, what the fucking hell did you think you were playing at?'

'Acting on my initiative . . . sir.'

'You were lucky, Alec. Bloody lucky. It might have turned out very differently, very differently indeed.'

'I thought, sir, that it was a fair gamble. An even bet—'

'No you bloody didn't, Alec, that's my whole point. You didn't think. You just acted. Going in there like some one-man army. It's the kind of thing . . . the kind of thing Joe Jackson would have done and there's no room for that sort of jingoistic, maverick stance in today's police force.'

Alec was silent for a while and then: 'Maybe you're right, maybe you're not,' he said. 'I acted as I saw fit in the situation.'

'Without the consultation or the approval of a senior officer. Without reference to procedure or to officer safety.'

'What officer safety?' Alec's voice raised angrily again. 'With respect, the only one I put on the line was me and that's something you could never say of Jackson.'

'Which doesn't make your actions any more acceptable.' Phillips sighed and then continued in a more conciliatory tone. 'I could have you suspended, Alec, but I won't and I won't force your hand over taking time out. But step out of line, just one fraction of a bloody inch out of line again and so help me, Alec, I'll see you go down.'

He left then without even telling Naomi goodbye.

Alec had then spent the early afternoon giving a full account of himself. Naomi was outraged that he'd been so stupid. Patrick, predictably, was impressed.

He had eaten lunch, tried to shake off the imminent need to sleep and managed to get an appointment at four o'clock with Penny Jackson's solicitor.

Mr Ian McKintry. Was a middle-aged man who, so he told Alec, had worked for the same firm since qualifying. He had known Joe Jackson as a personal friend and was puzzled as to the nature of Alec's visit. He was destined to stay that way.

'There's not much I can tell you,' Alec apologized, 'but Miss Jackson informs us that she collected some papers from you about a fortnight ago. I'm wondering if you could tell me what these entailed.'

Ian McKintry looked at him over the top of heavy glasses. 'Why don't you ask Miss Jackson?'

'I have,' Alec lied. 'Or at least, she told me about the extension plans and some other documents that had been left with them. The difficulty arises in that Miss Jackson can't be certain which of several documents she collected on that particular visit and which came into her possession at an earlier date.'

McKintry's pursed lips told Alec that he didn't believe a word of it. 'Might I enquire,' he asked, 'as to what kind of documents you may be referring?'

Alec shook his head. 'I'm sorry, I'm not at liberty to say.' He sat back in his chair and spread his hands in an expansive, placating gesture. 'Mr McKintry, I realize that you have to consider client confidentiality. We're both used to using our discretion in these matters. If you have any worries, I suggest you telephone Miss Jackson.'

'If I had any intention of telling you anything, I would do just that,' McKintry told him. 'Inspector Friedman, I'm very sorry but there's nothing I *can* tell you. Miss Jackson came to inspect the deeds, she took the plans for the house extension away with her together with an envelope, which I assumed contained other pertinent documents, and the photographs which had also been stored with the plans.'

157

'Photographs?'

'Please, Inspector, I really can't go into detail and in any case, I didn't really see them. There were photographs of building work, I believe. We glanced at them and Penny, Miss Jackson, commented that her father must have kept a record of the building work. And a photo of her father with a young policewoman. It looked kind of official. Anything else and you really will have to visit Miss Jackson again.'

He rose to indicate that the interview was at an end, but Alec was happy to go by then. Pictures of the building work, he wondered. Yes, but which house? Jackson's own or 43 Lansdowne Road?

Twenty-Six

Penny Jackson did not look too happy to see Alec.

'You remember me?' he asked her. 'Detective Inspector Friedman. We met the other night.'

She nodded slowly. 'I remember you. Is this an official visit?'

'Yes,' Alec told her. 'Yes it is. May I come in, Miss Jackson?'

She stood back to let him come inside, not commenting on the fact that he had returned to formality when he had called her Penny that night at Mari's.

'Come through,' she said and led him from the surprisingly large hallway into one of the rooms that led off it.

The room had a large bay window looking out on to the overgrown front garden. It was a pleasant room, spacious and well proportioned, but it had about it an air of neglect and underuse and damp. Yes, definitely damp, Alec thought, as though it had not been used or heated in quite some time.

He had been to Joe Jackson's house a few times before the man retired. Strictly business visits, usually conducted as swiftly as possible closeted in the small room at the back that Joe used as his study. Alec had never been in here, but he imagined it had changed little since Penny's father had died.

The grey carpet was patterned with leaves and reminded Alec of one in his gran's house that had been there since Alec was a boy. The three-piece had been fixed up with loose covers. Pink and floral and Alec could not imagine either Joe liking them or their even being his daughter's choice. Embossed wallpaper covered the walls that had no other decoration and on the heavy tiled mantelpiece, a pipe stand remained from the days when Joe still occasionally smoked.

It could, Alec thought, have been a room in a second-rate boarding house for all the character or sense of home it had.

'Sorry it's so cold in here,' Penny told him. 'I only heat the rooms I'm using. This place is like a mausoleum in the winter. Mother always hated it for that but Dad always insisted that he needed the space.'

She smiled wanly. The other night when he had seen her, Penny had at least been animated. Now she seemed as pallid and lacklustre as the room.

'Maybe you'd be more comfortable if we talked somewhere else,' Alec suggested. The chill seemed to be coming off the walls and seeping through the glass, yet he could have sworn it was a mild September day outside.

'No,' she said. 'No, I don't think so. We can talk in here.'

'All right,' Alec said. 'Miss Jackson, I've just been chatting with your solicitor.'

'Oh?' she said sharply. 'And why would you do that?'

'Because,' Alec said as soothingly as he could, 'I thought you had enough to contend with right now without me asking what must seem like trivial questions. Unfortunately, Mr McKintry wasn't able to be of much help.'

She frowned at him. 'I don't see . . .' she began. 'Inspector Friedman, I'd appreciate it if you came to the point.'

A small noise out in the hall caused her to jerk her head around. Was there someone else here? Alec wondered.

'Are you all right, Miss Jackson? If you already have guests, I promise I won't keep you from them any longer than—'

'What makes you think I have guests?' she said sharply. Then she sighed and seemed to be trying to relax, as though aware of how sharp and irritable she must be sounding. 'You must forgive me,' she said. 'It seems strange to have someone to visit. No one comes here. No one at all.'

'It must be lonely,' he offered. 'It might be better when you've moved.'

'If, I move.' She smiled tightly. 'The purchasers might not be so keen on living here when the story breaks. Who wants to live in the house of a murderer?'

'That's not been proven yet,' Alec said gently. 'Miss Jackson, Penny, there might well be other explanations . . .'

160

But she was shaking her head. 'You don't believe that any more than I do,' she said softly and the wealth of longing in her voice touched Alec for the first time since he had encountered her. Then she squared her shoulders and sat upright in her chair, all business again. 'Now, what was it you wanted to know?' Penny Jackson said.

Alec left ten or so minutes later having learnt very little, except that Penny claimed not to remember where she had put the photographs that came from the solicitor's office.

'I was upset,' she told him. 'Far too upset to take any notice of a few photographs after I'd seen that other thing.'

'I can imagine,' Alec told her, 'but maybe, if you could think now. What you did when you came home, where you might have put them?'

'What does it matter where I put a few photographs? Look, there were pictures my father must have taken of the extension being built and one . . . one of Naomi Blake in uniform. It must have been taken when she first joined the police.'

She broke off for a moment and Alec got the impression she was trying not to cry. There was another deep breath, a further squaring of shoulders that were already sergeant major straight. 'If you must know, it upset me,' she said softly. 'There was a message scrawled across the back from Naomi. She called my father the best friend anyone could ever have and said she hoped that he was proud of her.' She sighed. 'I know he was.' The corners of her mouth twitched into a small sad smile. 'He saw Naomi as a big success story. Something he'd done right, helping her, you know, after Helen had disappeared. Naomi blamed herself and I think her parents thought she was headed for a breakdown. Joe . . . my father . . . he spent hours with her, talking and so on. Getting her back into school. Helping her to face life.' She smiled at him again, but it was clearly an effort for her. It never reached her eyes.

He spent hours with her, Alec repeated to himself as he drove away. Hours, it seemed to him, that could have been spent with Penny, but that was something that Penny Jackson could not bring herself to say.

Gary Williams had been interviewed again. Travers having

161

the pleasure this time, but nothing new – apart from the odd combination of insults – had emerged from the hour spent in Williams' plush hotel room.

The paper, which had run his story, had paid for a week in the Majestic, a hulking piece of late-Victorian excess set on the cliff top ten miles up the coast from Philby, as part of their deal with Gary Williams and his new girlfriend.

Travers guessed that Williams had probably doubled the cost of the suite in what he'd imbibed from the mini bar. But then, that was their affair, not Travers'.

Back at the station he ran into Alec, fresh from his session with Penny Jackson and looking about as sour as Travers felt.

'Phillips catch up with you?' Travers asked

'He did, so you can consider me reprimanded . . . sir,' he added as a sort of afterthought.

Travers took his arm and stopped him in his tracks. 'Alec, if we weren't so undermanned he'd have had you suspended. You know that. And with good reason.'

Alec said nothing. He looked away, suddenly fascinated by the typists in the next office, drafting interviews into the computer.

'And I'd have backed him,' Travers added. 'OK, enough said. I'm about to run the reconstruction tape again. You want to join me?'

Alec nodded. 'I've just seen Penny Jackson,' he said, glad to get the conversation back on to a normal footing. 'And Penny Jackson's solicitor.'

'Oh? Anything new?'

Alec hesitated. 'Yes and no,' he said. 'But I don't quite know how it fits in. The solicitor said that Penny took some pictures with her, photographs, he thought, of the Jackson extension when it was being built.'

'But you wonder if they were pictures of Lansdowne Road?'

Alec nodded. 'But she claims not to know where she put them after she got home. Said she was too upset by discovering the confession, so she put them somewhere and doesn't know where.'

'And you don't believe her?'

162

'Not so much I don't believe her . . . I mean I can accept that finding a confession written by your father would kind of put everything else out of your mind. It's her reluctance to look for them that I find somewhat harder to accept. She says they're lost and as far as she's concerned, that's an end to it.'

Travers nodded.

'The other thing is, she was dead jealous of Naomi.'

They had arrived in Travers' office and Alec slid the tape into the machine. He perched on the edge of the desk with the remote, fast forwarding to the scene where Gary first appeared. They watched in silence as Gary pushed his way to the front of the crowd, to where he seemed to be smiling, almost laughing at the proceedings.

'What's he looking at?' Travers questioned. He let the tape run further on, watching as the camera angle changed, showing the crowd from another view. Gary Williams was staring and the woman he was staring at returned his gaze with as much intensity. The woman was Maggie Clarke.

Twenty-Seven

The next few days passed quietly. Alec spoke to Maggie Clarke who admitted that she remembered Gary standing in the crowd and that she had eventually remembered him as the father of one of Sarah's friends.

'I don't see why you're asking me about him,' she said. 'I thought he'd been released. I saw all that stuff in the paper.'

'He has,' Alec confirmed. 'Maggie, how well *did* you know him?'

The hurt expression in her eyes tore into him, but he persisted. 'I can understand maybe that with all the controversy about Williams you don't want to be seen to be involved with him.'

'I was never *involved* with him.'

'I didn't mean it that way,' Alec told her, but it got him thinking.

'How did you all meet?' he asked.

'How do you think we met? Our kids went to the same school. Look, it was a silly thing, the older ones were doing some family history thing at school. A family tree and it came out then, when they were talking. Williams was my maiden name. It got us talking, that's all and their little boy was in Sarah's class. They played together.'

She was getting impatient now, unable to see what use this irrelevant questioning could be.

'Haven't we been through enough,' she demanded, 'without you coming here and asking your stupid questions? You should be out there, looking for the bastard that killed my little girl.'

He got nothing further from her then, nor, to be honest, could he blame her for her reaction.

*   *   *

164

The Radleigh had quietened down. A few youths hanging around on the street corners, but nothing out of the ordinary and a week passed with little of consequence happening anywhere. Mari had asked again if Helen's remains could be released to them and again been told that while the investigation was still ongoing this could not be done.

She seemed to need something though, some way of marking the fact that her daughter had at last been found and some way, Alec guessed, of mourning the little deaths they had all been through. The death of faith, Naomi called it in an odd, almost poetic moment and Alec knew what she meant.

A memorial service had thus been organized to take place in the local church on the Tuesday, just over a week since the Radleigh riots. The family had asked for it to be a quiet affair, but despite this, the entrance to the church was lined with sombre, silent crowds and the opposite side of the road with journalists.

Alec accompanied Naomi. Penny Jackson came alone, and late, standing uncertainly in the doorway and then slipping into a seat right at the back. Sergeant Lyman had asked Alec if it would be out of order to turn up and Mari, when asked, had extended her welcome, though he too kept clear of the family until the end. He also steered clear of Penny, Alec noted, glancing her way only once and then studiously avoiding her.

At the end of the simple service, the family filed out slowly from the dour red brick church that had been so much a part of Helen's childhood landscape.

'Would you make a statement,' someone shouted from across the road. 'Mrs Jones, if we could just have a word or two.'

Harry had taken his mother's arm, was leading her on towards home, but to everyone's surprise, Mari stopped and looked around. Then she released herself gently from Harry's grip and crossed the road.

She was a small figure in her dark grey mac and her best black shoes; shoes that only made it out of the wardrobe for weddings and for funerals. Her quiet dignity brought a hush to the waiting crowd.

'I wanted to lay my child to rest,' Mari said softly. 'But it might be some while yet before I can. So I thank you all for coming. It was a nice service and for now, that'll just have to do.' Then with the same stiff dignity, she turned back towards her home.

'Oh, Mari,' Naomi whispered, her hand tightening on Alec's arm. 'Alec, what are we going to do?'

'You never told me,' she said later as Alec drove her home.

'Told you what?'

'Why you hated Joe.'

'I never said I hated Joe. I didn't like him, that was all.'

'And why was that?'

Alec sighed. 'Joe always had his own agenda. He was secretive; a maverick as Phillips would say.'

'And you're so different?'

'Oh yes,' he said. 'I am so different, Naomi. I've never laid anyone on the line, except myself. I've never put anyone at risk. If I'm working with a team, then I make sure I know the position of every damn member of that team. What they can handle; what they can't.' He looked irritably in her direction. 'You've worked with me. You know that's true.'

She nodded slowly. Alec might be impulsive on his own account, but it could never be said he was neglectful of his duty where others might be compromised.

'And Joe?' she asked.

'Joe was careless with other people's lives,' Alec said. 'At least, that's the way I read it. There was one time, Naomi, when Joe nearly got an officer killed, he was so damn sure of himself. So damned certain he was right.'

'Oh?' Naomi questioned. 'Who?'

'It was me,' he told her.

'I was young and green, at the end of my first post-probationary year. I'd been given this opportunity to work with the famous DI Jackson. Plain clothes, surveillance, the works. Joe said I was an unfamiliar face and he needed that. Me, I was keen as mustard. Wanted to prove myself. I was

166

young, impressionable, eager to impress and Joe had every right to be proud of me. I'd got myself a courier's job and the courier office was right next door to the warehouse that Joe was sure was the centre of operations. We're talking vice here. Porn mainly and Joe had been seconded to divisional because he was the one who'd uncovered the local side.

'Oh, he was a great detective. Committed, single-minded and that was just the trouble.

'I'd managed to get up into the roof space above the courier's office. They used it for storage mainly and off between calls we played darts and sat around in one of the big rooms upstairs. One floor higher and our building was separated from the next by studding, that was all, and guess who was tasked with getting the surveillance equipment into next door.'

Naomi was horrified. 'You were a kid,' she said. 'You didn't have the experience for that. How the hell did he get clearance?'

'He didn't. As far as anyone else was concerned, I was on a watching brief. Who came in, who went out. That was meant to be that. And there was me, thinking I must be doing a great job if Joe had persuaded our superiors I was capable of taking this on. Promotion glittered on the fast track and all I could see was my sergeant's stripes and a move to CID.

'Then it all went down. I knew it was coming – the raid on the warehouse – but I didn't know when and Joe had me on obs, supposedly keeping the intel flowing on who was in and who was leaving. The trouble was, Joe hadn't told anyone precisely where I'd been posted and there was me, stuck up in the roof space of this building when the shit hit the fan and our lot moved in, armed to the teeth, and their lot started to fire back.

'There was a way out on to the flat roof and across on to the next building and down their fire escape. And some of the gang decided to make a run for it. Armed officers followed and yours truly was stuck somewhere in the middle. God, Naomi, I have never been so scared. A bullet hit the wall two inches from my head and all I could do was curl up in a ball and pray. Next thing I know, I've got a gun pointed

167

at my head and some joker telling me to keep still and lay flat on the floor with my hands on my head. Fortunately, he was one of ours, but the fact is, Joe should have pulled me out long before.'

'Naomi, if I'd had a bullet up my arse I couldn't have moved then. I've never felt so scared or so . . . I suppose so stupid.'

'You never told me,' she whispered. 'Why did you never tell me?'

'You really have to ask? Naomi, how Joe covered his back, I never did find out, but the official record has me outside of the building keeping point all the time the gun fight was going on. It had me reporting to Joe when some guy left ten minutes before and him telling me to hold my position. That's it.'

'And you never challenged that?'

'Oh, get real. Only a handful of people ever knew the truth anyway and I was a rookie. Green as grass. I was commended for the undercover stuff I'd done working for the courier and I hadn't got it in me to challenge the official line. If I had, Joe would have just piled the responsibility back on to me. The eager youngster trying to make a name and I'd have been disciplined, maybe finished. I wanted in, I wanted CID more than anything.' He laughed. 'It seemed important back then. Now, I wonder if I'd have been better off working as a courier. A lot less hassle.'

Naomi said nothing. She had no reason to disbelieve Alec. It all fitted with what she knew of Joe, but did not consciously like to recognize. He had always focused more on getting the job done than he had on how to do it.

But she still found all of this so hard to accept. Joe had been a cornerstone of her life, one of its few firm foundations, and now she could feel the ground shifting beneath her feet. So much so, that she felt physically sick with it.

They were back at home and Alec followed her inside.

'Can I stay?' he asked.

'I don't know, I think I want to be alone.'

'OK. If that's what you need.' She heard him turn around and walk back towards the door, leaving a cold void in the space beside her.

168

'Alec?' She felt ashamed of the desperation in her voice, but then, as he turned back, she didn't care.

'Stay, please stay. I couldn't bear to be alone. Not really.'

He came back, wrapping his arms around her and holding her very close. Naomi clung to him, afraid that she might drown.

Twenty-Eight

The press conference had been scheduled for the Thursday morning so as to allow time for analysis on the lunchtime news. Patrick had phoned Naomi the night before to tell her they would be leaving for a while and taking Mari with them.

'I'm not allowed to tell you where we're going,' Patrick said. He sounded well impressed by this. 'But I'll phone you. I can always use my dad's mobile, even if they don't have one where we're going.'

'I'll miss you all,' she told him, wondering if the picture she had in her mind's eye of the boy was anywhere close to the truth. She knew he had soft dark hair which he wore rather long and his father despaired of keeping tidy. Alec told her that he had grey eyes and rather an angular, pointy kind of face. And that he wasn't tall for his age, a fact which rankled with him and his family were careful not to mention. But she would have loved to see if her image of him was anything like accurate.

'You want to talk to Dad?' he asked and handed over to Harry without waiting for a reply.

'It's all going to happen,' Harry said. 'I don't know how to feel.'

'At least it should be over soon,' she told him. 'There'll be a splash for a few days and then some other story will come along.'

'Will it?' Harry asked her and just for a moment he was a child wanting to be reassured, not a full grown man. 'You know, I never thought that normal things like going back to work would seem so appealing. It's such a bloody boring job, but just now, I think I'd like to just be bored.'

She laughed and sensed that he was pleased at that. Harry, who never considered himself funny, trying his hand at a joke.

'We will keep in touch,' he said at last as though he were planning a voyage from which they would be a long time returning.

'Do,' she said. 'And I meant what I told Patrick, I will miss you all.'

The press conference was set for eleven. Naomi was alone as Alec was at the conference and she felt his absence keenly.

Phillips' statement presented the cold hard facts as they understood them to be: 'On the 22nd of September this year, a document was brought to our attention which caused us to reactivate the inquiry into the disappearance of Helen Jones in February of 1979.

'Although no body had been found, Helen's family had long since reconciled themselves to the idea that their loved one was almost certainly deceased. When this document arrived on my desk, I had no way of knowing whether or not it might prove genuine or just another piece of misinformation of the kind that a case like this inevitably generates. However, because of the source of the information, we felt that we had no choice but to follow the information given in the document and to dig for Helen's body in the location mentioned, this being number 43 Lansdowne Road on the Bellingham Estate, which as some of you might know, was under construction at the time that Helen disappeared.

'Remains, later identified as those of Helen Jones, were found at the site.'

He paused briefly and cleared his throat. 'Um . . . as I'm sure you will appreciate, we did not wish to disclose the source of this new information until such time as the truth of the statements therein had been verified. We believe that this has now been achieved and after consultation with those concerned, both within the police force and those family members most affected by this matter . . .'

He's hedging, Naomi thought. Oh, God, why doesn't he get it over with? It's just making it worse.

'. . . it was decided that the best way of handling this was to make a statement. After which a further statement will be made from . . . well . . . from a member of the family.' He paused again, and Naomi could imagine him taking a deep breath before plunging on. His voice shook slightly as he announced, 'It seems likely, pending further investigation, that the statement we received was indeed a confession to the murder of Helen Jones in 1979 and that this confession was made by a police officer.'

Naomi heard the ripple of shock that ran through the assembly. She gripped the arm of the sofa so tight it made her fingers ache. Knowing what was coming didn't make it better.

'The statement appears to have been made by Detective Inspector Joseph Jackson, of Ingham Division, a man who we all considered to have an impeccable service record and to . . . to have been a great colleague and good friend.'

Phillips' voice cracked and broke over the last words and Naomi leaned back into the sofa, her fingers finally relaxing their grip on the fabric of the arm.

There, she closed her eyes. It has been said. It was finally out in the open. Now the storm would break, hit them full force for a few days, a week or two even, then it would begin to go away.

Such was her shock, relief, pain – she wasn't certain how to separate them any more – at hearing this, that it was several seconds before she heard the second speaker being announced. Alec's voice of all things, striving to be heard above the din that had greeted the end of Phillips' statement. Then Penny Jackson began to speak.

'What?' Naomi shrieked out loud to the empty room. She could barely believe it. She was struck simultaneously by admiration for Penny's nerve and outrage . . . though that particular emotion was harder to figure.

'My father left this statement amongst his possessions,' Penny was saying, 'but when he died three years ago, it unfortunately did not come with me. Instead, it had been filed with other documents that I had no reason to read until last month. I am only sorry that the family have been waiting

172

this long for news and I'm so dreadfully sorry that I could not have provided this information before. I hope that you will now leave us all in peace and allow us proper time to grieve.' She paused for an instant and the void of her silence was filled with questions.

'That's all I have to say,' Penny Jackson shouted above the din. 'That's all.'

Naomi sat staring at the screen, willing herself to see. When she could not, she shook her head at her own stupidity and then swore at Penny and at Phillips and anyone else who'd been responsible for putting on such an ill-advised and tasteless show. The phone rang, Napoleon whittered excitedly and shifted his tail upon the floor, telling her even before she lifted the receiver that it was Alec.

'Whose damn fool idea was that?' Naomi asked him without preamble.

He seemed unsurprised that she had known the identity of her caller without him speaking. 'Not mine,' he said. 'It's pandemonium here. Phillips said no questions and he's buggered off leaving the rest of us with the shit. Are you all right?'

'I'm all right. Shaky. I mean I've known . . . but hearing it out loud. Hearing it made official. Alec, it was just horrible.'

'I know,' he said softly. 'Look, I've got to go. I'll come round later?'

'Please,' she told him. 'I don't want to be alone tonight.'

Or any night, not really, she added to herself as she gently lowered the phone back into its cradle.

Twenty-Nine

A fter that it was all change. A cold case unit had been brought in to cover any final details in the Helen Jones case and focus switched back almost entirely to searching for the killer of Sarah Clarke.

Alec was assigned to the new team as, he complained to Naomi, 'a glorified collator', a job which tied him to his desk most days and which they both knew was Phillips' subtle punishment for Alec's actions on the Radleigh Estate. He was somewhat mollified, though, by the story circulating around the station of Alec single-handedly storming the flats and rescuing the two trapped officers inside. The story had grown with the telling and he'd become something of a hero in the ranks.

'Just like Joe,' Naomi told Napoleon. Just like Joe.

If it hadn't been for the dog she would have holed herself up in the flat and not gone out until the storm had passed, but Napoleon had to be walked no matter what and, to her relief, no one camped on her doorstep asking for a statement, nor did anyone in her local shops seem to make a connection.

'Why should they?' Alec asked her. He didn't like to tell her that a picture of the two of them had appeared in one of the nationals which ran a follow up piece – a mere sidebar really – comparing the Clarke murder with that of Helen Jones. It had made him think though, about where this relationship with Naomi Blake was going. It seemed that lately he slept in her bed, ate his meals with her, talked and argued and made love with her far more than he spent time alone, and it was growing in his mind that he'd rather like to put this arrangement on a permanent footing. But he had not yet put these thoughts into words that Naomi had been able to hear. The discussion had been one that had gone on strictly inside Alec's head. And now did not seem like a good time to broach it. Not until they could once and for all get away from the Joe Jackson dilemma.

And right now, Naomi couldn't escape from it. It was talked about everywhere. Wherever she went, she encountered the same sense of outrage and pained disbelief that a police officer – one who had received a commendation for bravery at that – should have so savagely murdered a child. And then gone on to investigate her killing.

That, of all things, seemed most cold, most callous, even to Naomi herself.

Alec read out the headlines to her and some of the articles. Not that she wanted him to, but he seemed unable to stop himself and she seemed unable not to listen.

'"Is this the face of a killer?"' he read. 'God knows where they got this picture. "Joe Jackson, in happier days, congratulates some new recruits",' he read and then frowned, something Penny's solicitor had said coming back to him.

'What?' Naomi asked.

'Just something McKintry said.'

'The solicitor?'

'Hmm, yes. He mentioned photographs. Penny collecting photographs and one of them showed Joe with . . . a new officer.'

His hesitation had given him away.

'With me,' she said.

'Penny said you'd written something on the back, about him being a good friend?'

Naomi frowned. 'That was years ago, Alec. I'm not sure I can remember.'

She closed her eyes and frowned harder, the way she always had when trying to pull a memory out of hiding. 'I said something like, I hoped that he was proud of me,' she said. 'Something along those lines.'

'Yes, that sounds about right. Naomi, do you have a copy by any chance?'

'I don't know. Maybe. Some of my albums are here, some are still at my parents,' she smiled. 'Bringing my photo albums didn't seem like such a big priority when I moved here. Is it important?'

'Probably not. It just rang a bell.'

'I'm not in this picture? The one in the paper?'

'I couldn't tell you. They've done that checkerboard thing with the faces. Just Joe shaking hands with a bunch of faceless uniforms.'

He frowned, folded the paper and dropped it to the floor and slipped an arm around Naomi's shoulders. Music was playing in the background; some easy jazz that wove itself around the room, the sax sidling up beside them in that sexy way it has.

'He talked about you a lot in his notes,' Alec said thoughtfully. 'Endless notes about you. What you did, what you said, the way you walked to school.'

'He was working the case,' Naomi shrugged.

'I know, but trivial stuff. I bet I could tell you what your favourite colour was back then.'

She laughed and leaned her head against his shoulder. 'You know my favourite colour. It's that deep kind of royal blue, like Mari's curtains used to be.'

'But not back then. Oh, he mentions blue, even mentions the curtains, but that year you were into lilac. Not purple, not even lavender, but a particular shade of lilac and your favourite clothes were a lilac shirt and a pair of embroidered jeans with butterflies on the legs.'

She sat up, turned her gaze towards him, as ever unable to shake her sighted body language. 'He recorded stuff like that? Why?'

'Lord knows. Maybe he had his reasons. But he seemed obsessed. You know, Naomi, I'll bet he knew more about you that he knew about his own kid. A whole lot more.'

Penny Jackson had retreated inside her own little world. She had let no one through her front door since the day of the press conference and she had not been outside. She had lived on the food she had stockpiled in the freezer. The milkman delivered what fresh food she needed, milk and eggs and even bread. She was grateful that he ran the gamut of photographers each

176

morning and was considerate enough to open the storm door and slip things inside the porch for her so that she did not even have to venture outside for the merest second to collect her delivery.

The papers arrived too; the boy enjoying the attention, she saw, as she watched him from the upstairs window. He stood talking to the crowd of news people and media types, his hands thrust down into his pockets, rocking forwards and back on his trainer-clad feet, the bright green bag slung across his shoulders, full of words about her father and speculation about her.

'Is this the face of a killer?' the headlines ran.

'Don't do this to yourself,' Bill said. 'Don't read it. It'll only make you cry again.'

But she had to read it. Had to see what they had to say as they speculated about Joe Jackson's home life and his family and the fact that Penny had been an only child and that her mother had left with another man and then come back, then left again. That time for good, and Penny with her.

They wondered, in careful tones: if her father might have killed before . . . since . . . ever; if the confession was some kind of hoax; what the implications were for policing in Britain today; if our children could ever be safe when those placed in such a position of trust could be found so wanting.

And when she had read them, she pinned the stories – each and every one – to the wall in her father's study, like a gallery of shame. When the walls were full, she overlaid the first reports with others until the words became a jumble and the stories flowed out, one into the other and made no more sense.

Only two spaces did she keep clear and free. The confession had been reprinted many times, but she chose the clearest image and gave that a place of honour above the empty grate where her father had loved to light the wood fire in winter. The second was one of the photographs she had collected from the solicitor that day. One photograph of her father she had sent to the local paper, anonymously, without being really clear as to her motives. She had acted upon impulse, regretted it almost instantly and been shocked to find it syndicated in

177

several of the nationals. The other, the one of her father and Naomi Blake, she pinned beside the confession.

Sometimes, against all reason, it felt good to have a way to keep the pain alive.

Thirty

By mid-October the sea breezes of September had changed tack and brought the first of the autumn gales. Perversely, Naomi loved this wild weather. Her walks still took her on to the promenade with a slightly less enthusiastic Napoleon leading faithfully despite his obvious wonder at what had happened to his world. The wonderful playground of summer beach was now a cruel and biting place that sprayed him with cold water and tugged painfully at his fur and ears.

Naomi knew that she would have to take pity on him and switch their daily walks to kinder, inland domains – such as the local park, like any sensible dog owner.

Harry and Patrick were due back soon. They had almost come back to normality, moving from the privacy of the safe house back to Harry's, and Mari had stayed with them. The plan was for Mari to make the final move when the schools closed for half term. Harry, who had lost too much time at work already, would probably have to commute each day.

'Dad's talking about selling up and moving to Ingham permanently,' Patrick told her in one of his frequent calls. 'I'd like that.'

'Wouldn't you miss your friends?'

He was silent about that, then moved on to talk of other things.

'He's still no happier at school, then?' Naomi asked when Harry came on for his usual quick chat.

'No, he's not,' Harry confided. 'You know, I think there are some kids who are just not meant for school. I don't honestly know what to do with him.'

'He's a good kid,' Naomi said softly. 'A bright kid, too. Just a bit different, I suppose. We'll help him through it, Harry.'

She heard his moment of hesitation on the other end of the line before he said gratefully, 'It helps – really helps – you saying that. Naomi, I really don't know . . . how I'd cope without a friend like you.'

Coming from Harry that was a major declaration and Naomi was both touched and troubled by it. How much had Patrick said to his father? she wondered. Did they talk about her when they were alone? And what did they say?

'Penny came round again today,' she said.

'You spoke to her?'

'Yes. She still insists that Mari gave her my address. This is five visits in just over a week and she seems to have my routine down pat. I can't even pretend not to be in when she rings the bell. I have to answer the door in case it's something important.'

'Have you spoken to Alec?' Harry asked her.

'Well yes, but what can he do? I can hardly have her arrested for calling round to see me, can I? And I feel sorry for her, Harry. She's obviously lonely.'

'So are a lot of people,' Harry said with more feeling, she was certain, than he had intended. 'I just hope she doesn't start the same thing with us when we get back home. I really don't think Mam could take it.'

'How is Mari?'

'Not too good. Stress, the doctor says. Like we needed him to tell us that, but her blood pressure's up and he's putting her on tablets for it. She just needs to get back to normal. We all do.'

Naomi couldn't have agreed more.

Alec spent most evenings with her at the moment. The desk job at least allowed him to work regular hours, though Naomi knew he was champing at the bit and practically making excuses to get out and interview people, whether he could really justify the time or not. The simple fact was that, as far as the authorities were concerned, Helen's killer had been found and the only reason that any kind of investigation was continuing was down to internal affairs. Such a high profile case as this one would automatically beg questions and those questions had to be answered. Primary among these was, did

180

any of Joe Jackson's team have reason to suspect all was not what it seemed with their boss. And with men like Travers, who had worked the case, now in positions of authority within the division, the internal investigation had to take place and the investigators had to prove that everyone was squeaky clean.

So far, they had found nothing, though Alec still resented his part in all of it. He felt that he was being set apart, made to work against colleagues who had long since earned his respect and he didn't like it one little bit.

She had just finished talking to Harry when she heard his key in the door. The door key was a recent thing, partly born of the fact that twice now she had thought it might be Alec at the door only to discover Penny Jackson standing there.

'Good day?' she asked as he kissed her. She leaned against him, relishing the warmth of his body and the scents of cinnamon and cedar she had come to associate with him, as well as the faint citrus tang which told her he had used her shampoo that morning.

'Strange day,' he said, letting go of her far too soon and heading for the kitchen, bending to fuss the dog on the way.

'I think you give that dog more attention than you do me.'

'Come here and I'll play with your ears.'

'I might like that.'

'Ooh, kinky!'

'You sound happy. What do you mean, strange day?'

She heard him fill the kettle and plug it in, then turn to lean against the counter in typical Alec fashion. She could picture him looking at her with his arms folded and his feet crossed at the ankle so that all the weight rested on his left foot.

'We've been working through the case files as you know, and it struck me a couple of days ago that there was something familiar about that confession, but I couldn't place it. You remember me mentioning it?'

'Sure.'

'Well, Bob Saunders and I have been sifting through all the calls and letters; all the usual stuff, including the other confessions.'

Naomi nodded. Any murder case or suspected murder attracted these bits of correspondence from members of the public either convinced in some way of their own guilt or playing some elaborate game. These were filed, checked where possible and given as much weight as any other information that came in. They were a sore point amongst any officers involved in such a case due to the man-hours wasted on false leads which often outpaced those which actually led somewhere.

'Well I found two letters written several days apart and delivered at a week's space from each other. This was a month or five weeks after Helen disappeared. I had this vague memory of seeing them when I first flicked through the evidence boxes, but I'd not seen the confession at the time and then we got distracted by other things. You know how it is, the memory was there but I couldn't have told you what it was or how important.'

Naomi laughed, they'd all been there, chasing down some fly thought in the back brain that often turned out to be nothing. But just occasionally . . .

'And,' she said.

'And, I'll bet what's left of my pension they were written on the same machine. They've been sent to Documents for comparison, but I'm confident, Naomi.'

'What did they say? Did they confess to killing Helen? Were they signed or anything? Maybe Joe, maybe he was trying to confess all along. Maybe . . .'

'Hey, steady on,' Alec told her. 'We've been kicking around ideas for the last three hours or so. Neither Travers nor Phillips remembers them coming in but that's hardly surprising. It's twenty-three years and a hell of a lot of cases later. Phillips was a sergeant and Travers a young PC doing door-to-door. Chances are neither of them ever saw the letters.'

'Letters, not confessions.'

'Letters *and* confessions.' He broke off and she heard him unhook the kettle and the chink of the teapot lid as he made tea. 'But two things we were decided on and we believe the experts will agree: same machine with the same fault on the letter A, but different author.'

182

'Joe had an accomplice?'

'If he did then it was a kid. And a kid who couldn't spell.'

'A child! Oh my God, Penny.'

'That's jumping to very big conclusions.'

'And you're telling me you didn't make the same leap? Come off it, Alec.'

'It was mooted, along with a dozen or more theories,' Alec confirmed. 'Naomi, when that bracelet was left on your doorstep, we wondered if maybe there had been a witness to the murder. What if Penny saw her father kill Helen? Can you imagine what that would have done to her?'

Naomi fell silent. She nodded, her mind reeling at the implications.

'But why not come forward? Why not tell someone? Why wait till now?'

'People do it all the time, you know that. If a truth is too big, they hide from it. If it's too painful they wrap it up in more lies and hope that it'll go away. And he was still her father and we know from what she's said, and more to the point what she's not said, just how important his approval was to her.'

'So, maybe she tried to tell someone without telling them: she wrote the letters. She left the bracelet now, or had those kids leave it because she wanted to tell you, or me, or anyone, that she knew the truth; that she had seen it happen.'

'Then why not come straight out and say it? What does she have to lose now?'

'Think about it,' Alec told her. 'She's had to confront a really nasty truth about her own father. A truth she's maybe been hiding from for years. Maybe she has to do it a little at a time. God knows, I'd want to cut myself off completely from it all.'

Naomi nodded. What Alec was saying made a kind of sense, but something kept nagging at Naomi's brain, much as the letters must have done Alec's. 'I don't know,' she said at last. 'Alec, my feeling is there's something else. This pop

183

psychology's all well and good, but does it fit Penny? The Penny we know?'

'The Penny we're doing our damndest not to know,' he corrected her.

Thirty-One

'Gary Williams has gone back to work,' Travers told Alec the following day. 'Phillips says you're to keep away.'

'My pleasure. Where's he working?'

'The warehouse. Seems the manager's up for giving him a second chance seeing as how there've been no charges and he's been victimised by "that poncy copper".'

'Oooh. Get him. I'm going up in the world, I am.'

Travers grinned. 'How do you figure that one?'

'Stands to reason. 'I've got my own bloody nickname. I'm not a filthy pig or a bloody wanker, I'm a poncy copper.'

'Nice to see you happy,' Travers told him. 'Good news is, we might have a lead on the Sarah Clarke murder.'

'Really? What?'

'Well, as you know, we ran another media request for film and holiday snaps and one finally came up. Rigby Waite. Known paedophile and all round nice guy. He was on the promenade.'

'That day?'

'That day. The photograph was time-coded. Three thirty that afternoon.'

'And we have a location for this Rigby Waite?'

'Alec, I said we had a new lead, not a bloody solution. The Met have a recent sighting. We can only hope he's not completely gone to ground.'

It was potentially good news. It was also potentially nothing, but Alec preferred the former option, though there had been potential leads before, from the same kind of source; known faces showing up in the background of holiday snaps. And checking was a time-consuming effort, heavy on manpower. It involved isolating individuals in the crowd, often enhancing

185

the pictures and then comparing them to the database of known sex offenders.

Alec hoped that maybe this time they'd get lucky.

'Alec, I want you to go back and talk to this Phyllis Mole.'

'Any particular reason?'

'We've had another call alleging abuse. A woman, quite out of the blue, wouldn't give her name and the call taker said her voice sounded muffled as though she was trying to disguise it. I've heard the tape, in places it's so unclear that the woman had to be asked to repeat herself.'

'Doesn't sound like Phyllis Mole.'

'No. We've compared this with tapes of her calls. It definitely isn't our Mrs Mole, but if she noticed the bruising, the chances are someone else may have and Phyllis Mole might be able to point us in the right direction.'

Alec frowned. 'I thought the family checked out?' he said.

'So far. It's almost certainly malicious but the timing's off. The really nasty ones usually come in the first few days when the case is highest profile.'

Alec nodded. Generally that was true. 'OK,' he said. 'I'll welcome the chance to get out of the office at any rate. Any chance of me hearing the tape before I go?'

'In my office already set up in the machine.' Travers glanced at his watch. 'Got to love and leave,' he said. 'Meeting with the great and good.'

Alec laughed and headed for Travers' office.

He was right about the tape, Alec thought. Definitely not Phyllis. The caller, though muffled, was quite insistent. She demanded to be put through to someone in charge and when told that at ten o'clock at night that might not be possible became almost abusive.

'How the hell do you expect to solve anything working like part-timers?' she'd said. 'Well, you'd better listen. Those kids were abused. The father was a right bastard. Now the girl's dead and you'd better look to the boy.'

Alec replayed the tape a second and then a third time. No, he had not been mistaken. 'Was,' Alec mused. 'Why the past tense?' Unless he had really been out of the loop these past

186

days, he'd not heard of Sarah's father being anything other than very much alive.

Phyllis Mole was surprised to see him.

'Well come on in,' she said. 'I don't expect this is a social call.' But she made tea anyway and Alec waited while she did things properly, dressing a tray with a linen cloth and bringing in biscuits on a rose-patterned plate.

'I'd like to play you something,' Alec said. He set the cassette player down on the little table. Phyllis listened, then rewound it and listened again.

'I hope you don't think that was me,' she announced finally. 'I don't hide things. I come out with them and I give my name.'

Alec smiled. 'No, we never thought it was you. What we did wonder is, if you'd recognize the voice. I know it's difficult to hear at times . . .'

'Sounds like she's talking through a handkerchief . . . But no, I don't think I know the voice. Why did she say *was*?' Phyllis wanted to know. 'That poor man hasn't done anything to himself, I hope.'

'That poor man? I thought you believed him to have abused his daughter?'

Phyllis shook her head impatiently. 'That's the trouble,' she said. 'People only half listen. I never thought that he did it. I never said so. It's the mother I wonder about.'

'The mother? Why?'

Phyllis thought about it. 'I couldn't give you a proper reason,' she told him. 'Not one that would make sense to you. It was just a feeling. Most mothers, even ones like me who didn't find it came naturally, they know that they should touch their children. Hug them, hold their hands. That sort of thing.'

'And Maggie Clarke? She didn't do those things?'

'Well, I didn't see her when she got home. But she didn't when I did see. Not even when she came to pick Sarah up from the Williams'.'

Alec frowned thoughtfully. 'Kids reach a certain age,' he offered, 'when they get embarrassed by too much public affection. Maybe that was it.'

187

Phyllis shook her head. 'Oh, the adolescent male,' she said and chuckled to herself as though remembering. 'Not little ones in kindergarten, and you must remember, that was all they were.'

'Did you ever see the boy, Michael? He must have been older so I don't suppose he came to play.'

'Oh, sometimes he did. A shy, quiet little lad he is. Or was when I had dealings with him. We used to play cards sometimes and if we all went to the park he'd push the little ones on the swings. Always a responsible child, as though he'd grown up far too soon.' She shook her head. 'I can't imagine what the poor child must be going through.'

Alec left a little after that with the names of other children she recalled playing at the Williams' house when Sarah was there. She didn't know their last names, but suggested that the head of the local school might be able to help there. Alec drove away thinking deeply about what Phyllis had said, about Maggie Clarke's distance from her children. He remembered the day they had met her on the beach, when the reconstruction was about to begin. Her obvious grief, the way she held herself, arms wrapped around her body as though to defend herself from the world. And the boy. Remote and silent, standing at her side.

'I don't know what you want, Inspector Friedman. I've already talked to what feels like an army of police officers.'

'I'm sure you have,' Alec commiserated. 'And I'm sorry to bother you. It's good of you to fit me in.'

She grimaced and glanced again at her watch. The third time, Alec noted, since he had been shown into her office. 'I've a staff meeting at twelve,' she told him. 'So I can give you ten minutes. I hope that will be enough.'

'More than enough. Mrs Pritchard, I've come about Sarah Clarke.'

'Obviously.'

'Mrs Pritchard. Maybe you're aware that there have been certain allegations made against the Clarke family. Allegations of physical abuse.'

'I've heard,' she said coldly. 'And I don't believe a word.

188

I had both children in my school, Inspector Friedman. I never had reason to think anything but highly of the family. Ben Clarke attended every parents' evening. When his shifts allowed, he met the children out of school and if problems ever arose he had the sense to come and see me.'

'Ben Clarke. Not Mrs Clarke?'

Mrs Pritchard sighed. 'In case you didn't notice, Inspector, women often work these days and if they have families, it's often the twilight shift or nothing. It makes it difficult to attend evening events when you're stuck on a production line.'

'I'm sorry,' Alec apologized. 'Was it never possible to take the evening off?'

'Can you always get time off when you want it?'

'No,' Alec admitted. He didn't think it wise to suggest that his job was a little less predictable than Maggie Clarke's.

'I've a list here of names of children who might have played at the Clarke's house, or played with Sarah at her friends'. You know that she played often with the Williams children.'

'I know.' She looked at his list and then handed it back. 'First names are not much use to me.' She jabbed a finger at the list. 'Emma, for instance. We have, I believe, four in Sarah's year. I already gave your people a list of contacts. Don't you lot ever consult one another?'

'Mrs Pritchard, as I explained, I've been seconded to this case rather late in the day. The list was given to me this morning by a material witness. But I'll check out records as soon as I get back.'

'Is that all?' She glanced at her watch again.

'No, if you could just bear with me.' He produced the tape recorder again. 'If you could just listen to this. It's the reason I'm trudging over what must seem like old ground.'

'Sordid ground.'

'Perhaps, but we have to follow these things up. I'm sure you can appreciate that. This call was made last night, just after ten.'

She listened impatiently, then shook her head. 'I don't know her. It would be hard to say for certain even if I did with the voice all muffled like that.' She frowned angrily at Alec. 'You come here because someone who hadn't even got the moral courage to leave their name makes accusations about a family who have already been put through hell. Will they have to listen to this?'

'That isn't up to me,' Alec told her. Interestingly, he thought, she had not picked up on the change of tense.

Mrs Pritchard got to her feet, signalling that the meeting was at an end and glanced for a fifth time at her watch, just in case Alec didn't get the point.

'Well, thank you for your time,' he said and added, just for devilment, 'I'm sure we'll be in touch.'

The wind had dropped that morning and it had turned into one of those wonderful October days when the sun shines with an unexpected warmth and the world is golden, bathed in filtered light the like of which Poussin would have been proud of.

The fact that she could not see it only took a little of the edge off Naomi's pleasure. The sun warm on her face after days of chill winds was more than welcome – even Naomi had her fill of dramatic weather after a week of it – and she could imagine the wealth of gold that touched the trees lining her little street and sparkling on the water making it much too bright to look upon for long.

Things are getting back to normal, she told herself. It had become a familiar refrain, marked by the passage of days and the little changes each one had brought. First had been the day she had gone shopping and no one had mentioned Joe Jackson or Helen Jones. Then there had been the news that Patrick and Harry had gone back home and Patrick, reluctantly, back to school.

Then, the visits from Penny, who, she confided to Naomi, had not dared go outside of her door for more than a week. Although Penny's visits were a trial Naomi found hard to bear – and then felt guilty about her lack of sympathy – the fact that Penny came at all meant that media interest had died down enough to allow life to return to normal. Naomi welcomed its homecoming like she welcomed the spring weather.

Lately, with the foul weather, she had taken almost to jogging along the promenade, Napoleon taking her lead and scooting along at a great pace, eager to get out of the wind. Today, their pace was leisurely and they strolled.

Naomi's habits had become so regular of late that she often met with the same people on her walks. In the last few days their greetings had been hurried, heads down, muffled behind scarves, their voices snatched away in the wind.

Today, this too was back to what Naomi called normal and her walk was punctuated by their voices and familiar footsteps.

'Good morning,' a voice said.

'Morning.' Woman with small dog. Yappy little thing, but she sounded nice.

'Mornin', love.' The candyfloss seller on the promenade. He'd hold out until after the half term, then shut up shop for the winter.

'Hello, Naomi?'

'Hi, Grace. How are you?'

'Off to see my son.' Old lady with walking stick. Naomi could hear the tap-tap of it alongside the rather shuffling footsteps. Grace had been one of the first to start exchanging conversation with her and often they would stop and talk. Not this morning, though. 'Sounds like your bus,' Naomi told her, hearing the groan of ageing metal and screech of the air brakes as it pulled up at the stop.

'You're getting good at this,' Grace told her. 'Take care, my dear.'

Naomi paused by the promenade railing, reaching out to find it and then leaning on it as though looking out to sea. 'That bus goes to Mari's,' she told the dog, who nosed her hand expectantly on hearing a familiar name.

She had never caught the bus alone, but now she could identify the stop without too much difficulty; or at least, she'd be able to whilst the candyfloss stall was still there! The smell of it would tell her even if Gus didn't see her and shout hello.

'I reckon it's time we gave it a go, don't you?' she asked the dog. Napoleon leaned in against her leg. 'You don't care, do you?' she told him affectionately. 'No back chat, no arguments.' She fondled his ears. Harry and company would be back at the weekend, it would be a big thing if she could find her way there alone.

The decision gave her an immense feeling of satisfaction and contributed to such a golden morning. Suddenly, her mind was dragged back from its pleasant illusion of ordinariness by the sound of tinkling bells and a girl's voice calling out her name.

'Helen?' The name escaped from her lips before she even had time to think. The girl laughed and then began to walk away.

'Come on,' she said, and for an instant Naomi was sure that she was addressing her. Then, in the next, as another child replied, the illusion was broken and she tried to convince herself that this was nothing to do with her.

But the voices were the same. Naomi was certain of it. The same children she had heard that night when they'd left the bracelet at her door.

'Wait!' she called out, but her voice brought only more laughter and this time the sound of skipping feet as the children hurried away.

'Wait for me, please wait.'

She set off, clinging tightly to Napoleon's harness, steering him towards the place she had heard the sounds, just a little further along the promenade.

Had this been summer then Naomi would have had little hope; in summer the crowds would have drowned out the noise of the children's laughter and their hurrying feet. As it was, Naomi could hear them – or thought she could – only a little distance up ahead.

'Wait for me, oh please wait.'

'Are you all right?' Someone touched her arm.

'Yes, thank you, I'm fine. I just thought I heard a friend.'

Whoever it was let go. 'You be careful now.' Naomi stumbled on.

She had lost them.

In that moment when the stranger stopped her, she had ceased to hear their voices, footsteps or the distant sound of tiny bells and she had lost her bearings too, she realized with a shock. Left her normal route and had not a clue where she was going.

Think, Naomi, think. She could not have gone more than a

few steps from the promenade rail. She listened hard to try and get her bearings and picked up off to her left the sound of video machines across the road in the small arcade.

'Just keep me on the path, OK?' she told the dog, trusting that he would do what he had been so well trained to do. So she took her courage in her hands and walked straight on, hoping to hear the sound of the children again.

'There.' She caught the faintest sound, off to her right and not too far ahead. The crowds had thickened here and other sounds were reaching her from the fairground at the end of the promenade. 'Helen?' Naomi called. 'Helen?' Why there should be any sense in calling out her name Naomi was not sure. But she got her answer.

'Naomi. Na-o-mi . . .'

'Wait for me. Please.'

What am I doing? This is insane. She stopped suddenly and drew breath, aware that her heart was thumping so hard she could hear the blood rushing in her ears. It isn't Helen. No, my Helen's dead. What the hell are they trying to do to me?

She took a few steps forward and the dog sat down. Feeling with her foot, Naomi found the edge of the kerb about to fall from beneath her feet.

'Good dog, wonderful boy.' She turned away from the road, feeling the rush of air as a bus rolled by her on the road. She turned back towards the music and the wailing of the siren that told her the Waltzers in the fairground had begun to spin at their fastest. The kids must have gone into the fair.

Without much hope of finding them now, and not sure even if she could find her way back home, Naomi followed the growing noise towards the entrance, trying to visualize its position as the dog wove in and out of the crowd, guiding her on the best path he knew. The volume increased, swirling about her, confusing her senses by the second and piling sound upon sound, layers of it that wiped her thoughts clean and deprived her even of the power of reason. It was like the swimming pool, she thought. The echoing noises of voices and music, and children squealing and demanding and arguing, and sirens wailing and footsteps, so many footsteps . . . She didn't have a hope in hell of finding the source of one sound in all of this.

Sensing her confusion, Napoleon stood still, pressed close against her leg, waiting to be told what to do next. Naomi didn't know. She didn't even know for certain where the entrance was.

She took a deep, quavering breath, shocked at how unsteady she felt, how tight her chest had become, how hard it was to breathe. Please, she practised in her head. Can you tell me which way to go? But she felt ashamed. Ashamed of having to ask, ashamed of the wild goose chase someone had forced her to begin and ashamed too at the sudden thought that the children, the bracelet, the calling of her name might have been all inside her own mind.

'Naomi? Are you all right? You look dreadful.'

'Penny?' A familiar voice. It didn't occur to Naomi to ask what the woman was doing there; she was just profoundly grateful that she was.

'I'm lost,' Naomi told her. She laughed nervously. 'God, look at me, I'm shaking.'

'Like a leaf,' Penny confirmed. 'Give me your arm and I'll get you out of here.

Gratefully, Naomi did as she was told, surrendering to the moment and letting this woman she had lately so wanted to avoid, lead her back home.

'Are you sure it was them?' Alec asked her.

'Of course I'm sure. I wouldn't have followed if I hadn't been sure.'

'No, I don't suppose you would,' Alec agreed. He hugged her more tightly. She was feeling better, now that some distance had been put between herself and the events of the day. Better and somewhat angry.

'Penny walked me home, came in and made me a cup of tea and I'll admit, Alec, I was really grateful, but . . .'

'What was she doing there in the first place?' Alec finished for her.

'She said she was just cutting through the fairground, and I mean, maybe she was. I used to do it all the time, from the town centre to the promenade.'

'Still one hell of a coincidence.'

'I know. Alec, I should be really grateful she was there and I am. I'd have been glad of anyone familiar at that point. I was in a real panic.' She laughed nervously. 'What a wimp.'

'Wimp, nothing.' He kissed her, softly at first but with increasing intensity, pulling her more tightly into his arms and sliding a hand beneath her shirt.

God, Naomi, he thought, moving down to kiss the hollow of her neck and his fingers fumbling with schoolboy awkwardness at the fastenings of her bra. Do you know how much I love you?

Thirty-Two

'The letters were definitely typed on the same machine as the confession,' Travers confirmed at the morning briefing. 'We've got a psychologist looking at the content, but so far the general inference is that these were written by a child; possibly Penny Jackson, though that is just supposition.'

'We could apply for a warrant, look for the machine,' someone suggested.

'These were written twenty-odd years ago. It might not even exist now,' Travers replied. 'Anyway, we're holding for the psychologist's analysis.'

Alec reached out and plucked copies of the documents from the table and read them again. The text was familiar now and the style still struck him as odd. But then, how would you write a letter to the police telling them about a murder your father had committed? It seemed right that the style was strange.

'Dear Sir,' the first began.

'I'm writing to tell you that I know who killed that girl, Helen Jones.' Helen had been spelt Hellen at first, then the word scribbled over and the correct version typed next to it. 'I saw the man do it. I was there. I saw him when he strangled her and threw her bag into the canal.'

'The bag was never found, was it?'

Travers shook his head. 'They sent divers down but nothing pertinent to the case turned up. There are no lock gates on that stretch and the water flows fast towards the mill and down over the top of that damned weir. They searched below it, I believe, but nothing.'

'Why was no notice taken of these, sir?' The question was put by a young PC. 'I mean with the detail and all.'

'Because they were among the hundreds of tip-offs, confessions and "my neighbour did it" information that came in over those weeks. And that's not including the phone calls and the witness statements,' Alec told him. 'I've had the pleasure of sifting through boxes of the stuff, and the number of claims that Helen was strangled has to reach maybe fifty. That her bag was thrown into the canal, or that she was, are also popular. Along with the dozen or so who reckoned she must be buried on the allotments under someone's potatoes or stuck under a compost heap. Back then, there was nothing to set these apart, not even the fact that there were two of them, and that might not even have been noticed at the time.'

The letter ended 'yours sincerely', Alec noted, as though constructed by a child who'd been doing letter writing in her English class and it was signed off 'a friend'. They had talked about that yesterday and speculated as to how well Penny and Helen knew each other. That they went to the same school meant very little. Ingham Grammar was one of only two secondaries in the immediate area. It would have been more worthy of note had they not.

Penny was younger by a year, so it was unlikely they had known each other really well, Alec thought, remembering the friendships he had formed in his own school days; strictly peer based. Naomi had not recalled Penny in any great detail from that time; only after Helen and during the Joe Jackson era had she realized who she was.

'Did you try to make friends with her?' Alec asked. It would to him have seemed a natural extension of the Joe Jackson network.

Naomi shook her head. 'No, I lost a lot of time at school after Helen. I'd just got settled in again when Penny left. I think that was about the time that Lydia and Joe separated for a time, though I sort of remember that Penny hadn't been around much before. I get this feeling it wasn't the first time Lydia walked out, but I'm sorry Alec, I don't really recall.'

The second letter was somewhat similar. 'Dear Sirs,' it began this time. The letter-writing class must have moved on to business letters. 'I wrote to you a week ago, but you have not done nothing.' It was the first major slip in grammar, but entirely in keeping with local language. 'I told you that the man strangled her and buried her and threw her bag into the water. She's buried in the new houses. I saw it happen.'

This time it was signed 'yours faithfully', but nothing more.

'The pattern's definitely different,' Alec commented. They had discussed this the day before, but it struck him afresh now. 'It's more hurried, impatient.'

'What about the reference to the new houses?' someone asked. 'Was that ever checked out?'

Travers shook his head. 'I couldn't tell you without going back through the records,' he said. 'But it could mean any of a half dozen locations being built around that time. My guess is that priority was given to the Mamby development closest to Helen's home.'

When the meeting broke up, Travers called Alec back. 'We've traced the mother and she's agreed to talk to you.'

'Good. When?'

'Not until Monday. Lydia Jackson remarried apparently about six years ago. She says she and Penny don't keep in touch and she never talked to Joe. I don't think she was all too happy to be found, and they're away visiting friends for the weekend. But she'll see you on Monday. I said around ten thirty. Here's the address and I've got the video footage from the CCTV cameras you wanted.'

'That was quick.'

'Efficiency is my middle name.'

'How many hours do I have to trawl through? I guess it's too much to hope it's digital . . . time-coded . . . No, thought not.'

'Have fun, Alec. And Alec, I think you should tell Naomi to take care. I've got an odd feeling about this. The coincidence is just that bit too much this time.'

Thirty-Three

Half-term had begun and Naomi had an invitation to tea at Mari's house. Harry had offered to collect her, but Naomi had declined. Her experience the day before had unnerved her considerably and she knew that the best way to deal with it was to get back on the metaphorical horse. Or in this case, to catch the bus. She knew that the bus stopped at the end of Mari's road and now she was reasonably certain she could find the bus stop on the promenade, it should only be a matter of counting the stops, though just to be certain she asked the driver to tell her when she'd arrived.

It was a triumphant woman and happy dog that arrived at Mari's door. She had worried slightly about finding the right house, but Patrick saved her the bother. He had been watching for her from the upstairs window, which gave the clearest view over the parked cars and down the street, and he had the front door opened before she was halfway there.

Patrick hugged her. Mari kissed her cheek and told her how well she looked. Harry took her hands and stood awkwardly for a moment before kissing her almost on the mouth and telling her how good it was to see her again.

'It seems like you've been gone forever,' she told them, the wriggle of dog beside her and thump of tail against the door a sign that Napoleon thought so too.

The afternoon passed too quickly and they talked of nothing in particular. Patrick's rendition of how well he was doing on his latest game merged with Mari talking about a trip to Chatsworth they had made while they were away. Harry said he had grown used to boredom once again, but that he had not settled back to it as well as he had thought he might.

'Are you still thinking about moving?' Naomi asked him.

'Oh yes, in fact I've got some viewings lined up for later in the week. If you'd like to come, I'd enjoy the company.'

'Who the devil's that?' Mari asked as a knock came at the door. 'I thought we'd seen all the neighbours.' She got up and went through to the hall.'

'Seen all the neighbours,' Harry said. 'They were waiting practically on the doorstep. Still it was nice for Mam. Next door had done some shopping for us and that.' Then he broke off. 'Oh,' he said as he recognized the voice coming from the hall. The pleasant atmosphere in the room seemed to evaporate as Mari led Penny Jackson inside.

It's funny, Naomi thought, just how stilted conversation gets when everyone makes an effort. It became more stilted when Penny asked how she was feeling after her experience yesterday and she had to go through the event for the benefit of Mari and company. Deliberately, she kept it simple, making no mention of Helen or the children.

'I got too ambitious,' she said. 'I walked too far and ended up in the middle of the fairground. I was feeling very lost and just about to shout for help when Penny turned up.'

'That was good,' Mari said. 'Naomi, don't try to push yourself too hard, love. She always did though,' she added, speaking to Penny.

'What were you doing there?' Patrick asked, voicing what Harry must be thinking, Naomi guessed.

'Oh, I often cut through,' she told him. 'It takes off that great corner at the end of Broadway.'

'Oh,' Patrick said and then fell silent. It was a silence that seemed to creep up on the others until it permeated the room.

Finally, Naomi broke it, unable to bear it any longer and eager to rescue Patrick who must by now be wondering if he could escape to his room.

'Napoleon needs to go out,' she said. 'Patrick, do you want to come?'

'Thanks,' the boy said as they were walking down the road.

'It's OK, but I feel horrid leaving the others and I feel cruel feeling the way I do about Penny. I mean, she's been through so much, but every time I meet her, I'm just so overwhelmed by it all again. I just can't handle it. Isn't that a cowardly thing to feel?'

Patrick shrugged. 'You said it was OK to be scared of things,' he said. 'I think you feel about Penny like I feel about swimming. I know it's all right really and I should be enjoying it and loads of people really like it. But, I'm just different, I guess.'

Naomi laughed. He had said it with a kind of triumph as though he had learnt this lesson well.

'Mind if we go down beside the canal?' she asked. 'I've not walked down there in a long while and I don't feel confident enough yet to try it on my own.'

'Sure. We need to cross over now, right?'

They talked little as they walked between the houses and down on to the towpath. Naomi's thoughts were full of the other times that she had come here. Fishing for tiddlers with brightly coloured plastic nets. Feeding the ducks with bits of old bread and watching the barges carrying the holiday traffic in the summer.

And those times with Joe, talking about Helen.

'Which way do we go now?' Patrick was asking her and from the noise of rushing water Naomi realized that they had reached the mill and the weir.

'Across the bridge, I think. Is that OK?'

'I guess.'

The bridge ran above the curve of the weir. A steel and concrete affair that replaced the slatted wood Naomi remembered as a child. She remembered how vertiginous it was, peering down between the slats and watching the frothing water flooding into the pool below. In this calm pool, narrow boats turned. These days just the holiday makers, but in times gone by merchantmen bringing wool to the factory and taking the bales away.

'Is it dark yet?'

'No, not really. The lights are coming on.'

'Are you all right?'

Patrick laughed. 'No, not really. You think I've got your arm to help *you*. You're all wrong.'

201

'We should be turning back anyway,' she told him, judging that they were something like halfway across. 'They talked about renovating the mill some while ago. Turning it into luxury apartments or something.'

'Doesn't look as if they got very far,' Patrick told her. 'It's all boarded up and there are keep out signs. At least I think that's what they say, it's getting a bit too dark to see.'

Naomi began to turn back. She paused, turning her head so that she could better hear the moil and bubble of the crashing flood.

'Joe rescued a child from there,' she said. 'A little girl who'd gone in off the bridge. In those days it was a rough old affair, all wood and holes mended with bits of twine. There'd been an incident, some flare-up in one of the waterside pubs and it was half dark like this when we were walking back to the car.

'We heard her scream and I just stood there thinking, oh my God, what do I do? I was still thinking it when Joe had his shoes and coat off and was in the water.

'They had dredged the basin when they replaced the bridge, but it was still full of six foot of mud and slime at the bottom and decades of rubbish. But he went out and he got her and he pulled her to the side. Got her breathing again before the ambulance arrived.'

'You still don't think he could have done it, do you?'

Naomi shrugged and began to move back across the bridge. 'I don't know that I don't believe, it's just when you've spent most of your life thinking one thing, it's hard to make the change.' She paused. 'It must be even harder for Mari?'

Patrick nodded. 'She can't,' he said. 'Nan's making herself ill just trying to work it out.'

Alec stretched and rubbed his eyes. He'd spent much of Friday, and then come in today, looking through more of the CCTV footage. This past hour or so, Travers had joined him and they had finally got a glimpse of what must be the two little girls.

They had been walking out of frame, having just circled a Hook The Duck attraction and for far too long had been blocked by a family playing it. Finding the next shot in sequence from the second camera position had been a long-winded nightmare.

'There,' Travers almost shouted. He froze the tape, then backtracked frame by frame. It was the first shot that showed both Naomi and the children; Naomi stood frozen a few yards from the entrance, her head moving from side to side as she tried to find her bearings in the cacophony of noise.

'My God,' Alec said as the older child turned and for an instant faced the camera.

Travers snorted in similar disbelief. From a distance, helped by the fuzzy quality of the video, the children looked like Helen Jones and Sarah Clarke, walking through the fair, hand in hand.

Penny had returned home not long after Naomi and Patrick had left on their walk and she was crying as she closed the front door.

'Penny?' He was there for her as always, taking her coat and leading her through to the kitchen where it was always warm.

'It didn't go so well, then.'

Unable to speak, she shook her head and slumped down in the nearest chair. Bill stood beside her, cradling her head and stroking her hair. 'Give it time,' he said. 'It's hard for everyone, you can't expect too much too soon.'

'I know,' she almost wailed the words in her despair. 'But Bill, if we could be friends, could help each other. It just hurts so much that they don't care.'

When Alec arrived at Naomi's with the tapes, Harry was there having just brought her back home.

'Good,' Alec said. 'Saves me doing this twice and you can help me with the commentary.'

'What is it?' Naomi wanted to know.

'CCTV footage of yesterday. She tell you about that, did she?'

Harry hummed his agreement. 'Naomi told us something,' he said. 'Penny filled us in with the rest of the facts and how you thought you heard Helen or something.'

'Penny?'

'She turned up this afternoon. And I didn't think it was Helen, not really. I told Alec, I thought it was the children who left the bracelet.'

She was irritated after making the effort to keep the more absurd aspect of the incident to herself that Penny should have let the cat so far out of the bag. She had almost forgotten that, being in such a state the afternoon before, many of her thoughts and feelings and, what she now told herself were her imaginings, had come flooding out, draining into Penny's ready, listening ear.

'Well, I know this may seem daft, seeing as how you can't see it,' Alec said. 'But I'm going to talk you through and you tell me anything you remember. Anything, no matter how trivial it may seem or how silly.'

She shrugged. 'OK. If you think it will do any good, but I'm not sure why you're—'

'Patience,' Alec commanded. 'It'll all become clear, I promise you.'

He sat back on the sofa with the remote control in his hand and began to run the tape.

'Right, Miss Naomi Blake's dramatic entrance complete with large black dog. We've had to edit several camera angles together to get the complete picture so it's pretty jerky, but as we pan left you see the kids for the first time just going out of shot.'

'There's Penny,' Harry said suddenly.

'Where?'

'Can you reverse it, frame by frame?'

Alec rewound instead and walked it through to give him a steadier image. 'Oh, yes,' he agreed. He shook his head. 'I've been looking at these things too long. She's only just in shot, but I still don't see how I missed her.'

'You were looking for the children,' Naomi guessed.

'I think she's with someone,' Harry commented. 'Look.'

'Is he with her? I'm not sure. Damn, she's dropped out of view.'

He let the tape run. 'Now watch,' he told Harry, 'next to the Hook The Duck booth and there –' he froze it for an instant – 'Naomi and kids in the same shot.'

He glanced sideways at Harry who was leaning forward staring at the screen.

'Amazing, isn't it?' Alec commented.

'What?' Naomi demanded. 'Tell me.'

'The oldest one looks like Helen,' Alec told her.

Thirty-Four

L ydia Jackson, now Lydia Reynolds was a woman in her late fifties but she wore it well. She had steel grey hair, cropped into a style that was fashionably spiky and did not look out of place with the grey blue eyes and fine bone structure that the years had left to her.

She looked nothing like Penny Jackson and, though he had not thought of it before, Alec realized just how much like the father was the child.

'It's good of you to see me,' Alec told her. 'I'm sure this is the last thing you wanted.'

She smiled, a slight smile that nonetheless crinkled the corners of her eyes, showing the lines. Alec liked her lines. They showed humour, he thought.

'It isn't what I want,' she said, 'but I've been expecting it, ever since the news broke. Come on inside.'

The Reynolds lived in a bungalow on the edge of a modern housing estate. It was small, but neat and furnished with an almost spartan simplicity. The floors were wood laminate, pale and clean and the walls unpapered, painted in light tones that set off the paintings hanging there. These mostly seemed to have come from the same hand and were vibrant and richly coloured. Semi-abstract landscapes that suggested the lie of the land rather than defining it were painted in such a way that at times the land dissolved slowly into sky and the sky swept down to penetrate the earth.

She caught him admiring them. 'You like my work?'

'Yours? I'm very impressed. Naomi would love these,' he added, then he caught himself, but it was too late.

'Naomi? Your girlfriend?' She bit her lip and the blue eyes

narrowed in thought. 'That wouldn't be little Naomi Blake, surely. Small world isn't it?'

'Small world,' Alec agreed. 'Do you sell your work?'

'Oh yes, I've got a growing market. Pity it took me a lifetime to find my niche.'

'At least you found it; some people never do.'

'True,' she nodded. 'Would you like some coffee, Inspector?'

'Please, and call me Alec. It seems silly to be so formal.'

Again that thoughtful narrowing of the eyes as she regarded him as though he were a painting whose composition didn't feel quite right.

'Alec,' she said at last. 'Alec Friedman. No, I don't recall you being part of the Joe Jackson menagerie.'

Menagerie. Naomi would just love that. Alec smiled. 'I worked with him on occasions. Not often though.' He glanced back at the paintings hanging on the living-room wall. Naomi would still like them, he decided. He could tell her how the colours flowed and the storm blended into silence all along those cruel hills. The way the spring colours of that one glided into autumn. He laughed at himself, silently, but she caught him, smiled in collaboration and he found himself thinking once again just how little mother and daughter had in kind.

'So,' she said at last. 'My daughter found that confession and handed it to the police.' They had stayed in the kitchen, drinking fresh coffee. Alec's attention wavering back to the paintings as she asked him if he needed sugar, if he had sufficient milk or would prefer the cream. She'd been procrastinating, Alec knew, but he didn't blame her. She had evidently made a massive effort to remove herself from the past and his coming here brought it all back. Must be difficult.

'You don't see your daughter?'

'No, I don't see my daughter.' She took a deep breath and began. 'You were asking about the time when Helen Jones disappeared. I'm not too sure I can tell you anything. About a month before that, I left Joe for the first time and I took Penny with me. It was a bad decision, Alec, but after all those years with Joe, I feel I'm entitled to one or two.

207

'I left him for another man and lived with this other man for a month or two, then he cleared off and left us and eventually I went back home. His name was Robert Williams and I'd been seeing him off and on for about a year before I took the plunge.'

'Williams,' Alec said. He put the thought away for the moment. It was a common enough name.

'Um, yes.' She smiled. 'Not a name most welcome to you, I don't suppose. I do read the papers, Alec.'

He laughed. 'I'm trying to break the habit. How did Penny get along with him?'

'Oh, well. Very well in fact. Joe, well Joe wasn't around very much and even when he was, well, I'm sure I don't need to give you a lecture on the effects of the police force on family life. But yes, she got on well with Robert. In fact, the funny thing was, it was Penny that introduced us in the first place.'

'Oh. How was that?'

'Robert had a child at Penny's school. Robert was divorced, but they had some kind of shared arrangement on care. We got talking . . . you know . . . things went from there.'

'And you say he just left?'

She nodded. 'We had this grotty little flat, and for a while I really thought we could make it work out.' She shrugged. 'I was wrong, but there you go. One thing it did teach me though, I couldn't stay with Joe any longer. We went back for a little while,' she laughed. 'I'm not even sure he'd noticed we had gone, or I'd gone anyway. Joe, if anything, was even more distant, but he was, well, kind of possessive too.'

'Understandable, I suppose,' Alec hazarded.

'I said that to myself. But it wasn't like that. I mean, he was never there, but when he did come home the first thing he wanted to know was where Penny was and if she wasn't in the house and I didn't know precisely where she was, he'd fly off the handle. Go berserk looking for her. I mean, she was at that age when she was stating to want her freedom, but Joe just couldn't hack it. So we left again, for good this time.

'We got a little flat, tried to settle down, but Penny was . . . I don't know . . . difficult. She lost interest in school, friends, everything really. The school advised counselling.

They thought it was the divorce, but when I spoke to Joe he would have none of it. Penny, she didn't seem to care.

'In the end, I took her to a few sessions in spite of Joe. He wasn't living with her, coping with her moods, her wandering off and not coming home for hours. Not telling me where she'd gone.'

'Did the counselling help?'

She shook her head. 'No. She wouldn't cooperate. Clammed up and said nothing. She said her dad didn't want her to go and I couldn't make her talk.'

Alec nodded. 'And when she was older?'

'Oh, she left home just after her eighteenth birthday. Lived in some kind of shared house and took a receptionist course at college.' She sighed and the eyes narrowed again as she caught her thoughts. 'You must think I'm a God-awful mother, but to be honest, by that time I didn't care . . . no, that's not true. I didn't want to know. There was no talking to her. No way of getting through. I kept telling myself, I'm here if she wants me, but I can't make her come back, and that's where we left it.'

'I don't have kids,' Alec said. 'It must have been hard to let go.'

'Not in the end. Isn't that dreadful? I heard she met some-one. Settled down, and I wished her well. Then I married again and here we are.'

Thirty-Five

N aomi had been unable to settle. Alec had left her early that morning and given her plenty of time to think until her session at the advice centre.

She had worked from ten till twelve thirty and been grateful of the distraction, but when the time came to leave and George Mallard had come to collect her, it was as if two and a half hours worth of thought suddenly clamoured for attention all at once and she knew she would have to do something about it.

Instead of going straight home she had George drop her at Mari's, assuring him that she would be able to get a lift home.

'I caught the bus on Saturday,' she told him. 'I'm dead proud of myself.'

George was impressed. 'Just don't get too independent,' he joked, 'or you'll be doing me out of a nice regular job.'

Harry listened to what she had to say and agreed there was only one course of action to take. 'We beard the lion in her den,' he said dramatically. 'Find out what she was doing there. Seriously, Naomi, I'm sure that woman was following you or something. On the tape, she's just standing there watching for a good few minutes before she comes over to you. I mean, that isn't normal, is it?'

'It's possible she just didn't want to intrude,' Mari suggested. 'We all know how independent you like to be.'

'Playing devil's advocate never did suit you,' Harry told her. 'Let's do it now,' he added. 'You know where she lives, don't you?'

'Joe Jackson's old place on the Sileby Road.' She shuddered slightly. 'It's going to be strange going there.'

'You make it sound as if you've never been,' Harry commented as he led her out to the car and settled Napoleon in the rear seat. 'I thought with you and Joe being so close . . .'

'I haven't. Not inside. Joe always met me somewhere else and even when I joined the force, he was never one to invite people home. He'd meet them in the pub or whatever. Lydia had gone by then, of course. Oh, she must have left during the investigation, though I'm not sure when.' She frowned, trying to recollect. 'I think it was the autumn after Helen disappeared that she left for good, but I gather things had been pretty rocky for a while. You know, Harry, I remember finding out where Joe lived and going there sometimes, just to look at the house. I'd stand outside and watch the lights come on and people closing the curtains or moving about inside the rooms and I'd fantasize about Joe coming out and finding me. Inviting me inside. I had this fantasy idea of what living with Joe Jackson must have been like.'

'I think we all have those,' Harry said quietly. 'Fantasies about other people's families. Sometimes it takes us a lot of growing up before we appreciate the value of our own.' He cleared his throat nervously. 'You know, I was the first of our lot to go to university. Mam was that proud and when I graduated she and Dad came to see. Naomi, I'm ashamed to say, I didn't want them there. Here was I with my friends from uni and their mams and dads in posh suits and posher cars – well, that's what I was looking at anyway – and there was Mam and Mac, come up on the bus; Dad in his best suit.'

'He was like my dad: only ever had one.'

'True. And Mam in this awful floral . . . thing. All clashing colours and roses and . . . God, it was gaudy. And me with a chip the size of a baking potato stuck on my shoulder. God, I was a stuck up little pig.'

Naomi laughed, she knew Mari's taste in clothes. 'But they were there,' she said. 'And you know better now. That's all that matters.'

'I wish I could take it back though,' Harry said feelingly. He hesitated for a moment and then he said, 'You know the funniest thing. I mean funny peculiar, not funny ha ha.'

'What?'

211

'When I saw them walking into the hall that day . . . I swear, even now, that there was Helen, hanging on to Mac's hand.'

Penny was not pleased to see them; uncomfortable, it seemed, to have them on her territory, as they had been to have her on their own.

'You'd best come in,' she said and led them through to the cold front room where she had entertained Alec a few days before.

'I could make some tea,' Penny said, but it was not much of an invitation. She stood, hovering in the doorway as they sat down, as though hoping that if she didn't follow suit they might quickly leave.

Naomi shivered. The room was chilly. It seemed to rise up from the floor and seep through the walls. The upholstery of the chair in which she sat felt clammy, damp to her touch.

Was it like this, she wondered, when Joe lived here and she had watched them from outside?

'It's been bothering me, Penny,' she said, deciding to come straight to the point. 'What were you doing there that day? Had you been following me?'

'Following you? What day? The day you got lost? Of course I wasn't, why on earth would you think that?'

'Alec showed us some film,' Harry told her. 'He got it from the CCTV cameras in the fairground and you're there, all the time Naomi is. Watching what she does.'

'Of course I was watching her. I wondered if she was all right. She came in and then stopped and I thought, is she going somewhere? Can she find her way on her own? I certainly didn't want to break her train of thought if she had her route set out.'

It sounded reasonable. Too reasonable.

'Were you with someone?' Naomi asked her. 'A man. About your height with short dark hair, wearing a raincoat. Grey, probably.'

'I wasn't with anyone. Naomi, what is all this? What on earth is Alec playing at, feeding you these ideas?'

'Alec isn't feeding me anything. Penny, I don't want to seem

212

difficult or to upset you in any way, but, if you were following me, I feel I have a right to know.'

'Have you asked yourself why on earth I would? Naomi, I have tried hard to be friendly. I have put myself out, exposed myself to all the degradation and the foul lies and the invective to make sure that the truth finally comes out. I didn't have to do any of this. I didn't have to let Helen's family know what had happened. I could have let them go on believing that my father was an honest man and never let them have their daughter's body back. I could have left them in the dark for ever more and never said a thing. But I didn't. I told, and since I told, I hoped . . . I hoped that maybe, between us, we could share the grief.' She broke off and took in a long quavering breath as though to stop the tears. 'I'm sorry, but I want you to leave now. Please.'

They left in silence and didn't speak until they reached the car.

'I feel like a right shit,' Naomi said. 'She's right, isn't she? We've been so wrapped up in ourselves.'

'Maybe. I don't know, Naomi, I still don't think it's right. She's hiding behind the words and if you'd let yourself be a detective again for just a moment, and stop letting her get to you with her emotional blackmail, I think you'd agree.'

Alec arrived back to find the place in uproar. 'What's going on?'

Travers was hurrying through to the back office. 'Alec, good, don't settle. You can come with me. They've found another body.'

'What? Where?'

'Lansdowne Road.'

'I thought the digging had stopped there.'

Travers shook his head. 'It had. Yesterday evening the editor of the *Ingham News* received a call.'

'The *Ingham News*. The free paper with all the ads in?' The *Ingham News* was a community publication for local businesses to advertise and local events to be given a bit of coverage.

'Yeah, I know it seems like an odd choice. Graham Harris,

the editor, describes the informant as a male, he thinks mid-thirties, forties. Local accent. Refused to give his name.'

'Naturally.'

'He told Harris that Helen Jones was not the only one and we should be looking under the patio of the house next door. Harris called us last night and was put straight on to Phillips. He had no choice but to organize the dig. With all the bad press and this being the most exciting thing ever to happen to our Mr Harris, we knew he'd be out there talking about it. We thought, OK, another hoax call, but at least the caller said the patio and not the bloody living room.

'So we dug under the patio. And there it was. Body number two.'

Body number two was almost certainly male though the pathologist would have to confirm that. And it was not a child.

'Jewellery,' Travers said, handing the evidence bags to Alec for inspection. 'A man's watch and one of those godawful sovereign rings.'

Alec turned them over in his hands, peering through the plastic at the heavy ring and the watch with its expanding bracelet, now tarnished and grey, showing only traces of the gold plating that had once been there.

'Not expensive stuff,' he commented. He glanced over to where the team in their white overalls were carefully excavating the grave, scraping back the earth in thin layers and recording as carefully as any archaeologist.

'We knew who we were looking for when we dug next door,' he commented. 'Who the hell is *he*?'

Thirty-Six

A lec had not been pleased about Naomi's visit to Penny and a few sharp words had been exchanged.

'You're being overprotective. It's not as if I went alone.'

'This time, no. But what other damn fool ideas are you going to get?'

'I'm blind, Alec. Not stupid.'

'I never said you were.'

'No, just that I'm a damned fool.'

'I said the idea was a damned foolish one.' He took a deep breath. 'Naomi, I just worry about you. I'd worry about you no matter what. That night, that night when I heard about the accident. I thought you might be . . . might not have made it.'

'Dead, Alec. The word is dead,' retorted Naomi, but she didn't want to argue either. 'There was a time I wished I was. Isn't that just so . . . so . . .'

'Yeah,' he said softly. She felt his hand on her hip. A conciliatory, let me get closer gesture, and she lay her forehead against his shoulder.

'I just wanted to have it out with her and I ended up feeling like shit,' she told him. 'I'm losing my touch, Alec. Losing that edge, that detachment. Harry said I was letting the emotional blackmail get to me and I should start trying to see through it. Start thinking like a detective again.'

The second hand crept around her waist. 'Much as I hate to agree with anything Harry says,' he admitted, 'I think he has a point.'

She lifted her head and squinted at him as though trying to observe closely. Her expression reminded Alec of Lydia, Jackson's ex-wife. 'What you got against Harry?' she questioned.

'Against Harry, nothing. Against Harry moving in on my territory, everything.'

'Your territory? I'm not territory, Alec.'

'No.' He let go of her so abruptly that she felt suddenly bereft. 'No, you're not. I know that.'

Naomi frowned. 'You're jealous of him?'

'No, I'm possessive of you.' He laughed, but the sound was mirthless. 'I think there is a difference.'

'Is there?' She sighed and felt behind her for the sofa, flopped down and grabbed one of the cushions, hugging it to her, wishing he'd come back and sit down.

'Alec, let's not argue. I've already had enough emotion for the day and I don't know what to make of what I've got.' She reached out a hand towards where she thought he was. He came over and took it, sat down on the floor at her feet and leaned against her leg. He reminded her suddenly of Napoleon.

'I'm sorry,' he said finally. 'Maybe I'm a bit uptight, but this just got bigger than any of us thought. We found a second body. In the house next to number 43. I'm not certain where this is leading any more.'

The Wednesday morning found Alec reviewing the video tapes of the fairground once again. He had gone in early to work, snatching a couple of hours before the day officially began.

Travers stuck his head around the door. 'Are you still on that?'

'Trying to get a better look at the man. The one we thought Penny might have been with.'

Travers came over and perched on the edge of the desk. 'And?'

'And, I think she definitely was. Look here, they're standing close together at this point, watching Naomi. She touches his arm and then he moves away.' He grabbed another tape, shot from an alternative angle. 'Here, the kids come into shot, he's moved to the shooting gallery. The kids walk by him, now tell me what you see.'

Travers watched. 'The older one speaks to him,' Travers

216

said. 'Pity he's not clearer . . . grab the frame, get it enhanced. Or are you already ahead of me?'

'Thought I'd make an early start. I've got a time slot at the lab in –' he glanced at his watch – 'half an hour.'

'Best get going then. Naomi OK?' he asked as Alec headed for the door.

Alec nodded. 'We had a few words last night. She went to see Penny Jackson. Took Harry Jones with her, but I still don't like it.'

Travers' smile was wry. 'Don't like which part, Alec? Her going to see Penny Jackson or her taking Harry Jones?'

Naomi was still trying to be irritated by what she described as Alec's overprotective attitude, but in her more honest moments she was glad that Harry had been there and didn't like to even think about visiting Penny alone.

The more she had thought about it, the more she had the vague sense that someone else had been in the house. There had been an atmosphere of tension which had nothing to do with the conversation and the nearest Naomi could get to it was that Penny had not wanted them to meet this other person or even know that they were there.

She almost dismissed this as overactive imagination. Almost, but not quite.

She didn't think that even Alec could object to her seeing Geoff Lyman again, though this time she had called ahead to make sure that the ex-detective sergeant was at home and able to fit her in.

She arrived just after eleven and heard him opening the door as she let herself and Napoleon through the gate.

'Your roses are still in bloom.'

'Yes, we're sheltered here.' He took her hand. 'Careful of the thorns now, that's it. Feel how soft that is.'

Gently, he placed Naomi's hand on the petals of the rose, closing her fingers carefully around the flower. It felt like silk, with velvety edges and the scent almost overpowering.

'What colour is it?'

'Colour? Oh a deep, deep red, the edges of the petals turn almost black before they fall. I think it's Fragrant Cloud, but I

217

bought it with the label lost the day I retired. A really scrubby specimen it was too, but it's fattened up nicely.'

She laughed, stepping inside the house, feeling for the small step she remembered from her last visit. 'It if was so scrubby, why did you buy it?'

'Foolishness,' he said. 'It looked like I felt. Useless and abandoned. I didn't take to retirement easy but in the end it thrived and I learned to cope with it. What have you got to ask me this time?'

'I promise, next time it'll be a social call. You know, I'd like a garden. Not that I knew a weed from a plant even when I *could* see.'

'Weeds *are* plants, you great ninny. You could grow things that smelt and felt nice, I suppose, and damn what other people told you.'

'I might just do.'

He took her arm and seated her by the window. She could feel the weak October sun on her face, its heat amplified by the glass, giving the illusion of summer.

'Tell me about Penny,' she said. 'When did her mum and dad divorce? What kind of child was she? What did Joe say about her?'

There was a long silence while Geoff Lyman considered her questions. 'I barely knew her,' he said. 'For that matter, I barely knew the wife. Lydia, I believe she was called, though I don't think I met her above once. She was younger than Joe by a good few years and they only ever had the one child. I got the impression that Joe thought one was enough and his wife didn't have all that much of a say. Impression, mind. There may have been all kinds of reasons that Joe didn't talk about.'

'Did you ever meet Penny?'

'Once or twice. She was a plain little thing. I remember that because of the saying, you know, "Penny plain, tuppence painted". Long dark hair, I seem to think. Straight as a yard of pump water, but with these fierce grey eyes. Hawks' eyes, you know, like her dad on occasion when something riled him. Tall too, where her mum was small. You know, really small, like those women who joke they shop in the kiddies' department.'

218

'I was out of kids' clothes by the time I was nine,' Naomi said feelingly. 'Used to drive my mam daft. She said she wouldn't have me dressing like a teenager 'til I was one, even if I was tall enough.'

'I never had children,' he said. 'Wife couldn't and we never felt we wanted anyone else's. She's off at her pottery classes this morning.' Naomi could hear the smile in his voice. 'You know I don't think we see any more of one another than we did when I was working. She does these classes and I do my garden and my allotment and in the evening we sit and watch the box or have friends round, but we might go days and say not above a dozen words.' Naomi smiled back. There was no self-pity in his words. She gathered that he was comfortable with the arrangement and hoped his wife was too.

'Did Penny have many friends?'

'No. I don't believe she did. Joe was like a lot of our profession, choosy about who his kiddie hung about with. It's often hard on the children, their parents seeing all the dross and the idiots and the wasters day after day. It skews your vision of the world so it's sometimes hard to see what good there is in it.'

Naomi nodded. She'd encountered this before. 'Boyfriends? Or was she too young then?'

Geoff Lyman guffawed, the sound so loud it startled Napoleon and he lifted his head to stare at the man.

'Oh, she might well have been too young, but whenever did that stop them? Like I said, she was a plain little thing, but she looked older than her age and from what Joe complained about, she had the boys after her anyhow.'

This didn't tally with what Lydia had told Alec, Naomi thought. 'Anyone in particular?'

Geoff thought about it. 'There was one,' he said. 'Joe off on his high horse about him being too old. She was what, twelve or thirteen. Looked sixteen mind, especially the time I saw her with her war paint on.' He laughed again. 'Strikes me as funny,' he said. 'Girls spend all their teens trying to look older and from their twenties on buying all this muck to make them look sixteen again.'

'We sure do,' Naomi agreed. 'You remember his name?'

'I'm thinking, love. The old brain takes a bit of persuading these days. Bill, or William or Billy or some such, I'm almost sure. Joe scared him off, I do believe. Told him Penny was under age and he could be done for rape if he went any further. I don't know that there was sex involved. I'm just surmising from the temper Joe got himself in, that if there wasn't, he thought there soon would be. He thought her mum should be doing more to keep her in line. Even talked about applying for custody, but of course, he never meant it. Joe as a full-time father! Lord, that was never on the cards.'

For a while, Naomi thought. For a while, he was to me.

Naomi had still been there, the talk moving to other things, when May, Geoff's wife came home, proudly bearing her newest pot. Any doubt about their marital harmony was dispelled by that pot. Geoff cooed over and admired it as a parent might over a child's first painting, though from what Naomi could tell when she held it in her hands, it was somewhat lopsided and less than round.

She was invited to stay for lunch, pressed into accepting and regaled with talk about May's classes and the people she met there.

'Have you ever tried to pot?' May asked her. 'It's very tactile, so I'm sure you could get on with it.'

'I tried once, at school,' Naomi said. And there had been clay everywhere by the time she'd got it centred on the wheel.

But she left promising that she might well give it a go and May threatening to call her when the times of the winter classes were announced.

'Pottery or potty, eh dog?' She rubbed his ears and he grunted appreciatively.

She called Alec on her mobile and ran him through her conversation with Geoff Lyman. Her phone began to beep at her.

'Didn't you put that on charge?'

'Yes, last night, all night. I think it's had it, the battery at least.'

'Easier to get a new phone. OK, love, I'll see you soon. I'm intrigued by this Bill, though. I think Lydia needs another talking to. I can't believe she would have forgotten about this.'

Thirty-Seven

Penny wandered from room to room feeling the silence and the emptiness of her childhood home and trying to recall if it had ever felt so very different.

The house was cold. It had central heating but she never switched it on. It was expensive to run and she had to keep costs down now she no longer worked. Maybe when she moved, she would find a job. A receptionist maybe, like before. Meeting people, being efficient. She hadn't worked in the past year really, not since losing her last job. She'd lived off the money her father had left to her which she hadn't touched before. That and her own meagre savings. Her costs were few and she worked hard at keeping them down.

It was a big house and, thankfully, the buyers had not dropped out after finding out about her father. They had forced her to lower the price though, suddenly worrying about the possible cost of rewiring, and pointing out that no maintenance had been done on the place in years. All things the original estimate had taken account of.

She resented it, knowing that they could just walk away if she didn't agree and she would have a hard time finding someone else now. Joe still ruining her life for her even from beyond the grave.

Though she wasn't sorry. She had been looking for this kind of opportunity for so many years that when that document came into her possession, it had seemed like a message brought by fate. At last, everyone would see her father for what he really was, not as the flawed but lovable heroic figure everyone wanted to see.

Her wanderings took her finally into her father's study and she stood in the centre of the little room surveying her handiwork. The news clippings were stuck on the bare walls, so carefully arranged, layer by layer like a wall-bound book.

In the alcove between the fireplace and the window was a built-in cupboard and Penny opened it now. On the middle shelf lay her father's old portable typewriter, with its scored A and its clattering keys.

'You really should get rid of that,' Bill said.

She started, not having heard him enter the room. 'I couldn't, not this.'

'Why not, Penny? There's only bad things, bad memories tied up with it.'

She sat down heavily in her father's chair, remembering how as a child she had loved this captain's chair with its leather seat and wooden arms. She'd spent hours swivelling and spinning and leaning back as far as the design would allow it to go.

'I wanted to talk to her properly that day. That day when I went to see them all at Mari's. I thought after what happened at the fair, she might be glad to see me, be grateful that I'd been there. But no, she just made some excuse about the dog needing to go out and took that boy with her. It was the boy that made her go out. Patrick. He doesn't like me, Bill.'

Bill went over to her. He stroked her hair and rubbed her shoulders, soothing her. 'Kids are like that sometimes,' he said calmly. 'They take dislikes to people, you know that. Christ knows you were ready enough at that age.'

She smiled, allowing his kneading hands to ease the tension from her muscles. 'I always liked you, though, didn't I?'

He bent down to kiss the top of her head. 'Always,' he said. 'Look, forget what happened on Saturday, forget what happened yesterday. You're all under so much pressure that sometimes only the bad side of things comes out. I reckon she was as upset as you by what was said.

'Give her a call, arrange to meet somewhere neutral. Have a coffee and try to make it up.'

She nodded. 'Maybe you're right. Though not right now. I don't think I have the strength right now.'

Close to tears but determined not to cry, she took a deep

breath and held it for a moment. A childhood habit held on to all these adult years.

'You know,' she said at last. 'We've got so much in common. I resented her so much when we were both kids. All the attention Joe lavished on her while I felt I was only getting the leavings.' She shrugged. 'Stupid really. In the end he lied to both of us and I don't think there'd be much between us with who got hurt more.'

Thirty-Eight

L ydia was not entirely pleased to hear from Alec first thing on a Thursday morning, but she recovered quickly. 'I thought I'd answered all your questions,' she told him.

'You didn't tell me about Bill,' he said.

'Bill?' To his surprise, she sounded genuinely confused.

'I believe that he was Penny's boyfriend and that Joe disapproved.'

'Joe? Bill? Look, I'm sorry, when are we talking about?'

'When Penny was twelve, thirteen. It was the time you'd left Joe for good.'

She still hesitated and then said, 'I really am confused here. I told you yesterday, Penny didn't have friends, never mind boyfriends. She was an awkward little thing at that age.'

'But there was a boy,' Alec persisted. 'Lydia, he might have been someone older than her. Joe was worried about what she'd got herself involved in.'

'Someone's pulling your chain, Alec,' Lydia told him. 'Penny didn't have anyone. She was too bloody awkward.' She thought about it for a moment more. 'I think you're getting mixed up anyway.'

'Oh, what with?'

'Well, Bill wasn't Penny's boyfriend, at least not the Bill I think you must mean.'

'And who do you think I mean?'

'Why, Robert. Robert Williams. You see, his friends and workmates, they always called him Bill.'

Alec rang off, feeling very thoughtful. So what did Joe mean when he said he'd got rid of Bill? Did he mean Robert Williams? Had he taken some sort of revenge for the theft of his wife and child, albeit the temporary theft?

He frowned, not certain that made any sense at all, but he sent a note to the collator's office anyway, asking them to track down the dental records for Robert Williams who might have been logged as a missing person around the time that Helen Jones was killed.

There had been two children at the right school and the right time called Williams, but neither of them had been called Gary. One was a boy called Colin who had been ten when Lydia Jackson had met his father, Robert. The other had been a little girl. Margaret. Maggie. Maggie Clarke.

Maggie Clarke invited him into her kitchen. She was baking and needed to watch the oven. Her kitchen was tiny and Alec stood in the doorway so as not to get in her way.

'Maggie, do you know Penny Jackson?'

She glanced over her shoulder. 'Joe Jackson's daughter. I saw her on the news.'

'But did you know her before?'

The slight tightening of her shoulders told him he had scored, but what, he wasn't sure. Her voice was steady and unconcerned when she replied. 'Sure,' she said. 'She used to work at the health centre as a receptionist. I recognized her.'

'And did you also recognize her as the daughter of Lydia Jackson? The woman your father left your mother for?'

She stiffened. She had been creaming fat and sugar in the bowl, but she stopped for an instant, before beating even harder.

'He didn't leave us for her. He'd already gone. And I was glad. We were better off without the bastard.'

Alec raised an eyebrow, but she still had her back to him, beating furiously, creaming the mix until it turned to slurry in the glass bowl.

'Maggie?' Alec said. 'Talk to me.'

She slammed down the bowl and turned sharply to face him. 'She knew who I was,' Maggie told him, the sudden anger in her voice shocking him as much as the naked pain in her eyes. 'One day, she came up to me in the doctor's office and she told me who she was. It was like she wanted to be friends or something and . . . and for a little while, I don't know, I tried to like her. She seemed so . . . lonely. Lost.'

She hugged herself suddenly, hands clamping her upper arms, her body tense and rigid. 'She kept turning up. Here, when I was out shopping, at the school. It got so I didn't want to go and pick the kids up any more. Their dad started doing it for me when he could. He could see how worked up I'd got. She said she just wanted to be friends. Bought the kids sweets and toys. They liked her, I mean what kid wouldn't if you're constantly stuffing them with sweets? But I couldn't cope. She came on like we were sisters or something. Had all these things in common.' She wiped her eyes angrily with the palm of her hand and turned her back on him again, her hands moving now to grip the bowl as though it were a life belt. 'You know, one day I got so wound up. She'd been hanging round the kids, Sarah especially, bribing them, telling them that she loved them more than anyone else. Sarah wouldn't settle that night, she'd had too much sugar, too much of Penny. I made her go to bed and she played up, said she loved Penny more than me.

'It was too much. I couldn't bear it. I took the kid by the arms and shook her. I could feel my fingers digging into her arms and she had bruises next morning. I was so ashamed. So bloody ashamed. And I know she saw. And every time after that, whenever I met her, she just looked at me like I was dirt and she'd say things like it was a shame I couldn't control my temper, that it set the kids a bad example, but that she supposed she couldn't expect any different knowing who my father was.

'In the end, I told her I was going to call the police if she didn't stop hassling me and I moved doctors and when they asked me at the health centre why, I told them why. I *told* them why.'

She took a shuddering breath and then another.

'Maggie?' Alec said softly. 'When was this?'

The hands moved again, both of them this time, wiping angrily across her eyes. 'A year ago,' she said. 'About a year ago. She left the place then, the health centre and, you know, I hope they forced her out. I hope they made her go.'

* * *

226

The rest of the morning was less useful. He visited Geoff Lyman, wanting to talk more about Bill, but no one was home and when he called Naomi she wasn't there either. He remembered belatedly that it was one of her days at the advice centre. So he went back to report to Travers and found that Travers himself had news.

'The man with Penny Jackson. He's a private investigator, name of Edwin Tompkins. We're trying to track him down. His office says he's out working somewhere, but don't know where. I hear you've had a busy morning.'

'Oh?'

'Maggie Clarke called me.'

'There's a link between the Clarkes and Penny Jackson. A more recent link than their dad taking off with her mother.' He told Travers what Maggie Clarke had said.

'So, she lost her job?'

'I imagine it must have been difficult to continue. Her employers must have seen this as a breach of etiquette if not of outright trust.'

'The pattern of behaviour though. It's very familiar.'

'Very,' Travers agreed. 'Maggie called me after you'd gone. I don't know exactly what you said to her, but it had an effect. She told me that Robert Williams had a record. They divorced after his wife accused him of abusing the children.'

'What? But he still had access.'

'The kids got scared and retracted their statements. The judge ruled in their father's favour and gave him one weekend in two.'

'God Almighty.'

'But that's not all. The mother was so distraught she did some digging and eventually the access was rescinded. Trouble was, Robert Williams had already disappeared.'

'Joe. Getting rid of a problem.'

'It's looking like a possibility. What eventually came out was that Williams had been accused of sexual assault. He was nineteen at the time, the girl was ten, but again, the kid was scared, the case was discharged for insufficient evidence.'

Alec felt that things were slowly sliding into place, but he could not yet see the completed pattern.

'If Penny saw her father kill . . . If Penny saw her father kill Robert Williams. If Robert Williams assaulted her and her father knew. If Joe had killed Robert and buried him on Lansdowne Road and Penny knew. Tried to make someone realize without . . . without implicating herself . . . But why not come straight out and tell?

'If Joe had confessed . . . Dick, that confession, it doesn't mention Helen. The letters don't mention Helen, what if we've been getting this wrong?'

'It doesn't mean he didn't murder her as well.'

Alec's thoughts returned to Maggie Clarke and to her little girl. 'What if it wasn't a man?' he said.

'Sorry?'

'Sarah Clarke. We made the assumption that it must be a man. But there was no semen and anyone can sexually assault a child. The PM never described it as rape.'

'Go on,' Travers said, but his expression told Alec he knew where this was heading.

'Sarah would only go with someone she knew. Someone who gave her sweets and toys and maybe even told her she was her auntie. Maggie says she wanted to be like family.'

'Motive?'

'Who knows? Some kind of belated revenge? I'm not sure I can even begin to understand that woman's mind.'

Travers nodded. 'But Penny Jackson might well be our killer,' he said softly.

Thirty-Nine

The patrol car radioed back that no one was home at the Jackson house. They had banged on the door and gone round the back. A neighbour, attracted by the noise, told them she had seen Penny going out an hour before.

'Naomi wasn't home yet either,' Alec told Travers.

'Had she left the advice centre?'

'I tried there as well. Apparently she's gone out to lunch today. It's someone's birthday, but the woman at the desk didn't know where. Come to think of it, she did mention it last week, but I'd forgotten. Then, I think she's due to go to Mari's later this afternoon.'

'What about her mobile?'

'Battery won't hold a charge. She's been having problems with it all week.' He was dialling as he spoke. Patrick answered. He was on his own and had also been trying to get hold of Naomi.

'Nan's ill,' he told Alec. 'Dad called an ambulance and he's gone to the hospital with her. He went in the ambulance and I stayed behind in case Naomi turned up.'

'What's wrong with Mari?' Alec asked. 'Are you OK on your own?'

'Alec, I'm fifteen. Of course I'm fine. But I don't know about Nan. I heard the paramedics talking about a heart attack. She's been taking these blood pressure tablets and she was white and her mouth was all blue when they took her away. Dad phoned me from the hospital about twenty minutes ago, but he doesn't know anything yet.'

'OK, look, ignore the door unless it's Naomi. When's she due?'

'She wasn't sure, someone's birthday at the place where she

229

works. She was winding Dad up and telling him she intended getting pissed. I think she should be here by three, half an hour or so.'

'Call me, the moment she gets there.' Alec gave him the office number and his mobile. 'The moment. Promise.'

'Sure. What's wrong, Alec? Something's happened, hasn't it?'

Alec hesitated, not sure how much he should tell but anxious that the boy should be protected. 'If Penny Jackson turns up don't let her in. Call me straightaway. You got that?'

'Sure I've got that, but Alec . . .'

'Sorry old son, can't tell you more. Any worries, dial the nines.'

He rang off and Travers' worried gaze met his own.

'If she was having Tompkins follow her,' Travers said, 'she'll know exactly where Naomi is.'

Naomi hadn't carried out her threat. She'd had two celebratory glasses of red wine and discovered that Napoleon liked pretzels. Lunch with Cathy and the others had been fun and she had been shocked at how much she really needed the balm of laughter and unforced, unimportant conversation. It was the first time she had eaten out since the accident and she marked it down as another little victory.

Her mood, therefore, when she got off the bus at the end of Mari's street, was happy and mellow. She listened for the bus moving off and then shifted towards the kerb, but she never made it across the road.

'Hello, Naomi,' Penny said. 'I think we'll take a walk. I really need to talk to you.'

Patrick watched from the upstairs window. He was scared, more scared than he really wanted to admit. Already, before Alec called, he had been anxious about his Nan; frightened at how blue and pale she looked and how clammy her skin had felt. Alec's phone call with its warnings and implicit threat had only served to unnerve him further.

He saw the bus pull up and, though it was hard to see, was sure that he spotted Naomi moving along the aisle. Relief flooded through him and he prepared to run down and tell

Alec that his friend was here and everything was going to be all right.

Then the bus moved off and Patrick froze.

Penny. He watched in horror as Naomi turned from the road and began to walk away. Penny's hand on her arm. Penny holding tight to Napoleon's harness.

For a second or two Patrick stared, too shocked to move, then he ran down the stairs and wrenched the front door open, pausing only to snatch the telephone numbers Alec had given him from the table by the phone.

Then sense kicked in. If anything happened, Alec had said, call in on the nines.

He dialled fast, jiggling impatiently from foot to foot and he waited for the line to connect, the operator to put him through, the call taker to ask him for his number and his name.

'It's Patrick Jones,' he yelled. 'Look, I don't have time. Tell Inspector Alec Friedman that Penny's here and she's got Naomi.' Then he dropped the phone and took off at a run, not even pausing to shut the door.

Forty

'Where are you taking me?'

'I just want to talk. That's all. It's what I always wanted, but you'd always got something more important to do. Someone who needed your attention more.'

'I'm sorry,' Naomi said. 'I didn't mean it to seem that way.'

'Oh, I suppose I should be used to it by now. Being less important than everyone else. There are steps down. A handle on your right.'

So they were going down on to the towpath, Naomi thought. She'd guessed as much but the steps were confirmation. The rail was scaffolding pipe, cool beneath her fingers. Her hands were sweating and a trickle of moisture crawled down her spine, soaking into the waistband of her skirt.

She hesitated at the top step. The towpath was likely empty this time of day. Children didn't play there as they had in Naomi's childhood. There might be a fisherman, but that was all. She was reluctant to shift so far away from the houses; from potential help.

'I told you what I'd do,' Penny said. 'I've got the dog and I'd not hesitate, Naomi. This knife is sharp.' To prove her point, she jabbed Naomi in the hand, not deep, but enough to bleed. She yelped, more from shock than real pain, and Napoleon grumbled plaintively.

'Now, I suggest we all go down.'

'Why are you doing this?' Naomi asked again. 'Just what do you hope to prove? To achieve?'

She felt Penny shrug. 'Someone might at last take notice,' was all she would say.

They walked in silence for a while, Naomi aware of the

232

woman's fingers digging into her arm. The only sounds she could hear were the soft pad of Napoleon's feet through the fallen leaves that littered the towpath this time of year; their own shoes, shuffling through the same; the faint trickle of water. She strained hard to hear voices, other footsteps, wondering if she could take the risk of shouting and attracting someone's attention if she did hear anyone near; if she could risk Penny hurting Napoleon.

She must have him on a lead, Naomi thought, not using his harness or she wouldn't be able to free her other hand. She must have her wrist looped through the end of the lead, so she could keep the knife in her hand.

She tried to imagine the position of Penny's other arm. How far would the dog be from danger if Naomi risked pushing against her and tried to grab her arm, but she didn't dare. All Penny would have to do would be to jerk on the lead and the dog would be at her mercy. He'd been trained to stick close to Naomi and that's exactly what he would try to do.

The sound of rushing water impinged upon her consciousness. Which way would they go? Across the weir or the other path, further along the branch of the canal and back towards the houses? It would be the weir, she knew it, towards the mill.

She tried to talk again, remembering her training for hostage situations. Make yourself real, particular, personal. Not just the faceless victim.

'Let's turn back, Penny. I know this has all been hard for you. I know we haven't helped but let's turn back now. Go to Mari's, sit down and all of us talk this through. We can forget this—'

'Shut up and walk,' Penny told her bluntly and it occurred to Naomi that, although Penny had avowed her need and her intent to communicate, now she had her, here, where she wanted her, helpless and forced to listen, Penny could no longer think what it was she had wanted to say.

Patrick had guessed where they were going as soon as they had disappeared between the houses. He followed swiftly, reasoning that they would not be moving fast but knowing that once they had reached the towpath, it would be near impossible to follow and not to be seen.

They were a third of the way along the path when Patrick reached the steps. Penny had the dog still, not holding him by the harness as Patrick had first thought, but on a choke chain and lead. Napoleon was clearly unhappy with the arrangement, pressing close to the woman's legs in his efforts to turn his head back towards Naomi. Patrick thought of running at her from behind, wondering if he could run fast enough and silently enough to reach them before Penny turned. Then he saw the knife glint in Penny's hand as she once more lifted it and jabbed it towards Naomi. The choke chain pulled the dog up short and the movement of her arm nearly jerked the poor animal off his feet. Patrick understood now why Naomi had gone so easily with Penny and he knew that there was nothing he could do which wouldn't put Napoleon at further risk.

Patrick crouched at the foot of the steps, half-hidden by the bank and its tall grasses and shrubby growth. Every second he hoped to hear sirens. To know that help was on the way. But however hard he strained his ears, there was nothing. How long would it take them? Had they believed him? Had they passed his message on? The questions nagged at his mind as Penny and Naomi walked around a bend in the towpath and disappeared.

The route split into two at the weir, he remembered from his walk that night with Naomi. He had to know which one they'd take and get the message back to Alec.

Taking a deep breath, Patrick left the safety of the steps and trotted on.

'We're in the mill, aren't we?' The smell of old wood and oil and grease, urine and stale alcohol was a familiar one. The building had been derelict for years and Naomi had come in here often during her career to clear the drunks and drug users when local complaints got too insistent. She kicked something as she took another step. She heard a bottle roll across the floor and smelt the pungent stink of methylated spirits.

'Watch it,' Penny said. 'The floor's littered with that kind

234

of junk. Steps, straight ahead. They're wooden and rickety so go slow.'

Naomi reached forward. The steps, she found, were open treads and very steep. Glass crunched beneath her feet and she caught another bottle under her heel, her foot rolling on the glass and unbalancing her. There were handrails at the side, but when Naomi rested her hand on one of them, it gave way beneath her palm and the steps shook violently as the spindles tumbled to the floor. Naomi cried out in shock and lifted her other hand from the other rail, afraid that it too would disintegrate.

'Move,' Penny told her, pushing her from behind. Angrily, Naomi kicked back at her, the heel of her shoe making contact with something soft.

It was Penny's turn to yelp and gasp as the breath was knocked out of her, but then the choke chain rattled and the dog squealed.

'Napoleon!'

'Now move,' Penny told her again, she sounded breathless but even more determined. Naomi was forced to almost crawl up the flight of stairs, using her hands on the treads to find her way.

From across the bridge, Patrick saw them go into the mill. He wondered what to do. If he followed them, he would almost certainly be seen. The bridge was utterly exposed and there were still unbroken windows in the upper storey of the building that, filthy as they were, might still give a view to anyone inside.

Think, think, he told himself, trying to fix the geography of the area in his head. There was a telephone, he remembered, on the road that ran above the bank. Patrick turned around and began to climb, tugging on the bushes for support, his feet slipping on the wet mud and carpet of leaf mould. He was gasping for breath before he reached the top and stumbled into the road hoping that the call box would not have been vandalised.

He had no money to call Alec. His dad had taught him how to make a reverse charge call in an emergency and he did that now, giving Alec's office number, not sure they would connect him to a mobile.

Would he be there? Would he accept the call? Would they think it was a joke, a reverse charge call going to a police station, and just hang up on him? He was preparing to put down the phone and dial the nines again when Alec himself came on the line.

'Where are you?'

'Did you get my other call?'

'Just. I was about to leave.'

'They're in the old mill above the weir,' Patrick told him. 'I'm going back. Alec, I think Penny has a knife, I saw it in her hand.'

'OK, OK, where are you now?'

Patrick told him as best he could.

'Stay there. I'll be with you.'

Once Alec had hung up, Patrick stood on the road and tried to think what to do next. He couldn't just hang around. What if they left? What if they had already gone? No one would know.

He turned and ran back, sliding down the bank, the bushes tearing at his hands and clothes.

Then, as he landed on the path, someone grabbed him from behind.

'Patrick?' He heard Naomi's voice before he saw her. 'Oh God, what are you doing here?'

She was sitting on the floor in the corner of the upstairs room. A big room with windows all along one side, though many were broken and others boarded up. The dog was beside her and chirruped a greeting when he saw who it was. Ever the optimist, his tail began its slow beat upon the floor, raising little clouds of dust from the wooden surface.

There were gaps in the floorboards where the wood had rotted and as Patrick was thrust forward, he stumbled, falling with his hand reaching out and finding nothing but space. He lay there for a moment, hearing Naomi's anxious questions.

'I'm fine,' he assured her. He scrambled to his feet and picked his way over to Naomi. 'Half the floor's missing,' he said, then as he settled beside her, whispered, 'Alec's on his way. It's going to be OK.'

236

'What are you doing here?'

'I followed you. Some man grabbed me. *She's* downstairs talking to him. She called him Bill.'

'Bill? What does he look like?'

'I didn't get to see him very well. Brown hair, tall, I'd say, and about Alec's age. I caught one real look at his face, but that was all. Look, stay put, I might be able to see, the floor's half-missing, like I said.'

She grabbed his arm. 'Probably half-rotten, too. I could feel it swaying and groaning when I crossed it.'

'I'll be careful.' Gently, he eased her fingers from his arm and crawled forward on his belly to the nearest gap.

He could see Penny and the man below. They seemed to be arguing about something, but the angle was not good enough for Patrick to really see his face. He got the impression of someone tall and strongly built – though he knew that from when the man had grabbed him; clamping one large hand tightly over Patrick's nose and mouth and twisting Patrick's arm painfully behind his back with the other, he had marched the boy across the bridge with seemingly none of Patrick's worries about being seen. He had smelt of soap, Patrick remembered irrelevantly. His hands newly washed.

He crawled back to Naomi. 'Can't see much,' he said, 'and they're keeping their voices down.' He huddled as she was next to the dog and rubbed his ears, examining him carefully for signs of damage.

'Did she hurt either of you?'

'Just cut my hand,' Naomi showed him. The bleeding had all but stopped. 'She was trying to make a point.'

'What does she want?'

Naomi shrugged. 'I don't think she knows any more,' she said. 'I think she went past working that out long ago.'

Patrick filled her in on what he'd done. How he had been watching for her after Alec's call and followed.

'You did well to call the police,' Naomi told him. 'But Patrick, you should have stayed put when Alec told you. If anything happens to you I'll never forgive myself.'

'Nothing's going to happen,' Patrick assured her, with far more confidence than he felt. The stupidity of his action was really sinking home and he felt numbed and shocked now the adrenaline had diminished. 'I hope Nan's going to be OK,' he added.

Naomi slid an arm around his shoulders and held him tight.

Tompkins the PI had been found skulking around on the towpath. 'She only said she wanted to talk to the lady,' he protested. 'I don't know nothing else.'

'You've been following Miss Blake?'

'She paid me to watch where the lady went. Said it was something to do with a divorce case.'

'And of course, you believed her.'

'She's a client. I need clients.'

Alec looked across the weir towards the mill. Officers were in position at all exits to the towpaths and slowly moving in toward the mill from the other end, Travers in the front rank. And they had an Armed Response Vehicle on standby, just in case . . . In case of what? Alec thought. There was no way Penny could get out, so what the hell was she playing at?

A PC scrambled down the bank. 'There's no sign of the boy,' he said. 'I went up and down the road, but no one's seen him.'

'He followed them,' Alec nodded. In his heart of hearts he had never expected Patrick to stay quietly put. Would he have done at fifteen? Alec thought not. 'We'll have to assume he's inside,' he said. 'Better notify DCI Travers that we may have a third hostage.'

Tompkins was shifting uneasily. 'A boy, fifteen years, but small. White with longish dark hair. You saw him?' Alec demanded.

'It was nowt to do with me,' Tompkins protested. 'There was this big bloke, see, came out of them bushes and grabbed him.'

'And you did nothing?'

Tompkins mumbled something which sounded like, 'Not what I was paid for', but Alec had other things on his mind.

He didn't even look his way as Tompkins was led off. 'Tell

238

Travers we've got three hostages and two suspects. Penny Jackson and an unknown male,' he said.

'Three hostages, sir?' the PC questioned. 'Who's the third?'

Alec frowned. He had got so used to thinking of Napoleon that way. 'Two hostages,' he corrected, but he felt privately that he'd been right the first time.

Inside the mill the murmur of voices had continued; Penny and this mysterious man pursuing what seemed to be an argument. Occasionally, the volume would rise. 'Just what is it you want?' the man was heard to shout and once Penny shouted his name, her voice anxious and tense as though she was afraid that he would leave her.

Mostly, Patrick and Naomi could hear little. They talked softly, Patrick describing the upper room to her: the smashed windows, old blankets and papers rucked up in the opposite corner. More bottles, broken and unbroken, the smell of piss and old booze so strong Naomi figured the wood must be almost pickled in it. She wondered how they were going to escape.

'You might make it out,' Naomi told him.

'Not without you. I don't know what she'd do to you or Napoleon if I made a run for it.'

Naomi sighed. Where was Alec? Hopefully, not Alec alone.

She did not think that either Patrick or herself were in any immediate danger. Penny and Bill seemed preoccupied by some business of their own. And who the hell was Bill? she wondered. She remembered the day at the fairground. Harry and Alec had talked about Penny being with a man, but thought the man they had described had been short and small not the way Patrick had described him, even allowing for the fear factor; victims often making their assailants bigger and stronger than they really were.

They had just begun to believe that something had gone wrong. That Alec had maybe not been able to convince anyone that they really were in trouble when the unmistakable sound of someone shouting through a megaphone cut through the silence and echoed around the walls.

'They're here,' Patrick whispered fiercely.

239

'That's Dick Travers,' Naomi recognized the voice even through the distortion.

'Miss Jackson, come on out of the building. Please hold your hands in view and move slowly on to the bridge.'

'What do we do?' Penny's voice was thin and anxious. 'Bill? Oh God, don't leave me now! Bill, what are we going to do? Bill . . .' She sounded faintly puzzled this time, then. 'Yes, maybe you're right. Give that to me, then go.'

'What? Give her what? Right about what?' Naomi wondered. 'And how can he get out? There's nothing but the loading dock through the rear door.'

'Maybe he'll swim for it.'

'You've seen the basin, would you want to swim that? The water's deep and rough where it comes off the weir.'

'I wouldn't want to swim in anything, remember. But not everyone's so wet.'

She clasped his arm. 'You're anything but wet.'

Nervously, Patrick began to giggle, the tension getting the better of him and overwhelming sense. 'No,' he said, 'but he will be. Nomi, we've got to be ready. If she comes upstairs I'm going to make a run at her. You keep Napoleon out of the way and help me if you can.'

'This isn't a computer game, Patrick,' she told him, more sharply than she meant. 'Sorry. I'm scared,' she apologized at once. 'Look, let's hold on, she might go out to Travers.' What did Bill give her before he left? she wondered again. What did she think he was right about?

The voice on the megaphone sounded again, but Naomi did not listen to what was said, a faint smell of smoke had drifted up through the broken floor. 'What's she doing down there?' But Naomi was afraid she already knew.

'I'll see if I can see.'

She felt him crawl forward once again and the scrabbling movements as he shifted around on the broken floor, trying to see through the gaps.

'I can't see much,' he whispered, then, 'There's smoke! Naomi, she's set the stairs on fire!'

The broken bottles, she remembered, the meths, maybe other dregs of alcohol, enough to act as an accelerant. 'Patrick, run,' she ordered him. 'If you go now, you'll get through. God, this place will go up like tinder. Penny! Penny! No!' She was on her feet now, stumbling forward, shouting at the direction from which the fire now rose.

Patrick's footsteps echoed on the wood as he ran to the stairway and then back.

'Go!' she yelled at him again.

'No way. I'm not leaving you.' His voice was almost shrill with panic. 'The stairs are burning. The stairs.'

And Penny Jackson standing a few yards back from her handiwork, the lighter Bill had given her still between her fingers, with no discernable expression on her pallid face.

'Smoke,' Travers shouted. 'There's smoke.'

A light plume of it drifted out through the broken door and another from the ground-floor window. 'What the hell?' He began to run towards the building, dimly aware of the figure hurtling across the bridge from the towpath on the other side as Alec saw it too.

Penny Jackson emerged from the half-open door. She still held the lighter in her left hand. The knife with which she had threatened Naomi clasped loosely in her right. She stood calmly on the bridge, smoke now fluttering out behind her as the fire took greater hold. Flames licked at the door by the time Travers reached her. He grabbed her, mindless of the weapon she was holding, thrusting her aside into the arms of another officer then plunged through the door, Alec hard on his heels.

'Patrick, Naomi!'

But within seconds they were forced outside. The smoke had thickened, catching a pile of rags and paper some itinerant had one time made his bed.

Naomi shouted. They heard her voice above the crack and crash of timber as what was left of the stairs disintegrated. Glass shattered in one of the upstairs windows, the knife-edged rain showering down and driving them back on to the towpath. In the distance fire sirens echoed.

It was the shattering of the glass that really galvanised Patrick. The windows on this level had been set low in the wall and rose high towards the ceiling, designed to maximise daylight in an age when electricity was still an infant science. And he knew then that the only chance any of them would have was to break the glass and jump.

He took Naomi's arm. 'Come on,' he said, 'you've got to trust me. We're going out the window.'

'We're what?'

The room was filling up with smoke. Thick black smoke that smelt of oil and grease and choked them when they tried to breath.

'What about Napoleon?' The dog was terrified, whining and yapping at the strange noises and the choking smoke.

'We throw him out first,' Patrick said. 'He can swim, he'll be all right. Nomi, we don't have any other choice.'

She knew that he was right. She could hear the fire engines in the distance, their plaintive wailing the most beautiful sound that she had ever heard. But she knew too that they had to face reality. The smoke was catching in her lungs. She could barely breath and speaking hurt like hell. By the time the fire service reached the mill they might all be dead from inhaling whatever muck was in the toxic smoke.

Patrick was leading her and she held tight to Napoleon. She heard the first crash as Patrick kicked the glass.

'Where?' she choked. 'Tell me where, I'll help you.'

'Straight in front.' He coughed violently and she heard another crash as he hit again. Naomi kicked out. She was hardly dressed for this, the irrational thought came to her mind. Heels and a skirt. She felt the impact as she hit something that felt too hard to be glass, but the crash too loud and satisfying take anything else.

She felt Patrick push past her and take the harness from her hand. He took precious seconds unbuckling it, scared that it might catch on something. 'You'll be fine, you'll be fine,' he kept telling the frightened animal. 'I'm sending him out, Naomi.'

'Oh, God, oh God. No, don't. No!' Suddenly terrified that the dog might die out there, regardless of the fact that he would certainly perish inside, Naomi reached out to grab him back, but Napoleon was already gone. She heard what would have been a cheer from Patrick if he'd had the breath for it. 'He's swimming. There's policemen on the bank. He's swimming.'

He turned back her and took her hand. 'Our turn now,' he said.

The first Alec guessed of Patrick's plans was the bizarre and frightening sight of a black dog flying through the air and landing with, given the circumstances, quite extraordinary grace in the canal basin.

'Shit!'

He watched transfixed as the black head disappeared below the water, then broke surface and powerful legs struck out towards the shore. The cheer that went up from the officers on the bank took him by surprise and Alec laughed aloud, momentarily breaking the tension.

Then he looked back towards the building. Patrick climbing out on to the window ledge, Naomi at his side, feeling her way.

'Do it right, do it right. You can do it right.' His heart seemed to freeze and his stomach curdle. He remembered Naomi telling him about Patrick's fear of water as well as her own. It was, he thought, the single bravest act that he had ever witnessed.

'Don't hold there, it's broken glass. Hand down just a tiny bit. Right.'

He directed her in a voice that was hoarse as a raven's and barely above a whisper. Her hand caught on the glass, but she hardly noticed it. The fire at their backs had made it to the second level. 'Between the dragon and the deep,' Patrick whispered and she knew that in his mind's eye he was seeing something from his computer games.

For the first time in her life she was almost glad that she couldn't see. At the top of her fears list, the list she had told Patrick about that night, was a fear of heights.

'On three,' Patrick told her.

She was crouched on the window ledge beside him, one foot still in the room. She began to ease forward, her body stiff with fear. They went on one, Patrick hauling her after him as he fell. It was a close thing who screamed loudest on the way down.

Men dived into the water. Travers had run back to the

towpath and grabbed a lifebelt. He ran now, coming up beside Alec with the red and white striped object in his hand, looking for where best to throw it. Alec himself was ready to make the plunge. Travers held him back.

'Not this time. You're a crap swimmer, you once told me so.' He nodded towards the two men and one woman who were swimming strongly towards where Patrick and Naomi had splashed down and Alec was forced to watch, silently agreeing and hating himself for it, but he was first there when they were hauled ashore.

'Napoleon?' Alec was never certain which of them asked first; both Naomi and Patrick's voices were choked with smoke and foul water, lungs filled with both.

'He's just fine. The paramedics are looking him over, they reckon he dislocated his back hip when he landed in the water, but we've got a vet on standby.'

'I've got to go with him.' That was definitely Naomi.

Alec clung to her like a drowning man. 'Dick's going to take him,' he reassured her. 'You're going to hospital. And you –' he reached to include Patrick in his embrace before the medics took possession – 'you are . . . God, your dad's going to kill me!'

Forty-One

◄

A week later and Patrick was home, still fervently denying that the man who had grabbed him had been Tompkins the PI. The description he gave was definitely of a different man, but mostly it was mooted out of his hearing that he was mistaken; shock having changed his memory of things.

'Why would she call him Bill?' Patrick demanded and no one could really answer that one and, though it was undeniable that his memory of the man coincided with the description of Robert Williams, as Alec pointed out, he'd been buried under the patio at 45 Lansdowne Road for more than twenty years and was hardly likely to be in the running.

Patrick didn't seem so sure and neither, in quiet moments, was Naomi.

The two children who had left the bracelet had not been traced, despite widespread appeals. Tompkins denied all knowledge of them. When shown the CCTV footage, he claimed that they had only asked him the time. But as he also denied grabbing Patrick and taking him to Penny, no one gave his statement much credence . . . except for Patrick, of course, who *knew* it wasn't him.

'Penny killed Sarah Clarke. It's about the only sensible thing we can get out of her,' Alec told them one afternoon when they had gathered at Mari's to talk things through. Mari, too, had been released from hospital. She had suffered a mild stroke and was taking it as a warning and Harry's plans to move closer had taken on an increased urgency.

'She didn't say why?' Harry asked.

Alec shook his head.

'Jealousy, perhaps,' Naomi said. 'Or even revenge for Maggie Clarke's rejection of her. Maybe even anger because

Maggie made her lose her job. I wonder if Penny really knew what her own motive was. Did she set out to kill Sarah that night or did something happen to send her over the edge?' She thought about it for a moment. 'Maggie must have drilled into the child that she should keep away from Penny. She was distressed and hurt enough at Penny's influence to inflict actual harm on her own little girl. Sarah must have known she was wrong to go off with this woman her mother hated. Maybe she tried to run away, run back to her brother. If she threatened to tell her mum, Penny . . . reacted?' She shrugged. 'I'm guessing.'

'You think she feigned the sexual assault so that everyone would assume it was a man?' Harry questioned.

'That's the one thing that mitigates against my arguments,' Naomi said. 'If Penny had just, well, reacted out of fear, that's an impulsive act. The assault, the feigning of evidence, the attempt – which everyone fell for – to make it look like a sexual killing, speaks of a rational mind at work. Someone who is thinking this through, not just hitting out in panic. If she'd killed Sarah and then run away, that would have been one thing. To stay around long enough to strip the child and make it look as though her abductor had assaulted her, that's something else again.'

Harry sighed. 'Whatever her motive,' he said, 'it's still horrible, Naomi. And knowing on top of that that Joe killed Helen . . .'

'Then Robert Williams and buried him in what he thought was the same place,' Naomi added. 'I still can't believe it, Alec.'

'We have to make the assumption,' he told her gently. 'There seems no other explanation. But I still don't understand why. I mean, we're guessing he killed Williams . . . Bill . . . because of something he did to Penny. But Helen? I don't know why.'

'And chances are we never will.' Harry commented. 'Lordy, what a tangled mess.'

'I saw Gary Williams the other day,' Alec said.

'Oh? What wasn't he guilty of this time?'

Alec laughed. 'I'm still waiting,' he said. 'He'll slip up,

even if it's only a traffic offence. He was with his new girlfriend, in Sainsbury's of all places.'

'Did he speak?' Naomi asked mischievously.

'No, he was too busy having a blazing row about spaghetti hoops.'

'You're joking.'

'No, I kid you not.'

'You know,' Naomi said quietly. 'I still feel sorry for Penny.'

'She tried to kill you,' Harry objected.

'Maybe.'

'No. It was for real,' Patrick told her. 'I was there, remember?'

Naomi smiled in his direction. 'I don't think she knew who she was trying to kill by then and you know what else I think? I think all these years she's still felt that Bill, Robert Williams, was maybe the one man who took notice of her, even if it was probably the wrong kind of notice, and then when she found the confession and realized what her father had really done, not, as she thought, just made him go away . . . it must have destroyed her. She knew the confession wasn't about Helen, but it gave her what she needed to smash her father's reputation. It must have felt like the ultimate victory. Revenge for him never having been there for her. As well as for having killed Bill.'

'And that's another thing I don't get,' Patrick said. 'How did she know that the confession wasn't about Helen? If he confessed about killing Robert Williams, then why not about Helen too?'

That, Naomi thought to herself, was a very discriminating question.

Penny Jackson sat by herself in a room which looked out over a little garden. This was meant to be a communal sitting room but at this time of the afternoon most people were involved in therapy or some such thing and Penny was left more or less alone. Watched, of course, but more or less alone.

She remembered that day with Bill, playing hookey from school but not knowing where he was taking her. And that

247

chance meeting with the kid that Bill had had his eye on all winter. The plump little thing with the pretty face and the long blonde hair. Helen Jones.

Penny had seen him with others, watched him play, encouraging them to talk to him, kiss him maybe, maybe other things. He liked to have an audience did Bill and Penny knew, then, that she wasn't pretty enough for him. Not small enough, or blonde enough and with her bony ribs and awkward joints too skinny and gangly to be of any real interest. Not in that way.

She had resented it, of course. It was like her father all over again: other people much more interesting, much more needful of him.

But Bill had liked her as she had grown older. She knew that. Bill had come to her and stayed, almost to the end.

She remembered that day with Helen Jones. Bill had become impatient with the girl after he'd got her into the woods. He hadn't meant to kill, he'd told Penny that. Not meant to choke the life from her the way he did.

Penny remembered the big hand wrapped around the blonde girl's throat and that bracelet, dancing and jingling on her plump little wrist. The sweet sound of silver bells.